A Pure Heart

Rajia Hassib

SCEPTRE

First published in Great Britain in 2019 by Sceptre
An Imprint of Hodder & Stoughton
An Hachette UK company

This paperback edition published in 2020

1

A CIP catalogue record for this title is available from the British Library

B format ISBN 9781529317381
eBook ISBN 9781529317374

Printed and bound in Great Britain by Clays Ltd, Elcograf S.p.A.

Hodder & Stoughton policy is to use papers that are natural, renewable
and recyclable products and made from wood grown in sustainable forests.
The logging and manufacturing processes are expected to conform
to the environmental regulations of the country of origin.

Hodder & Stoughton Ltd
Carmelite House
50 Victoria Embankment
London EC4Y 0DZ

www.sceptrebooks.co.uk

'A profound and deeply affecting examination of fate and free will, family a... ...ond between sisters ... ...cited About'

4 4 0106093 4

Rajia Hassib was born and raised in Egypt and moved to the United States when she was twenty-three. Her first novel, *In the Language of Miracles*, was a *New York Times* Editors' Choice and received an honorable mention from the Arab American Book Award. She holds an MA in Creative Writing from Marshall University, and she has written for the *New York Times Book Review* and the *New Yorker* online. She lives in West Virginia with her husband and two children.

In memory of my mother, Laila

For my father, Raafat,
and my sister, Dina

O my heart which I had from my mother, O my heart which I had upon earth, do not rise up against me as a witness in the presence of the Lord of Things; do not speak against me concerning what I have done, do not bring up anything against me in the presence of the Great God, Lord of the West.

The Egyptian Book of the Dead
The Theban Recension
Chapter XXXA

Part One

SUICIDE BOMBER KILLS 9 IN EGYPT

A suicide bomber detonated an improvised explosive device at a security checkpoint outside of the police headquarters in Cairo, killing three police officers and six civilians and injuring dozens more.

Egypt's police spokesman said the bomber had an arrest record and had gained some fame two years ago, when an American journalist interviewed him for a series of profiles that appeared in *The Times*. The bomber is not known to have ties to larger terrorist groups and is believed to have acted alone.

The bombing is the latest in a series of attacks that have occurred sporadically since Egypt's 2011 revolution. Previous incidents have mostly targeted military personnel stationed in the Sinai Peninsula, where militant groups loyal to ISIS are present, but attacks on police checkpoints are also common. Militants in Egypt blame the state's security apparatus for the crackdown on extremists.

A statement issued by the Ministry of Interior Affairs vowed that tightened security measures are being put into effect.

On her last night in Egypt, Rose waits for her parents to fall asleep and then sneaks into her sister's bedroom. She sifts through the clothes strewn on the back of the chair, examines the contents of each desk drawer, picks through every nook of the armoire, then slides the mattress to the side and goes through the things stored under her sister's bed. Her own childhood bed, still standing in the room she used to share with her sister years ago, is covered with clothes, books, CDs, and papers, and Rose goes through those, too. The items on the bed seem to be some of the ones her sister recently used—Gameela was never one for order—and from that pile Rose picks out a pastel-colored scarf, blue and green with Impressionist flowers that remind her of a painting of Monet, and drapes it on top of her head and across her face, inhaling deeply: her sister's favorite perfume, flowery and fresh. She ties the scarf around her neck and continues with her search. She sets aside two T-shirts, a small box of jewelry, and a string of black prayer beads engraved with the ninety-nine names of Allah, one name on each bead. Anything that seems potentially significant, she tosses onto the growing pile of things she intends to steal.

She assures herself that she is an archaeologist, not a grave robber.

She works as noiselessly as possible, and when the mattress grinds against the bed frame as she tries to lift it back in place, she pauses, mattress poised in the air, and listens. Her parents are former heavy sleepers turned insomniacs, who now resort to sleeping pills to get them through the night, and she hopes the effect of the pills will mask whatever noise she inadvertently makes. Rose, on the other hand, is still jet-lagged seven nights into her visit to Egypt, her biological clock stubbornly clinging to Eastern Daylight Time. Gently, she lowers the mattress in place and glances at her watch: 1:00 A.M. in Cairo; 7:00 P.M. in New York. She can stay up all night.

Under the bed, behind the desk, into each of the six dresser drawers, Rose looks, combing through papers, setting aside everything that seems potentially important. She takes the cup of fine china with the butterfly motif; the newspaper article featuring the boy with dark, piercing eyes; the turquoise stone on a delicate gold chain; the stack of unopened mail; the notebooks filled with scribbles; all the photos she can find.

She goes through the entire room in just over four hours.

By then, dawn has already broken, and Rose walks up to the window and pushes the wooden shutters open, letting the daylight in. Already people are stirring, walking up and down the narrow street below. Rose leans out, resting her elbows on the sill and letting the warm breeze caress her face, toying with Gameela's scarf, still tied around her neck. The room does not have the best view of Cairo her parents' apartment offers—that view is shared between the living room and dining room, both overlooking the Nile—but Rose still looks out, a bit nostalgically, at the alley below, which seems a lot narrower than she remembers. Dustier. Only five stories up, she can clearly see the faces of the few people walking down the alley, and she catches the eyes of a young man looking up, watching her as he walks. Reflexively, she takes a step back. Her tank top is stretched tight across her breasts and deeply cut, and Gameela's scarf does nothing to conceal her cleavage. Rose's first instinct is to reprimand herself for forgetting that she is in Egypt, that women here are not supposed to lean out of windows half naked, but then she steps closer to the window and looks out, and when she sees that the man is stopped, still staring up, she flips him off. He walks on.

Rose watches his back as he strolls away. For a moment, she is proud of herself, but then fear creeps up on her: What if he noted which floor she was on? Which apartment? What if he is so offended he comes back in a day or two, after she is gone, breaks into her parents' apartment in the middle of the night, and kills them? What if she just flipped off a psychopath?

She steps away from the window, her heart racing. Jet lag notwithstanding, Rose has been awake for over fifteen hours, and she knows exhaustion is partly to blame for her irrational fears. But then again, for the ten days since her sister died, she has had the butterfly effect on her mind, has been obsessed with minor events that lead to major ones.

An interview leading to a suicide bombing, for example.

Or her own marriage leading to her sister's death.

She looks at the pile of things she is taking out of her sister's room and all the way to the U.S. with her. Theoretically, the things could help her trace the events backward in time, from the tornado all the way to the butterfly, and the butterfly may prove to be something other than her marriage. She hopes this is true, but suspects it is merely wishful thinking. Even though everyone keeps repeating that Gameela's death is the result of being at the wrong place at the wrong time, a freak accident similar to standing in the middle of a field only to be struck dead by a Cessna making an emergency landing, Rose finds that such a coincidence is highly unlikely.

The pile of things on the floor is pathetically small, and Rose tries not to think of how she is distilling her sister's twenty-eight years into a heap of possessions. Noiselessly, she carries her suitcase from the guest room where she has been sleeping to Gameela's bedroom and, one by one, places her sister's things among her own, tucking them in, hiding them from sight.

She wakes up disoriented, takes a few seconds to remember where she is: in the guest room, staring at her mother, who has one hand on Rose's forearm.

"It's nearly noon, *habibti*. You need to get up," Nora whispers.

Rose sits up in bed, nods.

"I'll make you some breakfast," Nora says, heading out of the room.

"No, Mama, wait," Rose croaks. "I'll do it."

"Your dad and I are sitting on the balcony."

"I'll make us all some tea, then."

Nora stands in the doorway, looking at Rose. She has one hand resting on the door frame, and Rose stares at her mother's delicate wrist.

"Are you done packing?"

Rose glances at the suitcase, finds that she has brought it back into the guest room and closed it before she fell asleep. She remembers the things she took from Gameela's room and swallows to clear the knot in her throat.

"Yes."

Nora nods. "We'll be on the balcony," she repeats. She lingers at the door, looking at Rose, and then lifts one hand and touches her collarbone. Reflexively, Rose lifts her hand to her own collarbone, and is surprised to find she still has Gameela's scarf tied around her neck. She tries to pull it off, but it is tangled. Rose tugs at the knot, looking down, trying to see it—so close to her chin—and when she looks up again, her mother is gone.

IN THE KITCHEN, Rose waits for the water to boil, watches the lid of the copper teapot quiver under pressure, and munches on a triangle of pita bread stuffed with feta cheese. She scoops three full spoons of loose-leaf black tea, twirls them in the teapot, and gazes at the whirlpool. Once steeped, the tea will be black and syrupy, sweetened with sugar to mask its bitterness. Rose inhales the rising steam, opens a ceramic canister and pinches out a few leaves of dried mint, and tosses them into the teapot. Every time she reaches for something and finds it in its place, she is momentarily disoriented, unsure where she is or what year it is, the familiarity of her childhood home constantly jarred by the fact that, except for short, sporadic visits, she has been away from this home for six years. When she discovers that things have moved in her absence—the sugar is not where it used to be—she feels cut off. Foreign.

She pours the tea through a strainer into three cups placed each on its saucer on a silver tray, adds two cubes of sugar to her mother's cup, five to her father's, a dollop of milk to hers, then carries the tray to the balcony. Her parents are sitting on two of the wicker armchairs with their backs to the glass sliding doors and their feet propped against the low wall supporting the wrought-iron railing. They do not hear her coming. Rose pauses behind the glass and watches them in their silence, noting how similar their stances are, as if they are the mirror images of each other, with the line of symmetry running through the middle of the balcony and cutting the glass-topped coffee table in half. The only difference is that Ahmed is reading a book, while Nora has the fingers of both hands laced and resting on her stomach, her head tilted back, her eyes closed.

Rose pulls the sliding door open and places the tray on the table, handing her parents their cups. She drags one of the two remaining armchairs closer to the center of the table and sits there, imagining the line of her parents' symmetry running through her, splitting her in equal halves.

"You still make the best tea, Rose," Nora says, slouched in the armchair, the teacup held in both hands.

"*Belhana*, Mama," Rose says, wishing her mother would enjoy the drink in good health—the traditional reply. Rose feels everything about her mother has shrunk: her ankles are narrower, her legs skinnier, her arms and hands emaciated, covered in liver spots and contoured with raised veins. When Nora reaches up to pull off the rubber band holding her ponytail in place, her hair, usually a massive halo of silver curls, falls limply to her shoulders. She smoothens it down and tucks it behind her when she rests her head again on the back of the armchair. Rose wishes she had used honey to sweeten her mother's tea instead of sugar, because the healing powers of honey were mentioned in the Qur'an, because honey has antibacterial properties, and because, inexplicably, she remembers a papyrus in the British Museum:

The god Re wept and the tears
from his eyes fell on the ground
and turned into a bee.
The bee made (his honeycomb)
and busied himself
with the flowers of every plant;
and so wax was made
and also honey
out of the tears of Re.

The bees remind Rose of butterflies, which remind her of the fine china cup now hidden among her clothes in her suitcase.

She picks up her own cup, lifts it to eye level, and examines the miniature golden dots chasing each other on its rim.

"How long have you had this china, Mama?"

"Since I got married."

"I remember it since forever, but I wasn't sure. Have you ever had any other designs? I vaguely remember cups with yellow butterflies etched on the edges."

Her mother frowns. "Maybe you're thinking of your aunt Omneya's set?"

Ahmed puts his book down. "Omneya's cups have flowers on them, not butterflies."

"Didn't know you paid that much attention to fine china," his wife smiles at him.

"I pay attention to everything," he whispers.

Nora laughs—a small, soft chuckle. Rose reaches over and puts a hand on her father's shoulder, squeezing it, and he pats her hand in response. She wants to say something to make her mother laugh, too, but she cannot think of anything. Her plane heading home takes off in just over twelve hours, and it seems to her they are all biding their time until she leaves, the remaining hours too short to fill with anything other than small talk. The chance to discuss what they should have talked about—her husband, his work, the events leading up to her sister's death—is now gone, and Rose is torn between gratitude to her parents for sparing her this pain, and anger with herself for her cowardice, for failing to ask the questions she should have asked and to answer the ones her parents never posed.

Slowly, Rose withdraws her hand, pushes her chair back, and starts rocking it on its hind legs, her feet resting on the table's lower shelf for balance.

"You're going to fall down, Rose," her mother says.

"No, I won't, Mama."

"You'll break the chair."

"I won't."

Her mother sighs and murmurs something to herself. Rose runs a finger along the golden dots decorating the edge of her teacup. They are raised, tiny bumps.

"So you don't remember who has cups with butterflies on them?"

"Ask your dad, the one with the excellent powers of observation."

Ahmed shakes his head. "No one I know of."

Rose wonders where Gameela acquired that one cup of fine china, old and certainly used, its edge marred by a minuscule chip, its rim decorated with yellow butterflies. Her memory of the various things she confiscated during the night is so vague that she suspects she may have dreamed the cup up, but then she remembers how it was wrapped in tissue paper and placed in a cardboard box up in the corner of the armoire, and she doubts she could have imagined such details. Now Rose sees Gameela carefully tucking that box out of reach, and she feels a tenderness toward the cup, and, inexplicably, toward all fine china. Slowly, she lowers the chair, places her cup on its saucer on the tray.

A car honks, and Rose gets up and steps to the railing, looks at the cars crammed in the narrow, two-lane road below, at the Nile ahead with its traffic of sailing boats and floating restaurants, at the crowded bridge visible in the distance to her left, at the high-rises on the other bank. Once, when they first met, Mark took her on a boat ride down the Nile, and when she told him of the saying that claims those who drink from the Nile's water are destined to return to Egypt, he reached out of the small sailboat and scooped a handful of water, gulping it down despite her protests that the saying referred to purified, not raw, Nile water, and that he will now certainly die of dysentery. Resting her elbows on the flat, wrought-iron handrail, her fingers laced, Rose looks at the water flowing below and thinks not only of Mark, but also of Osiris, the ancient Egyptian god whose brother, Seth, trapped him in a coffin, nailed it shut, and sent it floating down that same river. Osiris's sister and wife, Isis, sought her betrayed husband, found him, only to see Seth kill him again, this time hacking him into fourteen pieces and sending the parts floating to each of ancient Egypt's provinces. Isis, faithful sister, faithful wife, roamed Egypt collecting Osiris's dismembered body, sewed him together, and brought him back to life. With Isis by his side, Osiris went on to reign as god of the underworld, of resurrection, as the ultimate judge of the dead.

Rose sees herself as both Seth and Isis, killer and redeemer. She imagines that by collecting Gameela's things she will put her sister together again and then instate her as queen of the underworld, empress of resurrection. She imagines Gameela whole again.

2

R ose insists that Mark does not meet her at the airport. She texts him
from London during her layover, repeats that meeting her would be
irrational. Her plane is delayed—a computer glitch is grounding all
flights—and she will most likely arrive in New York early the next morning. He must leave work if he is to meet her, which is foolish.

> I'm not a child. I can find my way home.

She stares at her phone's screen, the three quivering dots indicating that
her husband is typing something.

> I know you can. Not a matter of ability.

She waits to see if he will add anything. He does not.

> I'm exhausted. I'm going straight to bed once I'm
> home. I'll call you when I get there.

She clicks SEND and waits. The three dots appear, waver, and then disappear. He doesn't write back, and she tucks her phone away.

SHE IS TOO TIRED to take the subway, heads straight for the taxi line in
front of the terminal, and avoids looking around just in case Mark has

decided to come meet her against her wishes. In the cab, she glances out of the window, waits for the city's skyline, finds, as she always does, the approximate spot where she went for her PhD, the other spot where she, a year ago, started her curatorial fellowship at the Met's Egyptian Art Department. She has always had a soft spot for the Empire State Building with its concrete walls, square and heavy, like the temples of the Pharaohs, but she has fallen for One World Trade Center, too, for its facets of alternating triangles which, again, seem to her like glorious, modern pyramids. She loves that building, but it's a guilt-ridden love that she hardly allows herself because she feels that this site should evoke nothing but sorrow. She looks away.

The cab crosses the Greenpoint Avenue Bridge before dropping her off in front of the four-story apartment building where she and Mark have lived for five years. Entering, she is careful not to make too much noise lest Mrs. Kumiega, her landlady, hear her and step out to chat. Mrs. Kumiega lives on the first floor, and Rose, rather than roll her suitcase into the building, lifts it up, hauls it to the second floor, and opens her apartment's door, and closes it with the softest click.

The apartment looks the same but feels different. Rose knows that nothing physically changed, but she cannot shake off a feeling of foreignness, as if the universe she is now stepping back into were a cleverly forged copy of the one she walked out of when she left for Egypt just over a week ago. She suspects it's the jet lag, the effect of lack of sleep on her eyes, perhaps. Somehow, the colors have changed. The sun shining through the windows of the kitchen, open to the living room, is bright but cold, making the edges of the cabinets and the glass-top breakfast table glisten. The bookcases lining the walls seem more cluttered than she remembers. When she and Mark first moved in, she decided to take the right-hand side of the bookcase, he the left-hand side. They called it their East-meets-West arrangement, a visual representation of their marriage, where her books on

Egyptology, archaeology, and literature slowly blended into his books on politics and foreign affairs. The middle bay, originally featuring souvenirs of their various travels—a handmade urn from Spain; a wood carving of a cedar tree that Mark picked up in Lebanon; some figurines in the pharaonic style from Egypt; rocks from their hikes in West Virginia; a framed photo of them on the New River Gorge Bridge—has, over the years, started filling up with their books, and was now a mangle of mismatched volumes, an ambiguous territory. Rose walks up to the bookcase and runs her fingers on the edge of the books sitting on the shelves. She inhales, taking in the midday calm, the dust particles illuminated by sunrays. She is home—she knows she is home—and yet she feels out of place. Alien.

She takes Gameela's things out of the suitcase, finds a plastic bin to put them in, then walks into her bedroom where she shoves it in the closet, hiding it under a pile of sweaters. Then, dissatisfied, she pulls it out again and pushes it under the bed, concealing it behind her rolled-up yoga mat. She is exhausted but cannot fall asleep without showering first, and when she finally walks out of the shower, her hair dripping and in her underwear, she slips between the covers, pulling an eye mask over her eyes to shut out the light seeping in through the blinds. She has not called Mark, she realizes, but she is too tired to do it now. Within minutes, she has drifted away, dreaming that everywhere she goes, the walls are covered in pharaonic reliefs, images of people in profile, among them, of course, Gameela.

SHE WAKES UP TO a knock on the door. Opening her eyes, she is disoriented again and glances around her. The clock by her bed says it's past four in the afternoon. The knocking persists, soft but determined. She gets up, fishes for a pair of jeans and a T-shirt, and wobbles to the front door.

"You're back!" Mrs. Kumiega's smile spreads from ear to ear. Rose looks at the Tupperware box in her landlady's hands and smiles.

"Hey, Mrs. Kumiega. I missed you." Her voice is thick and sleepy. She clears her throat.

"I woke you up?" The statement a question; Mrs. Kumiega's eyes wide in concern.

Rose shakes her head. "Don't worry about it. I overslept. I should have been up hours ago. Please, come in."

"No, I'm not coming in. I know you're tired. But I brought you food."

"Thank you, Mrs. Kumiega. You're an angel."

They linger. Rose accepts the box her landlady hands her with one hand and holds the door open with the other. Mrs. Kumiega is short and stout, her hair a dusty blond forming a compact, curly halo around her head, and Rose, just over five feet tall and quite a few pounds heavier than she would like to be, feels she is looking at an older, whiter version of herself.

"Your parents are okay?"

"Yes. Thank you."

"I'm sorry about your sister, Rose. I'm very sorry."

Her landlady reaches one hand and touches her forearm. Rose nods. Her eyes are starting to water on cue. She is too self-aware to wipe her tears, so she tries to blink them away.

"Thank you for the food, Mrs. Kumiega. I'm quite hungry. I think I'll have some right away."

"Yes. Do that." Mrs. Kumiega's eyes shine with excitement. "I made you some golabki but I didn't use pork, just beef. It will be good for you. Make you stronger." She pumps her fists in the air, signaling the impending strength the meal will invoke. Rose looks at the cabbage rolls and nods. She wants to tell Mrs. Kumiega of the very similar Egyptian dish, different only in being a bit smaller and having more rice and less meat in the stuffing, but she remembers how much Gameela loved this dish and decides to say nothing. When Mrs. Kumiega leaves, Rose walks up to the kitchen and puts the Tupperware in the fridge for Mark.

———

ROSE CHECKS HER PHONE for messages from Mark, finds several as well as two missed calls. She texts him back.

> Sorry. Was asleep and had the phone on silent.
> When will you be home?

Immediately, he replies.

> Trying to get out of here as soon as possible. Have
> to finish editing an article for online publication
> tonight then will go. Probably need another hour.

She looks at the clock, estimates that she has close to two hours. She heads to the bedroom and pulls out the bin, lifts it up to her bed, and sits down next to it.

Carefully, she pulls the items out one by one and sorts them into stacks, divided by category: photos, documents, books, clothing, jewelry, miscellaneous. The items cover up half the surface of her bed. When she is done sorting them out, she walks over to the kitchen for Ziploc bags and a marker, then returns and puts the smaller items into bags and labels them with the location she found them in and a serial number. Rose's desk stands in the corner of her bedroom, and from there she grabs a notebook and starts labeling the pages, each with a number corresponding to a bag, and jotting down notes: *That's the necklace she bought at Khan El-Khalili that time we went there in high school. This stack of photos is probably work related: construction sites, dug up trenches, and freshly poured cement. That stack is personal, probably with friends or colleagues, a few at the offices of the construction company, a few at a restaurant (where?).* As she writes, she becomes increasingly aware of the triviality of some of the items she picked out: *A pink T-shirt with "All you need is love" stamped on it in black cursive font.* What did she think such an item will tell her? She picks the T-shirt up, lifts it to her nose, and sniffs it—it smells of laundry detergent, soft but impersonal. She puts it back on the bed. A couple of the items are her own and thus further complicate the sorting: her old, frayed book on ancient Egypt, the one she bought as a child and has kept because it marked the beginning of her fascination with this subject; the necklace with the turquoise stone; a photo album with snapshots of a high school trip to Upper Egypt. She puts the necklace on but leaves the book and photo album with Gameela's things. Her sorting system is already flawed, marred by cross contamination, but she still goes through with her work, the monotony of jotting down and labeling soothing. Whenever she is done with an item, she returns it to the plastic bin—larger items on the bottom, smaller ones on top, everything in its place.

ROSE IS HALFWAY through unpacking when Mark arrives. She hears him open the door, hears his muffled footsteps on the carpet, but does not stop. Her suitcase is on the floor in their bedroom; Gameela's things are tucked under the bed again.

"Hey." Mark walks over and hugs her. She averts her eyes until the last minute, when he is standing right next to her, then she looks up and makes herself smile.

"I missed you," he says.

She lets him hug her and says nothing.

"How was your flight back?"

"Okay. Hate the delays, but otherwise fine."

He sits on the bed. She is aware of his eyes as she picks up her pajamas and puts them in the laundry bin, as she plugs the phone's charging cord back into the wall by her bedside table, as she pulls a pair of shoes out of the plastic bag she had packed them in and puts them on the shoe rack in the closet.

"How are your parents holding up?"

"As well as you'd expect." She pulls a couple of T-shirts out of the suitcase, can't remember whether they are washed or soiled, and tosses them in the laundry bin just in case.

"I'm glad you got to spend time with them. I'm sure you all needed it."

"Yes."

"Nothing new here. Ingrid called to check on me, which was nice. She and Ted wanted to take me out for dinner, but I said I'd rather wait till you're back so that we can all go out together."

Rose nods.

"She asked when you'd be back at work. I told her probably as soon as you arrive," he laughs a soft, low laugh.

"Yes. I'm going back tomorrow."

"That's what I thought."

She glances at him and sees him sitting with his head bent down, his elbows on his knees, staring at the floor. He is trying to make small talk, which is entirely out of character, and Rose almost feels sorry for him, starts to take a step his way, considers giving him a hug, but then she remembers her mother, sitting out on the balcony, fingers laced on her stomach, head thrown back, silent, all delicate joints and skinny limbs, and her sympathy for her mother floods over any sympathy she might feel for her husband. She remains in place.

She looks back at her opened suitcase, checks pockets for forgotten items, but the suitcase is empty now. She doesn't know what to do next. Finally, she zips it closed and tries to slide it under the bed, careful not to disturb her bin. The suitcase's top gets caught on the sideboard.

"Let me help you." Mark gets up.

"No. I've got it." She gives the suitcase a final shove and it slides in so suddenly that Rose hits her face nose-first on the bed's wooden sideboard.

"Ouch!" she yelps.

She leans back and holds her nose, which stings with a sharp pain that strangely comforts her. She doesn't try to hold her tears back.

"Let me look." Mark is sitting on the floor next to her, trying to pry her hand open.

"I'm fine," she lies.

"Just let me see."

"I said I was fine, Mark!"

She jumps up and heads to the bathroom, closing the door behind her. In the mirror, she sees that her eyes are shot red, her nose is equally red and bleeding. She runs the water and splashes her face, notices her hands trembling, and holds them under the water, examining them, marveling at the tiny tremors. Her hands will not stop shaking. She looks back up at her nose, still dripping blood, then at the dots of blood as they turn the water in the sink a variegated pink.

"Rose. Open the door, honey. Let me look at you."

She tilts her head back, pinches her nose, waits. On the other side of the door, she can feel her husband waiting, too. When she finally walks out, Mark holds her face in both hands, and she lets him do it. He seems so concerned for her safety that she is afraid she'll start crying again. His fingers are probing her face, gently pressing on her nose. Just two weeks ago, she would have found this funny. Endearing. She would have joked with him about it. Now she cannot joke, but she still caves under his touch. She reminds herself of how angry she is with him, but her mind seems indifferent. All she can think of is her husband's fingers touching her face.

"It's okay."

"I think you broke your nose."

"No, I didn't. It always bleeds when I hit it. You know that." She wiggles free and walks away from him.

"Let me take you to the ER to check it out anyway."

"No." She walks up to the fridge, pulls the Tupperware box with the cabbage rolls out. "Mrs. Kumiega made us some golabki."

For a moment, she is disoriented again, the mixture of the English she speaks, the Polish names thrown in, and the Arabic words in her head dizzying. She stands in place, the Tupperware in her hands, and it takes her a second to remember what she was doing. Carefully, she picks the cabbage rolls up, one by one, and places them in a casserole before pouring the sauce on top of them, covering the dish with foil, and putting it in the oven. The glass door shows the reflection of her husband standing behind her, his hands on his hips. His reflection is looking her in the eyes, mirrored in the oven's door, but she doesn't turn around.

شركة المقاولون المتحدون

إخطار بالموافقة على طلب الاستقالة

٢٩ مارس ٢٠١٦

المهندسة/ جميلة جبران،

تحية طيبة وبعد،

إشارة الى الطلب الذي قدمتموه بتاريخ ٢٢ مارس ٢٠١٦، والذي تطلبون فيه الاستقالة من منصبكم، نود أن نبلغكم أن السيد المدير العام/ المهندس أحمد المصري قد قرر الموافقة على طلب استقالتكم من العمل اعتبارا من تاريخه. على أن يتم التنسيق مع مدير قسمكم المهندس/ سامي البيومي لإصدار إخلاء طرف رسمي والقيام بمحضر استلام لجميع ما بعهدتكم من المتعلقات الخاصة بالعمل.

ونود أن نتقدم اليكم بخالص الشكر على ما بذلتموه من جهد طوال فترة عملكم في شركة المقاولين المتحدين. مع تمنياتنا لكم بدوام التوفيق والنجاح.

وتفضلوا بقبول فائق الاحترام،

مها العطار
قسم شئون العاملين

نسخة:
- المحاسبة
- الضمان الاجتماعي

THE NATIONAL CONTRACTORS

Notice of Approval of Resignation

29 March 2016

Engineer/Gameela Gubran

Greetings,

In response to your request dated 22 March 2016, in which you ask to resign your post, we would like to inform you that the general manager, Engineer Ahmed Elmasry, has decided to grant your request for resignation starting the date of this notice. Please arrange with the director of your division, Engineer Samy Bayoumi, to issue an official severance form and a record of receipt of all the company's belongings that are in your possession.

    We would like to extend our deepest thanks to you for your efforts throughout your employment time with The National Contractors.

With our best wishes for continued success.

Respectfully,
Maha Elattar

Employee Affairs
cc: Accounting; Social Security

3

The room Rose works in at the Met is saturated with odors of old wood and dry stone, which she believes is exactly how time smells. When she walks in, she doesn't take her jacket off. She knows the room is colder than most of the other sections of the museum, and she dislikes the cold, the way it pinches at her skin and makes her hands flake. Whenever she can, she keeps her hands tucked inside her pockets, warm against the fleece lining.

Dr. Winkenstein, one of the curators at the museum, is Rose's supervisor. She has been granted a postdoctoral fellowship so that she can assist him in preparing for a new exhibit on ancient Egypt, set to be launched in two years. Rose, sitting at her desk in the center of the room, looks at a sticky note she has tacked to her computer screen: The Daily Life of Ancient Egyptians. The exhibit is to focus on regular people, not on the Pharaohs who could afford to build monuments and commission sculptures to immortalize them. Rose's job is to help pick out artifacts that, when brought together, can depict the lives of the poor, silent masses, the ones who were not mummified and buried with golden slippers and gilded furniture, but who quietly slipped out of life leaving everyday artifacts behind: clay pots, folding stools, amulets on leather strings. This, she knows, is what inspired her to collect Gameela's things.

In the pocket of her jacket, Rose carries the severance letter she found among Gameela's unopened mail. The letter was one of several she had put in a Ziploc bag yesterday and sifted through this morning as she ate her breakfast, after Mark left for work. Now she fingers the letter and tries not to think of why Gameela quit her job and why her parents never mentioned it. She pulls her hand out of her pocket and attempts to focus on work.

She flips through a large folio containing reproductions of various papyri as well as images of wall engravings standing half the world away, inside some of Egypt's many pyramids, temples, and tombs. Before she took a week's break to go to Egypt, Rose had been immersed in studying the Met's own massive collection, figuring out ways to pull some pieces out and fit them into the new exhibit. She likes the idea of arranging pieces in new ways and listening to the stories they tell. Inanimate objects do speak, as she once told her father when he asked about her work cataloging artifacts, if they are only given a chance to do so.

The objects now speaking to Rose are bowls engraved with letters to the dead. The twin bowls are in a museum in London, and she wonders if the Met can arrange to borrow them for the duration of the exhibit, assuming that Dr. Winkenstein will approve including them. With less than twenty such letters to the dead discovered, and at least one of them destroyed during World War II, he may not want to pay attention to that particular Egyptian ritual—the act of writing to the dead spirits of recently deceased relatives in order to ask them to intervene on the living person's behalf. Rose herself had not thought of that until she was flying back from Egypt, when, half asleep and looking out the window just as the sun was rising and the clouds were gleaming in yellow and orange hues, she thought of the East and the West and remembered a line out of one of those letters:

> *A communication by Merirtyfy to Nebetiotef:*
> *How are you? Is the West taking care of you as you desire?*

The West, for ancient Egyptians, was the direction of the setting sun and, by extension, the land of the dead. Rose used to tease Mark about how ancient Egyptians associated the West with death, called the dead "the Westerners," placed their burial grounds on the west bank of the Nile and lived on the east bank. On the plane heading home, Rose had thought that she could include a couple of letters to the dead in the exhibit, demonstrating that ancient Egyptians believed in life after death and showing proof of the layperson's attempts at communicating with the spirits of loved ones. The imploring nature of the letters (the writer always had a favor to ask of his deceased relative) would shed light on a practical side of ancient Egyptian religion and ritual. It would tie the myth to solid life. Up in the sky crossing over the Atlantic, Rose was certain this would be a good addition to the exhibit.

Now, in the cold, crisp museum office, she is not sure anymore. Dr. Winkenstein is away at an expedition site in Upper Egypt and will not be back until mid-October. Rose emails him weekly with her progress, but she is reluctant to ask about the letters to the dead. She teeters between thinking the idea is brilliant and absurd. She imagines Dr. Winkenstein's possible reactions: He could reach up and hold his chin in the nook between his thumb and pointer, start kneading it, and then look down, scanning the floor, perhaps, for the reason why he had agreed to hire an imbecile such as her. Or he could start nodding as he reads her email, his eyes twinkling behind his rimless glasses, his bob of gray hair bouncing in that endearing way that always tempts her to reach out and touch his curls, an indiscretion that she has repeatedly struggled to resist. It could go either way.

In Dr. Winkenstein's absence, the only person Rose is comfortable enough to discuss this with is Ingrid. That morning, Rose had arrived at work and walked straight into Ingrid's open arms, staying there for as long as her friend held on to her.

"You're good?" Ingrid had finally asked, pushing Rose away but keeping both hands on her shoulders, looking her up and down as if in search of visible signs of affliction.

"Yes," Rose had lied, nodding.

Ingrid had narrowed her eyes, paused for a moment as if about to say something, then had given Rose a quick pat on the shoulder before walking back to her desk.

Rose looks up at Ingrid, staring at her computer screen with concentration so absolute that Rose is sure that if the statue of Amenhotep III were to walk into the room asking for directions to Egypt, Ingrid would either shush it or wave in the general direction of the East without lifting her eyes from the screen. Rose met Ingrid five years earlier at Columbia, where they were both getting their PhDs, Ingrid one year ahead of Rose. On the first day they met, Rose was sitting in the cafeteria when Ingrid, seated at the table next to her, knocked her coffee down all over her notebook and cursed, quite loudly, in German. Rose, who graduated from a German school in Egypt, had laughed out loud. They bonded over their mutual tendency to mumble *Scheiße* when frustrated.

Rose considers asking Ingrid about the merit of including the letters to the dead but decides not to interrupt her friend's work. She picks up a book instead.

Flipping through the pages, she finds another letter, this time from a man to his dead wife, written on papyrus:

> To the able spirit Ankhiry: What have I done against you
> wrongfully for you to get into this evil disposition in which you
> are? What have I done against you? As for what you have done,
> it is your laying hands upon me though I committed no wrong
> against you. From the time that I was living with you as a
> husband until today, what have I done against you that I should
> have to conceal it?

Rose reads the rest of the letter, brows knotted. The man is blaming his dead wife for some illness that has befallen him. Rose considers what this implies about ancient Egyptian daily life: a belief in the afterlife, of course;

a way of communicating with the dead; but also a belief in the influence that loved ones, long deceased, can still have on their living relatives.

If she focuses on how the living reach out to the dead, she could present this as a way ancient Egyptian culture held on to family relationships even after death.

If she focuses on how some of those letters ask the deceased for help, she could present this as a way of seeing the dead person as a savior, a pathway to greater powers, an ally with divine connections.

If she focuses on the way a letter such as this one blames the deceased for the evil that befalls the living, the deceased becomes a force to fear.

Three different narratives. But which one is true?

Now look, the man writes to his wife, *you don't differentiate good from evil.*

ROSE WAITS FOR lunchtime then walks out of the Met and straight to Central Park. She calls her parents.

"Fayrouz, *habibti*," her dad answers. "Back at work?"

Rose smiles at the sound of her old name, now permanently tinged with nostalgia. "Hey, Baba. Yes. Is this a good time to talk?"

"Of course. I'm making tea and heading over to the balcony. Your mom is already there. Just give me a minute."

Rose walks up to the first available bench, sits down in the shade of a tree. Around her, people are jogging, walking, or relaxing in the sun. One mother struggles with a crying toddler and, with obvious exasperation, parks her jogging stroller in front of a bench across the walkway, pulls her son out of the stroller, and sets him on the ground. Rose watches the boy sit up, look around, then start crawling while his mother hovers over him. For five years after she got married, Rose had imagined she would start a family after earning her degree; by then, she would be thirty-one—a perfect age to have two babies before she hit thirty-five. She had always liked to plan her life in advance, figure out when she will do what. She earned her PhD just over a year ago; turned thirty-two a few months later. She watches the crawling baby, thinks of Gameela, then of her parents, then looks away.

"Rose—you're on speakerphone now. Your mom is here."

"*Ezzayek ya Rose?*" her mom asks. *How are you, Rose?*

"Okay, Mama. I'm on my lunch break."

"Good. And how's Mark doing?" her dad asks.

"Okay." Rose looks at her watch—she is already ten minutes into her lunch hour. "Listen, Baba," she swallows, "I have a question." She regrets not having asked her father while he was alone in the kitchen, rather than wait till her mother can hear her. Too late now. "One of my colleagues wants to send out an email to the department telling them about Gameela." She chokes on her lie, coughs. "He asked what her job title was."

"Engineer at the National Contractors," her father answers.

"Explain to them who the National Contractors are," her mother adds. "Tell them it's one of the largest construction companies in Egypt."

"Yes," Rose says. She hesitates. "So she was still working for them?"

"Of course!" her mom answers.

Rose does not know how to proceed. She had thought up the question as a subtle way to inquire into Gameela's employment status, but had not expected her parents to know nothing about her sister's resignation.

"I just wasn't sure, so I thought I'd ask. I hadn't spoken to her about her work in a long time." She hadn't spoken to her sister about anything in a long time. She unbuckles her water bottle from the strap of her backpack, takes a sip.

"She was doing really well there," her father goes on. "They even started sending her on trips out of the city, to a new construction site they had in Rasheed."

"Oh," Rose says. "So she used to travel?"

"At least once a week for the previous four or five months, yes. You didn't know?" he asks.

Rose counts the months backward on her fingers, starting with August. Five months lands her in April—immediately after Gameela quit her job.

"No, Baba." Rose contemplates the variety of things neither she nor her parents know. "I didn't know."

On her way back to the office, Rose stops at a clearing, finds a shady patch of grass under a sprawling red maple, and lies down, looking up at the leaves. She knows she has skipped lunch and that her stomach will reprimand her for it by the end of the day, but she cannot fathom eating. Far above, the leaves occasionally rustle, shivering with a sudden gust of wind and then falling still again. Rose watches them: movement then stillness, movement then stillness.

She wishes she could fall asleep right now, right here.

Because she does not want to think about the phone call to her parents, she tries to think about work. Letters to the Dead, Bridges to the Afterlife. Perhaps she can expand on this idea and include other texts that tie the living to the dead. She thinks of magic spells engraved on the inside of coffin lids—spells to transform the dead person into a falcon; spells to open the gates to heaven.

The forty-two negative confessions, supposedly uttered at the Weighing of the Heart ceremony—the ancient Egyptian equivalent of Judgment Day—to declare one's heart free of malice and suitable for an eternity in the afterlife.

> *I have not caused pain.*
> *I have not caused weeping.*
> *I have not killed.*
> *I have not commanded to kill.*
> *I have not made suffering for anyone.*

Forty-two declarations of innocence of different transgressions, from lying to blasphemy to murder, from mistreating orphans to defrauding people, some even proclaiming that one has not harmed cattle or birds or fish. An almost hysterical insistence on having lived a guiltless life, all leading up to the last assertion:

I am pure, I am pure, I am pure, I am pure!

The right words, uttered at the right time, to produce a desired effect. Rose has always found this longing to be pure fascinating, has imagined people who lived thousands of years ago uttering that last line with desperate vehemence, probably hoping that if they believed in their own goodness, the gods would believe in it, too. As if declaring one's innocence were enough to will such innocence into existence.

She can still get excited about the prospect of work, and her excitement, now creeping up on her—so much she can do with texts linking the living to the dead, so many applications—makes her feel guilty.

Thinking of ancient Egyptian coffins and spells evokes her dream of the day before: the walls covered in profiles of people, including Gameela. Ancient Egyptians carved depictions of their daily lives on the walls of their tombs so that the soul of the deceased could remember how she lived in this world and continue the same lifestyle in the netherworld. Up until a few weeks ago, Rose would have thought it was easy enough to pick out a few scenes to represent each phase of Gameela's life: Gameela the child, playing the piano; Gameela the teenager, her hair long and curly, wearing her uniform of blue jeans, a graphic T-shirt, and sneakers; Gameela the college student, with that same hair covered under a head scarf; Gameela the engineer, the aspiring botanist, the devourer of mystery novels and TV series, the lover of mangoes and guavas, the participant in revolutions, the advocate for social justice, the defender of religion.

Gameela the idealist. The ideal. Gameela, who always played by the rules. Rose remembers the words of a cousin who visited her at her parents' apartment to offer her condolences: *Who would have thought something like this would happen to Gameela, of all people?* As if dying in a terrorist attack was a choice one made, and Gameela, by making that choice, had acted out of character.

Rose reaches into her pocket and pulls out the severance letter, reads it one more time.

Why did Gameela quit her job? Why did she tell no one? Where was she traveling to?

Rose holds the letter up in front of her face. The sunlight shines through it, merges the words on the front of the page with shadows of the tree above, and the distorted words evoke an ancient language, not Egyptian, but Sanskrit, perhaps, or ancient Greek.

Rose drops her hand.

Above her, the leaves rustle again, and she wishes they would all fall, rain gently down on her, bury her, hide her from sight for millennia, until some anthropologist finds her, digs her up, examines her bones, and, perhaps, theorizes about her life and death, publishes a narrative in a magazine where people can read her story and pretend to understand something about her.

For now, she watches, waits, and hopes for a rainfall of leaves.

4

Rose walks out of work half an hour later than usual and finds Mark sitting on the Met's front steps, munching on a hot dog. He does not notice her until she is standing beside him, casting a cooling shadow his way.

"The plan was to take you out to dinner," Mark says, mouth half full.

"How many hot dogs ago did that plan fizzle out?" Rose smiles.

"Three, but I'm still hungry. I'm sure I'll manage to eat some more." He gets up, shoves the remainder of the bun into his mouth.

"Now you've made me hungry for hot dogs, too."

She heads to the food cart parked at the foot of the steps and joins the line of three people waiting to be served. The man working the cart is new; he must have started while Rose was in Egypt. Rose takes one look at him and immediately recognizes a fellow Egyptian. She scans the cart, notices the trinkets hanging all around it: a framed verse of the Qur'an; a blue glass ornament to ward off the evil eye; a string of prayer beads; a photo of Umm Kulthum; a postcard of the pyramids. He is using disposable gloves, carefully picking up each hot dog with a pair of tongs and placing it in the opened bun. She has already made it to the front of the line when Mark joins her.

"Rose, let me introduce you to Safwan," Mark says, a palm extended toward the vendor. "Guess where he's from?"

Rose glares at Mark, but he doesn't get the hint. "Egypt!" he says, excited, joyful.

Rose looks at Safwan and nods.

He nods back at her, smiling. "So you're Egyptian, too?" he asks Rose.

"*Aywah*," Rose replies.

The man nods again but does not make eye contact with her. His face is flushed, but it could be the effect of the heat. Rose watches him turn the hot dogs around on the warmer, pick one up and place it carefully in a fresh bun.

"Safwan kept me company while I was waiting for you," Mark says. "Do you know he just arrived here from Egypt?"

Rose smiles, takes the hot dog Safwan hands her. "That's great. Thank you. Good luck," she tells Safwan, pulling Mark away.

For a couple of blocks, they remain silent, Rose eating as she walks next to Mark, who keeps his hands in his pockets and his eyes focused on the ground in front of his feet. The afternoon is not too hot, yet Rose starts to sweat. The light jacket that was barely keeping her warm at the office smothers her.

She stops. "Hold this for a second, will you?" She hands Mark her hot dog.

She takes her jacket off. Gameela's letter of severance is zipped up in the inside pocket. Carefully, Rose folds the fabric around it, making sure it does not get bent, then puts the jacket in her backpack.

"How come you didn't want to chat with Safwan?" Mark asks.

She takes her hot dog back, bites into it, and feels a dot of ketchup on the side of her mouth. She wipes it off with a napkin. "I didn't want to embarrass him."

"Why on earth would he have been embarrassed to talk to you?"

Rose huffs. "He speaks English with no accent, he is wearing food-handling gloves, and he is new here. What does this tell you, Mark?" She gives him a second to think about it but does not wait for his answer. "It means he learned English as a child, which means he went to a private school, which means he is middle class in Egypt. The food-handling gloves also imply that—no street vendor in Egypt stands on such technicalities;

you *know* that. Which means the man is probably college educated. He could be an engineer or an accountant or a doctor working to support himself while he tries to find a residency position. Definitely not someone used to serving others. Here, among Americans, it doesn't matter. Any work is honorable work. Once he faces a fellow Egyptian, a woman, too, someone who obviously has a better job than he does, he will definitely be embarrassed to be seen selling food out on the street." She takes another bite and resumes walking.

"That's just a load of crap. The man chatted with me for a good half hour while I was waiting for you and was perfectly friendly. Seemed excited to be talking about Egypt. He was very happy to know I lived there before."

"That's just what I'm saying: He'd be happy to talk to *you*, an American showing positive interest in his country and thereby stroking his ego. But he wouldn't want to talk to *me*. I would only remind him of how he is stuck doing a job he would never be caught dead doing in Egypt."

"That makes no sense. You're just superimposing your own anxieties on a stranger who, for all we know, thinks nothing of all that classist crap."

"Everyone in Egypt has that classist crap conditioned into them." Rose stops walking for emphasis. "How can you not know that, after living there for four years?"

"Everyone you know, perhaps. All your uppity, private-school-educated, multilingual friends who think they are better than everyone else." He does a little head shake that always accompanies his sarcastic statements, a side-to-side bobble-head effect that, right now, infuriates Rose.

"Oh. And you, public-school-educated West Virginia native, do not think you're better than everyone else?"

"Of course I don't!"

"Have you even read your own articles?"

"What's my work have to do with this?"

"Everything!" She is shouting now. A young woman in a suit and heels passing by glances at her. Rose glares at the woman, who speeds up her pace. Stepping up to a trash can, Rose tosses the last of the hot dog in it with such force it lands with a thud. "You take moral stands with such ease. You write about things like you can clearly see who is right and who is wrong. Don't you think that's just a bit of a superior attitude? Passing judgment on people like that all the time?"

"This is about Gameela, isn't it?" Mark stands in front of her, arms crossed. They are blocking the sidewalk, and people are streaming around them, diverging before them and converging again after they pass.

"It's not about Gameela." Hearing and then saying her sister's name makes Rose's heart race. She clenches her teeth and frowns at Mark.

"You never used to criticize my work before. Now suddenly my writing implies I think I'm better than everyone else. You bet it's about your sister."

"It's about how you think you know everything."

"I didn't know the boy would blow himself up."

"I know you didn't."

"And yet you blame me. You act like I'm the one who killed your sister."

A man passing by falters, glances at them, and then hurries past.

"This is not the time or place to discuss this," Rose says.

Before Mark answers, she starts walking toward the subway entrance ahead. A train pulls in just as she reaches the platform, and she hops on and walks to the end of the car. Only then does she turn around to check for Mark. He gets in through the same door she used, looks around, sees her, but stays where he is.

She watches him as the train moves, starting with a jolt, speeding, and stopping at each station with a screech. Mark remains in place, holding on to a pole with his eyes closed. She knows what he is doing: meditating, counting his breaths, listening to the train's hypnotic rhythm. She tries to do the same, but she is never able to meditate. Every time she closes her eyes, her thoughts race, and she sees images of her sister running under her eyelids in double speed, like a movie on fast-forward.

At Court Square, they both get out to change to the G train, walking next to each other but not talking. By the time they reach Greenpoint, it's early evening. They pass by the fresh produce stands, by the Polish deli, by the coffee shop, by the park at the corner of Nassau and Russell. Usually, they would grab two coffees and head to the park, sit there for half an hour to unwind before walking home. Today Rose trots past the coffee shop, and by the time they reach the corner of their street, her step is so hurried that Mark almost sprints to keep up with her.

At the door of their apartment building, they see Mrs. Kumiega watering her geraniums.

"Lovely day, right?" the landlady asks.

"Yes, Mrs. Kumiega," Rose says, walking up the stairs and past the landlady. "Beautiful day."

SHE WALKS STRAIGHT TO the kitchen, dropping her backpack on the living-room floor on her way in. Mark follows her, closing the door behind him.

"We need to talk."

She is filling the coffee carafe with tap water to pour into the coffee machine's reservoir. Either her grip on the carafe is too strong or her hand is shaking—she ends up splashing water all around the machine. She curses under her breath, snags a kitchen towel off its hook, which is nailed to the wall at the end of the counter. The violence of her pull tears the hook clean off the wall. It falls to the floor with a clang, leaving a quarter-size hole in the wall where it used to sit. Rose looks at the wall, the towel still in her hand. Then, slowly, she walks up to the kitchen table and sits down.

Minutes pass and Rose does not talk or look Mark's way. When she finally moves, she places the towel on the table in front of her. Mark, who had been standing in the doorway separating the living room from the kitchen, walks in and picks the towel up, dries up the mess around the coffee machine, and brews a pot. In minutes, the kitchen is filled with the smell of coffee. Mark pours two cups, adds cream to both, then sets Rose's cup in front of her and takes the seat across the table.

"Thank you," she whispers, wrapping her fingers around the cup. She lifts it to her nose and inhales the rising aroma.

"It wasn't my fault, Rose."

"I didn't say it was."

She does not look up for fear of what his eyes will reveal: that she has said that it was his fault, over and over, and that they both know it. First, when Gameela went missing for two days, Mark had joined Rose in her anguish, and they had tossed theories between them, groping for reassurance that she would be found alive: *Maybe she got in an accident and is lying in a hospital somewhere, unconscious; Maybe they couldn't find her ID—it could have been damaged; Maybe she ran away with someone—it's not like her, of course, but it happens, right?* Not once did they fathom a connection between Gameela and the news they read online and casually dismissed. But the moment they learned how she had died, their status as partners in worry vanished, and Rose turned on Mark, yelling at him with all the vehemence of her grief and anger. *She would not have died if not for you and your interviews, your articles, your obsession with meddling. Why did you have to bring her along? Why did you have to drag my sister into your work?* Useless, back then, for him to repeat that Gameela was the one who introduced him to the boy he interviewed. Useless to insist that no one could have predicted what happened next.

"But you're still acting like it's my fault," Mark says. "You're angry with me. You just fought with me because I wanted to chat with a vendor. Don't tell me that was all about the poor guy's feelings. And since when did my writing reveal a superiority complex?"

"I didn't mean it that way. You just write with such confidence. Just like you acted with that vendor. Like you know how he feels and what he is thinking."

"And that's a bad thing?"

"No, but it can be simplistic. People's stories never stand in isolation."

"Don't you think I know that?"

"You know it, yes, but on some level, you have to isolate their stories to make them fit neatly in a two-page article, don't you?"

"Please don't preach to me about my own profession, Rose."

"I'm not. I'm sorry if it came through that way." She takes a sip of coffee and lets the bitterness warm her mouth and throat. When she places the cup on the table, it anchors her hands in place and stops them from shaking. "You need to understand how monumental this whole thing has been for me."

"Of course I understand. I never—"

"Let me finish." She looks up at him and he falls silent. "I'm not only talking about losing my sister. I'm talking about . . ." She pauses, unsure how to explain. "History. I'm talking about history."

He seems puzzled but doesn't speak. She takes another moment to organize her thoughts. From where she is sitting, she can see the magnolia tree in the backyard, its branches reaching up to her kitchen window. She watches it while she speaks.

"I'm used to dealing with finished stories. That's what I do at work: I examine history after it has happened. Not just broad, cultural history, but individual history as well. The stories of Pharaohs, of kings and queens, and so on. I look at the way people lived thousands of years after their death. In a way, it makes it simpler to see things in context, even though so much remains unknown." She takes a sip of her coffee. Mark does not touch his.

"This is different," she goes on. "First, I have the problem of seeing Gameela's history cut short. It's extremely painful for me to think of her story as done. Finished." She pauses to clear her throat. "Then there is the added problem of how my own life may have affected hers. How yours may have affected hers. Because, regardless of how you both came to know that boy, the bottom line is your story intersected with hers at that point, and I keep tracing events back to this, and further back, to our marriage, and wondering how all of this influenced her life." She looks straight at him, tries to see if he has understood. She is not sure he has, but he is still listening. She pushes her coffee cup aside and puts both palms flat on the table. "This is her life," she says, pushing her left palm a few inches forward. "But it has stopped here. Now this is mine," she moves the right palm parallel to the left and lets it pass it, "and mine is still going on. And I can't stop thinking about how my own choices may have had an impact on hers."

She stops moving. Mark looks at her hands. Slowly, he holds each of her hands in his and brings them together at the center of the table. They stay still for a moment, watching their tangled mass of fingers and palms, his skin tone so much lighter than hers.

"Do you regret marrying me?" he finally asks. He is not looking at her, but his fingers are kneading hers. He brings the tip of his thumb against the tip of hers and holds them both in place, watching them.

She shakes her head. "No. I don't." She pulls her hands free and gets up, taking her coffee cup to the window, and sliding it open. She wants to explain to him that she feels the guiltiest precisely because she does not regret marrying him, but she is choked up and fears that talking will lead to tears.

It's close to sunset now. In the distance, a flock of birds takes off and flies away. Rose stays in place, leaning against the wall, looking out on the backyard. The magnolia tree stands perfectly still.

Mark moves next to her, wraps one arm around her shoulders. She rests her head on his hand but keeps looking out of the window.

"I wish I could go back in time and change things," Mark mutters. "Not write that interview, not go to Egypt, or at least refuse when she suggested taking me to that boy. But I keep telling myself that no one could have foreseen this. I certainly never did."

"I know. And yet—here we are."

Outside, a bird lands on the magnolia tree, shaking a branch and, with it, every single leaf attached to it, the bird's minuscule feet starting a shock wave that vibrates on and on, leaving hundreds of leaves trembling in its wake.

Part Two

5

Desert sand: dry, blistering hot. At this part of the Giza plateau, where archaeologists once used to dump loads of sand excavated elsewhere, unaware that they were thus burying the queen's pyramid deeper, the sand settled in layers, fine beige above coarse red, the constitution of clay embedded with white rocks. Rose, sitting on a rock in the narrow shade of one side of the five-foot-tall recently excavated pyramid base, grabbed a handful and let it filter between her fingers. A cluster the size of a dried-up date remained; she crushed it between her forefinger and thumb, watched it crumble.

"Bachelor of arts in Egyptology, American University in Cairo; followed by an MA in Egyptology and Coptology, also from the AUC, specializing in language, literature, and religion. Correct?"

Rose, startled, looked up, examining the American reporter more closely. When Tamer, her superior on the excavation team, had told her the reporter wished to interview her, Rose had assumed the American was the journalistic equivalent of small fry. Why else would he be satisfied with interviewing her, a junior archaeologist who, on paper, is supposed to be a linguist, but whose days are spent inputting data that her supervisors collect and interpret, reducing her role to that of an overqualified secretary? She had acquiesced, of course, agreeing with the same willingness she showed when asked to perform various insignificant tasks: run to the nearest stationery store to fax a form; drop off a specimen at the main office for analysis, spending half the day stuck in Cairo's perpetually congested traffic. Paying her dues in order to advance in the ranks. She had approached the waiting reporter with an apologetic nod, assuming he had asked to speak to one of the site directors and had to settle for her. The newly discovered pyramid behind them, Rose walked over ready to tell him the bare basics about the biggest archaeological discovery of 2008: that they had discovered a 4,300-year-old pyramid of an ancient Egyptian queen called Sesheshet; that her name evoked the goddess of history and writing, Seshat; that she was the mother of King Teti, a Pharaoh of the Sixth Dynasty. She had not expected him to know anything about her.

"How did you know that?"

He smiled. "Do you think I would come to interview you without knowing the most basic biographical information? I'm not that incompetent."

Rose blushed. "I didn't mean to imply any such thing. I just assumed you had wanted to talk to a member of the expedition regarding the recent discovery of the pyramid. I didn't expect you to know anything about me personally."

"I asked to interview you personally, not just any member of the expedition."

"Why me?"

"Because I need to talk to women in professions generally dominated by men."

"There are many women on site. Four of the archaeologists in charge of the Giza Plateau Mapping Project are women, for example."

"Yes, but they are foreign women. Europeans, mostly. I'm interested in Egyptian women. It's part of a piece I'm writing on sexism in Egypt."

She laughed. "That's a huge undertaking. You must be very ambitious. Or totally insane."

"A bit of both, I guess."

He sat across from her, out of the pyramid's wedge of shade, beads of sweat already forming on his temples, his hair—fine, blond—sticking to his forehead.

"What did you say your name was again?"

"Mark. Mark Hatfield."

He was wearing a white shirt and khaki shorts, both already covered with Giza's fine sand, looking like a character out of an old British movie about a group of aristocrats seeking adventure among Egypt's lost tombs. He squinted at her, the sun shining straight at his face.

"Here," she said, scooting to the side. "Share my rock."

"WHAT DREW YOU to the field of Egyptology?"

He had set a recorder on top of his backpack between them, but had still pulled out a notepad where he had written questions and where he was now jotting down notes as she spoke.

"I fell in love with the Pharaohs at a very young age, during a visit to the Egyptian Museum. I had never been that close to relics before, and I remember looking up at King Tut's mask and wondering what the writing on the back said. I became quite obsessed with it; had to learn to read hieroglyphs. Nagged my father until he got me a book on the subject. I started then and I never stopped."

She did not tell him about *The Curse of the Pharaohs*, the book she had read weeks before that visit, the nights she spent dreaming of the sordid fates and sudden deaths of many of those present at the opening of King Tut's tomb (all nonsense, she would learn much later, all medically explicable, much to her disappointment). She had wanted to decipher the hieroglyphs to see if they spelled any curses, if the Pharaohs had engraved words of protection and wrath on the young king's death mask. For weeks, she lay on the floor in her bedroom, a book opened before her, and copied the old hieroglyphs: the *f* a snake, the *a* an arm, two feathers for a *y*, the *r* shaped like parted lips, a dangling rope with a tie for a *w* or *ou* sound, a knotted rope for an *s* or a *z*. She wrote her name in hieroglyphs: Fayrouz. Rose, as she insisted people call her shortly afterward.

"Did you ever consider whether it was a career suitable for a woman based on Egyptian social norms?"

"Not really."

"Never crossed your mind? Not even when you got older?"

Rose shrugged. "Women have taken part in excavations for decades. Even this very team has two Egyptian women other than me; both just happen to be out of the country this week. That's why I'm the only woman working here now."

"It's still a profession that many people here would argue women can't do, isn't it?"

"I wasn't brought up to think of what I can or cannot do, just what I should or shouldn't do."

He looked at her, a bit puzzled, a bit surprised. She smiled, reassuring him, holding back one piece of information: how a German teacher at her elementary school, in an ongoing attempt to teach his students German grammar, had stressed the difference between *should* and *must: Man muss nur sterben.* The only thing one *must* do is die. The implication: everything else is a choice. And never use *must* when you mean *should.* Now, sitting in the blazing sun with an American journalist interested in Egyptian women and their relationship to freedom, Rose didn't want to credit a European with her most poignant revelation regarding what one must do versus what one can do. She hoped that, in her silence, he would assume that her parents had taught her that. To their credit, they had not objected when she had adopted this as her mantra. *The only thing one* must *do is die.*

"Did you face any opposition to your choice of studying Egyptology? From family or friends?"

He was sweating profusely now, and Rose, seeing one of the field-workers pass close by, signaled to him for two bottles of cold water, which he promptly pulled out of a cooler and brought over. She allowed Mark a minute to drink before she answered his question.

"My parents' only concern was financial profitability, which has nothing to do with sexism. In fact, it would have been sexist if they hadn't minded the income problem—it would have implied that they assumed I was bound for marriage and didn't need to provide for myself. But they did not; they hoped I'd be able to support myself. They would much rather have seen me become an engineer or a doctor."

He smiled. "Did they ever get over the disappointment?"

She stretched her lips in a dry smile. "My younger sister is studying to become an engineer. I let her handle the parent-pleasing department. She's better at it than I am."

She took a sip from her water bottle, looking away from him. She hoped he didn't think her last remark sounded bitter.

"How did you come to be on this excavation team?"

Evening at her parents'. Rose sitting in the corner of the sofa, shrinking into the fabric. Ahead of her, one of her mother's many acquaintances: Aunt Somayyah, sister-in-law to the minister of antiquities.

"Rose graduated top of her class at the American University in Cairo," Nora said as she handed her guest a cup of tea, placed three petits fours on a plate. "She can get a wonderful teaching position at the university, if she wants to. But she has her heart set on doing fieldwork. Cannot fathom why days in the burning sun would be preferable to a nice, secure, comfortable university position—but what can I do? The girl is stubborn. I keep telling her the sun will ruin her complexion and she will shrivel by the time she is forty, but there is no dissuading her. So I gave in and told her I'll talk to you, Soma *habibti*. Maybe there is somehow you can intervene on her behalf. I know I'm asking too much, but if you do me this favor, I will owe you for eternity."

Aunt Somayyah, plump, her hair coiffed in a large mass around her face, dyed a reddish blond, her hands weighed down by seven golden rings (Rose counted), smiled at Rose and then bit at a petit four. Rose smiled back, her face (which would age prematurely, according to her mother) painfully stretched. She glanced at the version of her mother sitting across from her, the one who cared about shriveling skin and who surfaced only in the company of women like Aunt Somayyah, the version so different from the Nora who refused to dye her hair and who was happiest sitting down with a book or magazine. Her mother made eye contact with her, gave her a stern look, and Rose looked down at the coffee table, concentrated on examining the motifs on her mother's fine china, golden droplets decorating the edge of the teacup, droplets that, soon enough, Aunt Somayyah partially covered with her lips as she sipped at the tea, its hot steam rising between Rose and her.

Rose brushed away the memory, focusing on the American. "I applied directly to the Office of the Minister of Antiquities for any opening on his various field endeavors, precisely the ones concerning the Middle Kingdom, since the literature of that particular era interests me tremendously. I think, at the end of the day, I haunted his staff so much that they offered me an unpaid internship." She laughed nervously; Mark smiled at her. "Old Kingdom, not Middle Kingdom, but I took whatever I was offered. I clung to this internship like my life depended on it, worked twelve-hour days, did everything I was asked to do and then some. At the end of eight months, one of his junior assistants quit—he was offered a position in Germany—and I got his job."

She paused. Mark looked down at his notepad, flipped the page. The small recorder he had placed between them was still running, but Mark continued to take notes anyway. Rose peered at his penmanship—large, rounded letters, open, confident. Honest. The penmanship of someone who doesn't have a lot to hide.

"Also: my mom knew someone who put in a good word for me to get that internship in the first place," Rose added, her voice softer than she had intended. Mark lifted his eyes from his notebook and nodded. When his article came out, it did not mention her mom's friend.

"How about your superiors here? What kind of responsibilities do they charge you with? Do you think you are treated differently than your male colleagues?"

Does she tell him that she is careful not to bend down in front of them?

Because, if they were behind her, she would expose her rear, and if they were in front, they might glance down her top? So she squats whenever she wishes to pick something up, keeping her knees close together, a picture of modesty.

Does she tell him about the male colleague who, just the previous week, had tried to explain her own field to her? The running jokes about how she, at twenty-five, is already a spinster? Rose glanced behind her, saw her immediate supervisor standing a few feet away.

"No. I don't think I'm treated differently. I'm not asked to carry heavy stuff around, but other than that, no."

She took a big gulp of water to wash down the lie, telling herself it's a matter of national pride. As the saying goes, we do not air our dirty laundry in front of strangers. If the American was preparing to depict the treatment of women in Egypt in a negative light, she, for one, was not going to help him.

"How come you're writing about sexism in Egypt? Why this subject matter?"

"It's very interesting, I think." He placed the cap back on his ballpoint pen, clipped it to his notepad. Rose wasn't sure if he was done asking questions, or if he was only taking a break to answer hers. "I've been living in Egypt for two years now, and I've come across many women who are strong willed, independent, and active. And yet . . ." He paused, the familiar, I'm-not-sure-if-I'm-going-to-offend-you pause that Rose knew from her dealings with so many Westerners. "They seem willing to take more than you'd expect of such strong women. Many of them seem okay with the subordinate position society has given them, regardless of their professional posts. I'm talking of powerful women, lawyers, for instance, whom I've interviewed and who had to glance at their watches nervously because they had to make it home in time to prepare dinner before their husbands arrived from work. Or doctors who laughed when I asked how come their husbands didn't help with the housework. It seems that Egyptian ideas of what women should and shouldn't do differ from Western ideas, even when it comes to those women who are considered liberated here." He ticked quotation marks with his fingers when he said the word "liberated." The gesture irritated Rose, rubbed a sore spot that a lifetime of dealing with condescending Westerners had created, a spot that, despite its old age, had not calloused yet. Rose remembered Herr Spaet, the German teacher who drove around Cairo taking photos of piles of trash and donkey-pulled carts and then brought the album to class, sharing it with the students. She was thirteen then.

"Did you consider that, perhaps, cultural norms are much harder to fight here than they are in the U.S.? That those women deserve more credit than you give them precisely because they manage to 'liberate' themselves"— she copied his air-ticked quotation marks—"while still performing the roles society forced on them and on those around them?"

"Of course. I didn't mean to imply the women were to blame. But don't you think a truly liberated woman should not be put under such pressures? Should not have to compromise so?"

"Everyone has to compromise. Women and men do. You're imagining an ideal situation, but reality is not always ideal."

"But it can be nudged toward being a bit more ideal, don't you think?"

"Through writing?"

"Why not?"

She shrugged. She refrained from revealing to him that his article, regardless of where it will be published, will most likely not result in a gender revolution in Egypt. She thought of her father, how he would pick up her mother's empty teacup and carry it to the kitchen, and how she, Rose, would view that as so kind of him, so considerate, how, if she saw him do it, she would rush to take it from him, carry it to the kitchen herself because it seemed like the right thing to do, because she, after all, was a woman.

She did not do the same with her mother. For some reason, the sight of Nora carrying cups to the kitchen did not offend Rose. Rose looked back at the American journalist, felt angry with him for making her notice things she would rather not.

"Do you still have questions? Because I have to get back to work." She kept her eyes on him, careful not to look away.

He flipped through his notebook again. Rose tapped one finger on the side of her water bottle.

"I have enough background information on the discovery here, so I don't need to keep you for that. But I would like to ask a couple of personal questions, if you don't mind." He looked at her, waiting for permission to proceed.

She nodded. "Sure."

"When I was researching you, I found out your given name was Fayrouz, not Rose. Is this correct? And why the change?"

"It's quite common for people to have nicknames and to go by them. Every second Mohammed you will meet actually goes by Hamada, for instance."

"Like John and Jack."

"Exactly. But my name change had to do with something I discovered as a child, when I first got interested in Egyptology. I read somewhere that every newborn in ancient Egypt had two names: a common name that everyone called him or her by, and then the *real* name, which only the mother knew and which was kept secret. They believed that casting a magic spell intended to harm anyone required the pronunciation of the person's real name, and if the name was kept secret, the person was protected against black magic. After reading that, I walked up to my parents and asked them to call me by my nickname, Rose, and not my given name, Fayrouz. I guess I hoped that, if they did it long enough, my future enemies would never be able to find out what my real name is."

Mark laughed. "And you would remain protected."

"Exactly," she nodded, smiling.

"But of course, if I publish your real name, everyone will know it."

Rose shrugged. "I stopped believing in magic after I turned fourteen."

"But you still go by Rose?"

"This part of my original plan worked: the name stuck."

Mark put the pen down again. "So the power is tied to the voicing of the name? To saying it out loud?"

"As part of a spell, yes."

"The power of words."

"The power of words, yes."

"Is that where your interest in ancient Egyptian writing and literature started?"

"Partly." Rose glanced away. In the distance, she could see the stepped Pyramid of Saqqara, built by King Djoser, the first Pharaoh to succeed in building a pyramid. To get there, he had failed two times, building structures that crumbled down on themselves or that sank into the ground. "Many of the funereal texts have an element of that: they would describe the dead man's afterlife, for example, giving details about his resurrection and favors with the gods and even his hunting and fishing trips, everything he hoped he would have in the afterlife. The implication is that if one said something out loud, it was bound to happen."

"Has that ever happened to you? Did you ever say something out loud and see it come true?"

She smiled. "I said I would become an archaeologist. I walked up to my parents and declared that at age twelve. How about you?"

He laughed. "Not yet. I did tell everyone back home that I was traveling to Egypt to dig for treasures and find an exotic, oriental wife who would dress up as Cleopatra on Halloween and have the genes to justify that."

"Was that part of your research for this article? An experiment in sexism and racism?"

The smile that had curled his lips vanished. "I was joking, of course. Sexism and racism not intended. And my friends understood that. It's just that some people find it strange that I choose to live in the Middle East. It's hard for them to understand the fascination. Usually I try to clarify how things really are, but sometimes, if I'm too tired, I just fall back on stereotypes to make it easier for them."

He cleared his throat, took a sip out of his water bottle, squinted at the pyramid in the distance. His face was already so flushed from the heat that she couldn't tell if he was blushing.

"So have you found her yet? Your Egyptian queen?" She looked him straight in the eyes.

"No. Not yet. Still single." He paused. "How about you? A husband or boyfriend?"

She watched him flip through his notepad.

"Cleopatra was Greek," she said.

He looked up, puzzled.

"Cleopatra was not of Egyptian origin. She was Greek, the last ruler of the Ptolemaic dynasty. A foreigner ruling Egypt, just like so many others. Nefertiti would probably be a better option for a Halloween costume, if you're interested in authenticity."

He nodded, wrote something down in his large, loopy penmanship.

"So—are you? In a relationship? You don't have to answer, of course, if you'd rather not. But it would help my interview." He spoke without looking up.

"What does this have to do with the interview?"

Mark counted the reasons on his fingers: "One: it's to complete the biographical info. Two: I'm writing about sexism, and it is therefore important to know if the man in your life is giving you a hard time regarding your career, especially considering how much travel must be involved. If you have his support or if you have to struggle at home to fulfill your ambitions."

"There is no man in my life. And if there were one and he harbored any illusions about controlling what I do with my career, he wouldn't last long anyway." The words rang true, even though she had not thought of them before. But they were true. She had broken up with two men in the previous three years, both times because they restricted her freedom, wanted to control how she dressed, whom she spoke to, where she traveled to. Her romantic experiences had taught her that she needed her freedom above all else.

"So you're free," Mark said, as if he had read her mind.

"Always, regardless of whether I'm single or not." She paused as he wrote her answer down. "Speaking of freedom, are you free for dinner, by any chance?"

Her question surprised her more than it did him. Later, she would wonder if she had simply wanted to impress him, to prove to him that Egyptian women were not as oppressed and helpless as he thought they were. She would never have asked him out if he was Egyptian, but that didn't seem to matter. An Egyptian man would have seen her forward move as a slutty approach with hidden intentions, a bait leading straight to an imaginary altar. An American, she hoped, would see just what she meant: a friendly meal out with one of the locals. A local who was female, who was not oppressed, and who was free to ask a man out to dinner without fearing the wrath of society. Perhaps this small gesture would influence his attitude once he'd sat down to write his article. She would be doing her country a service. Her motives, she assured herself, were firmly rooted in national pride.

He took his time finishing what he was writing before looking up. "Sure. If you're paying, that is."

"Of course I am. I asked you, didn't I?"

SHE DID NOT fall in love with him suddenly, like a dive in a pool, but gradually, like the way she used to waddle into the sea in Mersa Matruh as a child, taking one step at a time and pausing to marvel at the clarity of the water, to wiggle her toes and watch the sand around them cloud up, to contemplate a seashell, half buried by her feet. She may have taken her first step during that dinner, when she took him, somewhat defiantly, mean-spiritedly, she would later admit, to a sidewalk restaurant selling *koshari*. Rather than see him squirm at the grimy tables or shy away from the Egyptian carbohydrate bomb of a dish with its layers of pasta, rice, lentils, and fried onions, she watched with a considerable degree of awe as he dowsed his dish in fiery hot sauce and gulped it all up, all the while talking nonstop, seemingly more at home in these surroundings than she was. She paid for her misadventure with a night of stomach cramps and hourly bathroom runs, her intestines protesting her stubbornness in matching him fork by fork, as if they were in a competition to prove which one could embrace Egyptian food with greater enthusiasm. She had worried about him, that night. Imagined him lying in bed, sweating, twisting in pain, with no one to help him. She should have taken him to the Marriott next door to her parents' apartment, shelled out the five-hundred-pound charge to feed him USDA organic steak, imported all the way from America.

The next morning, she needed to make sure he was okay. It was both the charitable and the smart thing to do. After all, she didn't want him infusing his articles about Egypt with laments of food poisoning. Her relationship to him was that of an ambassador, a representative of her country and her people, and she had to make sure she made a positive impression. Still in bed, grateful that it was a Friday and she didn't have to go to work, she had fished his business card out of her purse, picked up her cell phone, and sent him a text message. He, of course, had been fine. He wondered if she would be willing to invite him to the exclusive Gezira Sporting Club, located near where she lived. He had never been there before, and was interested to see it. She, reminding herself of her national duty, said that she would be happy to, and then jumped out of bed and spent forty-five minutes trying on different outfits before realizing what she was doing and, in self-reprimanding defiance, donning her customary jeans and T-shirt.

In the following months, her steps into the waters of love followed steadily, stealthily. There was the way he looked at the donkey-pulled carts with their child drivers and saw not the poverty and filth her German teacher had noted, but the nobility in the genuine smile of a child forced to provide for himself and for his family. The way he devoured coal-grilled ears of corn as they walked by the Nile, and then stopped midsentence to watch a sailboat float by, his eyes gleaming with the same excitement she would later experience on first seeing New York City's skyline. She took a leap on the day he rescued a kitten to add to the two he apparently already cared for in his apartment. Driving him to the vet with the kitten dozing in a cardboard box in his lap, she had explained to him that he could not possibly save all of Cairo's stray cats, their population rivaling the 15 million inhabitants of Egypt's capital. He, in typical Markian simplicity, had agreed, but had retorted that he could rescue this one cat, and that he was going to.

Later, he would write an article on Egypt's stray cats, focusing on an elderly man called Ibrahim, whom Mark dubbed the Cat Whisperer. Mark had dug him up in Bolak, one of Cairo's poorest neighborhoods, living on the first floor of a decrepit apartment building and running a feline soup kitchen, placing dozens of plates of home-cooked rice mixed with bone broth out for the neighborhood's stray cats, feeding, according to Mark's estimate, at least four or five dozen cats daily. Ibrahim spent a good third of his income on the cats, and that earned him a glowing essay.

Mark, Rose would later find, viewed the world through a lens of impartial morality. When she was first getting to know him, she had found his moral compass fascinating, had genuinely admired his stances on society's ill treatment of the less fortunate. He had a marvelous ability to jump cultures seamlessly, to talk with the same vehemence about America's greedy capitalism as he did about Egypt's corrupt autocracy. Mark held moral stances. Fixed stances. Mark, Rose would later find out, knew what was right and what was wrong, and wrote about what he knew. Article after article came out during the months they first met, all infused with Mark's views on social justice, all focusing on personal, intimate stories that demonstrated such justice or the lack thereof. Rose would read his articles, sometimes in the hard copies he shared with her, sometimes online, and, with time, her skepticism turned into fascination as she, too, shared his conviction that writing about something could fix it, that putting words down on paper could affect history.

Mark, like the Pharaohs, believed in the power of words. That, perhaps, gave Rose the final nudge.

"MARRY ME," he said for what was perhaps the tenth time.

"You know I can't."

"Since when are you so religious?"

"I may not fit your idea of a religious Muslim woman, but that is a line even *I* can't cross."

They had finished eating dinner but were still sitting at a restaurant by the Nile, one of the small, inconspicuous nooks that Mark loved and that they had been regularly visiting for the previous nine months. Next to them, waiters cleared a table that had been occupied by a dozen raucous college students. Rose was grateful for the relative calmness their departure had allowed. Now the place was almost completely hers and Mark's, and she hoped would be for the next hour or so, allowing them to enjoy dusk and the city lights turning on before people started flooding the restaurant for a late Thursday evening dinner. Rose was always grateful for moments of calmness in the center of a sleepless city, a rare gift. They cleared her brain, allowing her to notice details that otherwise escaped her, such as the family of stray cats that now sat under an adjacent table. Rose watched the mother, an emaciated white-and-peach shorthair, groom one of her kittens.

"You know you will end up marrying me anyway, right?"

She lifted an eyebrow, glared at his cocky smile. He was right, of course, but she was not ready to admit that.

"You know I literally *cannot* marry you, right? I'm legally *not allowed* to marry you."

"We've been over this before. I'll convert."

Mark, who had been living in the Middle East for six years—in Lebanon, then Egypt—knew that Muslim women were not allowed to marry outside of their faith. In Egypt, interfaith marriages were legally permitted, except when a Muslim woman sought to marry a non-Muslim man. Even a civil court would not issue a marriage license in such a case, not unless Mark presented a certificate of conversion to Islam issued by an accredited institution. The alternative would be equal to living in sin—not a big deal to any Westerner, but in Egypt an offense that still warranted honor killing in some parts of the country. Not that Rose's parents would kill her, of course.

"My parents would kill me," she sighed.

"No, they wouldn't."

"Not literally, no. But close. My mom's family would ostracize her, and she would disown me."

"No, she wouldn't. You don't give your parents enough credit. Besides, I said I'll convert."

"Please stop. This is not a joke."

"I'm not joking. I mean what I said. All I have to do is say the *shahadah*: *I profess that there is no god but God, and that Mohammed is his messenger.* Here. I said it already. Now I'm a Muslim." He smiled.

"You know it's not that simple."

"It is, actually. I asked."

"You have to believe it, not just say the words."

"Believe that God exists? I do. Believe that Mohammed was one of his prophets? Why shouldn't I? Why is this less likely than Moses being a prophet, for example?"

"Believe that Jesus was not divine? That he, too, was a prophet?"

Mark shrugged. "Some of the earliest Christians didn't believe Jesus was divine."

"Your mother would kill you."

"It seems that one of us is destined to be the victim of filicide."

"*Please* stop joking about this."

He leaned across the table, reached out, and grabbed her hand. "You want me to stop joking?"

Rose nodded. Between his firm grip on her wrist and his eyes, wide and staring into hers, she knew he was serious.

"I've read about every single major religion in the world. I have long ago concluded that, at the end of the day, all religions are the same, just as all people are the same. You want to know if I'm certain that God exists and that Mohammed is his prophet? No one can be certain of this. This is the definition of belief—to *think* that something is true without having *proof.* Do I *think* it's true? Sure. Why not? I have no way of disproving it, any more than I have a way of disproving that Jesus healed the sick and raised the dead or that Moses split the sea. And while I'm being honest, I should probably tell you that I would be just as open to being Buddhist or Hindu or Baha'i. I believe in the validity of the religious experience, in the necessity of a spiritual life. And despite many rational objections, I do believe that God exists." He reached over and grabbed her other wrist. "Now, this is what I'm offering you. What I *know,* what I'm certain of, is that I love you, and I would very much like to spend the rest of my life with you. I respect your adherence to your religion. I would not want you to do anything that goes against your conscience and regret it ten or twenty years down the line. I'm not going to claim that I would have converted if I hadn't met you—that would be a lie—but I am going to reassure you that my conscience is clear, and that I'm open to Islam as much as I'm open to Christianity or Judaism. I think this is all you can fairly ask of me. What I'm asking of you is to answer one question: Do you love me?"

Rose turned her hands and grabbed his wrists, too, just as strongly as he was grabbing hers. "You know I do. Of course I do."

She pulled her hands free. She was tearing up, and she hated crying in public. From her purse, she pulled a tissue and blew her nose. If someone had asked her opinion on this same matter only nine months earlier, she would have had a clear, firm answer: Muslim women should marry Muslim men. Her entire life she had heard the arguments: children inherited the father's religion; if she were to marry a Christian, she would not be able to raise her kids as Muslims. How would she fast the entire month of Ramadan each year—a requirement of every Muslim, one of the five pillars of Islam—if her husband didn't practice the same faith? How would she raise her kids to do the same and to pray five times each day if their father didn't do it? The arguments against such a union went on and on. She could recite them all.

Theoretically, it all made sense. Any person of faith would apply the same arguments to his or her own religion and agree to their validity. But theoretical arguments gained an irritating level of complication once they tried to impose themselves on one's personal choices. Besides, who said she had to believe those arguments anyway, all of which were, at the end of the day, justifications for religious injunctions issued by mortal men interpreting a sacred text. Did she truly believe that Muslim men could marry Christian women, but that the rule did not apply the other way around? The prophet Mohammed married a Christian and a Jew, and as far as she knew, there was no clear verse in the Qur'an that forbade women from doing the same. What if all those arguments were merely another manifestation of the patriarchy's obsession with controlling women? What if they married and Mark promised to allow her to raise their kids as Muslims, regardless of his own religious beliefs or lack thereof? What if they married and decided they would remain childless? And which version of God did she believe in: the God who revealed Judaism, Christianity, and Islam and would therefore not prefer the followers of one to the followers of another, or the God who took sides that differed depending on whom you were talking to? Most people believed that God favored their religion, regardless of what that religion was, and that He would therefore certainly send the followers of all other religions to hell. Did she truly believe in that?

She knew of only two women who had had to make a choice similar to the one she was now struggling with: Hanan, a school friend who married a German convert and who took every opportunity to assure people of her husband's true Islamic faith, even carrying a photo of the beaming, bearded, blond man performing pilgrimage in Mecca; and Soha, a college friend who married an American, and who, when asked, calmly declared that neither she nor her parents cared what her husband's true religious belief was, even though he, too, had converted to Islam before marrying her. Rose was neither one of these women.

And Mark was unlike any other man she knew. In a country of 80 million souls, she had to fall in love with a foreigner. She looked at him, sitting back in his chair, watching her, smiling. She imagined him going to his parents and announcing that he had converted to Islam. She imagined herself going to her parents and announcing that she was eloping with him to the U.S. She imagined standing in front of God and explaining why she chose to marry an agnostic or an omnist or a deist or whatever Mark classified as.

"My parents will kill me, and your parents will kill you, and I may end up in hell," she said.

"Is this a yes?"

She put her head down on the table, her forehead resting on its edge. "I need to think about this," she said, speaking to the family of cats that now sat by her feet.

"Take your time," Mark said, grabbing a piece of bread and tearing it up into smaller chunks before feeding it to the cats. "I'm in no rush."

In her parents' living room two months later, Rose announced her engagement.

"Mark and I are getting married." A statement. Not a question.

Her parents sat next to each other, her father holding her mother's hand as if in anticipation of disaster. Rose saw his grip tighten with her words, saw his shoulders tense, but then he smiled. For his smile, Rose would forever be grateful.

"Married?" her mother repeated, bewildered. Her expression implied that Rose had announced the rebirth of the phoenix, some mythical experience that could not possibly happen in real life. "How?"

Rose was expecting this.

"He's converted to Islam, Mama. Don't worry."

Then and only then did her mother sigh in relief. "Oh, thank God. Your aunts would have killed me."

Ahmed wiped a tear. Nora hugged her husband. Rose watched them congratulate each other before either one thought of congratulating her. Neither one asked how Mark was willing to change his religion.

Gameela asked. Gameela, Rose had anticipated, would be counted upon to ask.

"Does he really believe in Islam, or is he just doing this to marry you? He has to genuinely believe in it, you know. You can't fool God."

She had been standing behind Rose as she announced the engagement to her parents, so Rose had not seen her expression. She turned around to face her sister. Gameela had just walked in from campus and had not taken off her head cover yet. The only covered woman in the entire family, rebellious in her conservatism, Gameela stood peeling off her scarf, unfurling the bun at the nape of her neck, running her fingers through her long, curly hair.

"So you want me to question his intentions? I thought only God knew what was in our hearts. He went to Al-Azhar. He pronounced the *shaha-dah*. What else do you want? If he were Egyptian, born a Muslim, would you have tested him on his faith? Are you really naive enough to think all Muslim-born men have true faith?"

Rose did not try to restrain the edginess in her voice. She had endured this censure from Gameela for the previous year: every time she got a text from Mark; every time they went out together. A silent, reproachful glance; a turning of the head; even a muttered *I hope you know what you're doing.* Gameela the missionary seemed a universe away from Gameela the sister. Rose could not remember the last time she had looked at her sister and not felt guilty. Now Rose looked at Gameela and saw only the embodiment of the judgment she would face once people knew she was marrying an American, a judgment she both resented and feared.

"I'm just asking, Fayrouz. You know I want only what's best for you. I'm glad you're happy, I really am, but I just want to make sure you're not doing anything wrong."

"Thank you for your concern." Rose turned away to face her parents. She ground her teeth, tried to swallow a thought, failed.

"Why are you the only one who still calls me Fayrouz?" She turned again to face her sister. "Everyone else calls me Rose. Even you used to call me Rose when we were kids. But then you became all religious and it's Fayrouz again. Something wrong with Rose? Too Westernized a name? *Haraam?*" Sinful?

"No, of course not." Gameela crumpled her scarf in her hands, balled it up. "I didn't realize it bothered you. I'm sorry if it did. I just thought Fayrouz was such a beautiful name. I like the sound of it. And the meaning."

For Rose's previous birthday, her sister had given her a turquoise stone wrapped in thin gold chains. "Fayrouz—like your name," Gameela had smiled, handing it to her. Rose had held the stone in her hand, felt the thin gold chains that wrapped around it, intersecting, keeping the stone in place, making sure it behaved. "Yes. Very appropriate. Thank you." She had given her sister a hug and worn the stone around her neck that day. In the evening, she had shoved it in the corner of her bedside drawer. She had not worn it since.

Now, Gameela looked at her parents, puzzled, imploring.

"Your sister didn't mean anything bad, Rose." Nora got up and embraced Rose, then pulled Gameela closer. "Here. Give your sister a hug and congratulate her. She is getting married! Can you believe that?"

Gameela stood in front of Rose. Rose, seeing her sister's eyes well up, pulled her in a tight hug that she held until her father, too, walked over and hugged them both, pulling her mother in with him. They remained standing, all entangled arms and awkwardly angled elbows. Rose felt one hand pat her on the back, another hand tousle her hair, but she couldn't tell whose hands they were.

6

The next morning, Gameela snuck out of the apartment before anyone woke up—an easy feat in a family that slept past ten on weekends. She needed to walk the Cairo streets at the time she loved them most: early on a Friday morning in October, when the summer's heat had finally subsided, replaced by a crisp breeze just cool enough to sting her nose, when the sprawling city was mostly still sleeping. Stepping out of the apartment building and onto the street and, crossing it, reaching the promenade that bordered the Nile, Gameela felt refreshingly clean, as if she had just stepped out of the sea and under the shade of an umbrella, like she loved to do when they used to vacation in Mersa Matruh years ago. She walked slowly down Saraya El-Gezira Street, occasionally glancing at the Nile below. Watching a boat float down the river, Gameela took a deep breath in and waited for that familiar sensation to fill her, the one that she got whenever she, as a child, strolled by the Nile with her father—the feeling of blissful belonging, an anchored identification with all that surrounded her: not only the running water, but also the Cairo dust that rendered everything a dull shade of gray, the suffocating heat that often prevented her from pursuing this same walk, the chaos of the streets crowded with peddlers and taxicabs and donkey-drawn carts and Mercedeses all maneuvering around each other with skill that decades of coexistence bred.

She could not believe how easily Fayrouz was giving all of this up, how easily she was leaping into a marriage that would inevitably take her away from her country.

She could not believe how easily Fayrouz was giving her family up.

Selfish of her, she knew, to mourn her loss instead of rejoicing in her sister's gain, as she should be doing. Childish and foolish, considering how marred her relationship with Fayrouz already was. She and her sister weren't best friends anymore anyway. That damage was done exactly two years and four months ago, when Gameela had put on the head scarf that magically, instantaneously transported her closer to God and away from her family, which was as fervently devoted to its secularism as any religious fundamentalist was to God. Suddenly she was not Gigi, who loved detective stories and pop music and spent hours whispering secrets to her sister at night—she was just Gameela: the Covered One; the Pious One; the One Who Is Judging All. The Other. That was how her family now saw her. That was a complication of her *hijab* that she had not foreseen.

Crossing the Qasr El-Nil Bridge, she stopped halfway across the Nile and leaned against the wrought-iron railing, looking down at a floating restaurant anchored close by. She wished it were nighttime, so that she could enjoy the sight of the illuminated city and of the floating restaurants decorated with string lights. Cairo, at night, seemed cleaner. Less dusty. Cairo, at any time of the day, welcomed her with a much warmer embrace than anyone in her family did anymore, the city's streets dotted with *hijabis* and women in tank tops, all cohabiting in a peace that her family still couldn't find. A peace that Gameela now found only at Marwa's.

Slowly, Gameela made her way toward the streets of Garden City, taking her time so that she did not arrive at her friend's apartment too early in the day for a visit. Once she arrived at the old neighborhood with its curvy roads, home to many foreign embassies, she continued walking in the shadow of the old villas and spacious apartment buildings and the newer, colossal office buildings that jutted in between them where other villas once stood. She arrived at Marwa's street a few minutes before ten, and, convinced that a visit in the double digits was more appropriate, stood in the crevice of one of the building's entryways, passing the time.

Marwa's apartment building, taking up almost an entire block, was beautiful. Balconies dotted its façade, their handrails supported by elegant marble balusters, their shapes echoed by Corinthian columns that, on some floors, surrounded the larger balconies, their crowns connected by delicately carved arches. The building dated back to the early twentieth century and boasted the typical high ceilings, a spacious, marble-tiled entryway, and stairways so wide that Gameela, Marwa, and Marwa's younger brother, Mustafa, could all walk up the stairs side by side. The kitchen in the Tawfiks' apartment opened to an atrium that in older, richer days used to be populated by servants walking up and down the metal stairs, hanging up clothes to dry on the various lines strung off the one continuous balcony that surrounded the enclosure, or chitchatting while they took out the garbage. When they were kids, she, Marwa, and Mustafa used to play hide and seek in that same atrium, much to Aunt Ameera's alarm. She would chase after them, warning them of ill-maintained balconies eaten by rust, so decrepit that the kids risked plunging to their deaths if they didn't *get back in there right now!* How Gameela loved that building—old and beautiful, despite the wrinkles that time carved onto it, with an air of bygone wealth that seemed exquisitely Egyptian.

The entire building belonged to Ameera's family, but, because of fixed rent laws that were set half a century ago and then never changed, the apartments that were rented out back in the 1960s had remained, stubbornly and irrevocably, in the possession of the families that had rented them. The owners of the building were not allowed to terminate the contracts or raise the rent, which meant that the current inhabitants of most of those apartments were the children or grandchildren of the original renters and paid a now nominal fee of twenty-two pounds per month for four-bedroom dwellings located in one of Cairo's most coveted neighborhoods. Marwa and Mustafa often ranted about the injustice of those laws—if they could only raise the rent to the actual market value or, better yet, sell the entire building, they would be millionaires. Instead, they controlled only their apartment and their cousin's, one story above, and could do nothing but glare at their neighbors, who, according to Marwa, were all thieving crooks, even if protected by the law.

Glancing at her watch, Gameela started her slow walk up the stairs to Marwa's apartment, rang the bell, and a moment later found herself violently pulled by the arm into the large foyer.

"What took you so long?" Marwa asked, kicking the door shut.

"It's barely ten in the morning!"

"You texted *an hour* ago and said you were coming over. I called *three times*! I thought the cabdriver kidnapped you."

"I had my phone on silent. And I walked." Gameela smiled.

"Putting your phone on silent negates the entire purpose of carrying a cell phone, doesn't it?"

"Not if your purpose is to reach people but not allow them to reach you!"

Marwa rolled her eyes. "Mama!" she shouted. "Gameela is here."

Aunt Ameera's head popped out of the hallway leading to the kitchen.

"Gigi, *habibti*," she said, blowing Gameela a kiss. "Welcome. Breakfast will be ready in a minute."

AN HOUR AND a hearty breakfast later, Gameela lay on Marwa's bed, her back resting against the headboard, her friend sitting across from her, both knees hugged close to her chest.

"So you were right. It's actually happening," Marwa said.

Gameela nodded. "Official and with my parents' blessings. They are getting married."

Marwa shrugged. "Good for her. If he converted, you can't fault her."

"It's not just that. How can she leave the country so easily?"

"Are you kidding? Half of Egypt wants to leave the country."

"But what if this is part of his appeal? You know—a life in America." Gameela pronounced "America" with an exaggerated, deep growl.

"I'd take that, to be honest." Marwa leaned over and grabbed a brush from the top of the dresser, running it through her long, thick, black hair, which she then weaved into a French braid as she spoke. "I'd marry him, go to the U.S., and live in a house on a cul-de-sac with a large fenced yard. Get two dogs and play yoga. And go out with my friends—who will all look like Jennifer Aniston—for lunch in New York while on break from my job in a shiny high-rise."

"You watch too many American movies."

"And you don't, Miss I'm-Obsessed-with-Mystery-Series?" She tossed the brush back onto the dresser, where it landed with a clank. "But seriously, why is this upsetting you so?"

Gameela looked down at her lap, wrapping the edge of her scarf around her finger and unwrapping it again. "I don't know. I just hope she's doing the right thing. I'm afraid she's so swept up in the romance of it all that she is not considering it carefully enough."

"Talk to her about it, then."

"I tried. Yesterday. But all I could think of saying was to ask if he was a true Muslim or if he converted only to marry her, and she lashed out at me."

Marwa winced. "I would have, too."

"It's a perfectly legitimate concern!"

"Yes, but it's one you cannot possibly test. Unless you are secretly in possession of a lie-detector machine, like Robert De Niro in *Meet the Parents*." Marwa chuckled. "And what's in his heart is none of your business anyway. As long as he says he is a Muslim, he is a Muslim. The rest is between him and God."

"I know. I don't know what I was thinking. Sometimes I feel like I play into the role they all put me in just to spite them. The religious one and all."

"You *are* religious, which is perfectly okay. And they don't put you in any role. You're just being too sensitive, Gigi."

Gameela glared at her friend. "My father calls me *hajjah*." She was surprised to hear her voice crackling at the title given to women who perform the hajj, the pilgrimage to Mecca. A title often used to address grandmothers in black shawls regardless of their level of religiousness. An honorary title when used to address older women; a sarcastic jab at her.

"You know your father," Marwa said softly. "He's just teasing you."

Reaching over to the nightstand, Gameela grabbed a tissue, blew her nose. "Your father never calls me that. He was okay with my *hijab*, even though no woman in your family wears it."

"My father takes liberalism to the extreme." Marwa stretched her arms, first to the right, then to the left, pulling at her wrist with her opposite hand. "He'd have the exact same reaction whether I walked out of the house in a bikini or covered head to toe in a black *abaya*. 'The girl is free to dress any way she wants,'" she imitated her father, her voice low, soft, melodic.

Gameela laughed.

"And Fayrouz is free to do what she wants, too," Marwa added, reaching over and placing her hand on Gameela's. "You need to accept that, *habibti*."

ON HER WALK BACK HOME, Gameela chanted her friend's advice, a mantra of tolerance: *I need to accept my sister's choices. I need to accept my sister's choices.* She was perfectly aware that she had not fully confided in Marwa, that she was embarrassed to admit how much of her reaction was rooted in her own needs. Absentmindedly, she lifted one hand and tucked a loose strand of hair back under the edge of her head scarf. So much of faith as she understood it lay in a constant struggle to improve oneself, in the true meaning of *jihad* as an ongoing striving to be better, to do better, to let go of egotistic, selfish notions, to strive to be the best person one can be, a truly good person, a kindhearted, pure person. But the harder she tried, the more aware she became of how elusive true goodness was. She had to do better than this. Crossing the bridge again on her way back home, she chanted a new mantra: *Stop being childish and self-centered. Stop being childish and self-centered. Stop being childish and self-centered.*

At home, the apartment buzzed with life. Nora walked around puffing up throw pillows, dusting shelves and figurines, and picking up stray books and magazines. Fayrouz vacuumed the living room, and Ahmed sat out on the balcony, apparently trying to stay out of everyone's way. Hosna, the elderly lady who had served Gameela's family for the previous two decades as nanny, maid, and all-around helper, was in the kitchen, pots, pans, chopping blocks, and knives all clicking under her capable hands.

"You're back. Good," Nora said when she heard the front door close. "Can you please set the table? Mark is coming over for dinner."

Gameela pulled a tablecloth out of the dining-room cabinet, then put it back in and dug deeper for the nice, hand-embroidered one that her mother had bought during her trip to India a few years earlier. The tablecloth, a delicate cream with miniature burgundy flowers that matched the dining-room walls, had been clumsily shoved in place after its last use, and rivers of creases ran through it. Gameela, determined to do her best—*I need to accept my sister's choices*—carried it to her room, set the ironing board up, and carefully pressed it, maneuvering around the delicate flowers, spraying the creases and going over them again and again until the cloth relaxed in immaculate smoothness.

She didn't notice Fayrouz standing at the door, watching her.

"It looks perfect, Gigi. Thank you."

Gameela looked up. The sound of her nickname pushed a lump up her throat, and she swallowed to clear it. "No problem, *habibti*."

"Here. Let me carry it with you so that it doesn't get creased again on the way to the dining room."

Each sister holding two corners, they carefully lifted the tablecloth. Walking backward, Fayrouz stepped out of the room and down the narrow hallway toward the front of the apartment.

"Mama is in full entertainment mode," Fayrouz whispered. "She's been ordering me around for the past two hours. She even called Hosna and had her run over here on a Friday, can you believe it? I kept telling her Mark is not expecting a meal, but she won't have it."

"You know how Mama is. She just wants to make you proud."

Entering the dining room, Fayrouz walked around the table and held the cloth high. Gameela did the same, and for a moment the sisters looked at each other under the cloth.

"You know what that reminds me of?" Fayrouz asked.

"The bedsheet tent." Gameela smiled. Fayrouz laughed, and they lowered the cloth down and over the table that, as kids, they used to cover with a bedsheet, turning the space below it into their supposedly secret hideout.

They centered the tablecloth and together set the table, pulling the plates of fine china out of the cabinet, setting the silverware, the crystal glasses, the napkins folded in neat triangles. Once done, they stood at the door to the dining room, examining the finished product.

"Looks okay to me," Fayrouz said.

Gameela nodded.

They remained in place, not looking at each other, not moving.

Gameela looked at her feet, waited, hoped that her sister would say something, that she would tell her how much she would miss her, once she was married, how much she wished she did not have to move away.

"I think I'll go see if Mama needs help in the kitchen," Fayrouz said instead.

Gameela, nodding, did not look up.

Stop being childish and self-centered.

Stop being childish and self-centered.

Stop being childish and self-centered.

As she had expected, Mark was charming. A bunch of long-stemmed pink roses for the hostess; smiles and eye contact and a general air of oozing happiness; infatuated gazes at Fayrouz whenever she spoke; an awed hush in his voice as he officially asked Ahmed for his daughter's hand in marriage, beaming at the acceptance that he knew was coming; a reverent look in his eyes as he looked down and recited *al-Fatihah*, the one-paragraph Qur'an chapter that was traditionally read to seal an engagement and which he did seem to know by heart (Gameela watched him, listened to him recite it); then, over dinner, immediate, witty comebacks to all her father's jabs; even a trip to the kitchen after dinner and a heavily accented *"El-akl momtaaz; shokran!"*—Food was excellent; thank you!—directed at Hosna, who stood giggling like a child. By the time they all returned to the living room for tea and dessert, Gameela was reluctantly, unbelievably, starting to think that he just might be okay.

In the yellowish light of the two tall table lamps on either side of the sofa where he sat next to Rose, Mark glowed, his whiteness and blondness emitting a golden sheen that obviously blinded her parents.

That was the first thing that bothered Gameela: how nervous her parents were. How complimentary. How eager to please the American, who, rightfully, was also trying to please them and should not have been catered to with such overbearing civility.

"So how can you handle all our spicy food? Rose tells me you love *koshari*! How come? Even I can't handle the spices," Nora said, her laugh a bit too shrill.

"Oh, that doesn't bother me at all. I'm used to the spices. I grew up eating spicy jerky and venison smothered in chili." Mark laughed.

"You eat *deer*?" Gameela, thinking of Bambi, shuddered at the thought.

"Yes. West Virginia has an enormous deer population. One deer can feed an entire family for a pretty long time."

"They actually hunt them with bow and arrow—isn't that interesting? Like Robin Hood," Fayrouz said.

"Fascinating!" Nora replied.

"Sounds like a good sport," Ahmed chimed in, leaning back in his chair. He sounded inexplicably British. Gameela half expected him to pull out a pipe from the pocket of his blazer and start tapping it on the side table, even though he didn't smoke.

"It's really quite environmentally friendly, if you think about it. People hunt their own deer, prepare it for storage, and freeze it, bypassing all the commercial meat-processing facilities."

"Wouldn't it be great if people cared about the environment that much here, honey?" Nora asked Ahmed.

"I'm sure they will once they can stop worrying about day-to-day survival," Gameela said.

"What are you talking about, Gameela?" her mother asked, smiling, tilting her head a bit to the side.

"Poverty? Survival? It's easy to be critical of people's attitudes toward the environment here, but this is a poor country. Very few Egyptians are as lucky as we are," Gameela said, waving a hand at their general surroundings. "You can't think of the environment when you're busy thinking about how you're going to feed your kids tonight."

"Gameela is a champion of the poor and downtrodden," Ahmed chimed in.

"No, I'm not," Gameela murmured. Her father's tone reminded her of the way he pronounces his derisive nickname for her—*hajjah* Gameela.

"It's okay if you are, Gameela," Fayrouz interjected. "Mark has written many articles about Egypt's poor. He knows exactly what you are talking about."

"Does he?" Gameela asked.

"I don't pretend to know as much as you do, of course. I've only lived here for a few years. But I have been around many of Cairo's neighborhoods. I've seen the contrast between wealth and poverty."

"I'm sure Mark knows all you're talking about, Gameela. Sometimes you see things better when you are not a native. Distance gives you a better perspective," Nora said, smiling at Mark.

"I think it's admirable, personally, that you can travel far away from home and care about people so different from you," Ahmed said. "I've always found Americans to be so open to other cultures. Much more tolerant than Europeans. Don't you think so, Nora?"

"Yes. I agree. It's probably the exposure to all the immigrants."

Gameela took a deep breath in, closed her eyes, and instead of saying what she was thinking (*Seriously? How many Americans or Europeans do you even know?*), she silently chanted a new mantra: *Strive to be a better person. Strive to be a better person. Don't be mean to your parents.* She knew how obsessed most upper-class Egyptians were with the West; how deferential their attitude toward it was. How flattered her parents were that an American had chosen their daughter to be his wife, thereby indirectly complimenting them as equals, as desirable, as something better than the inferior Other that they felt they were, even though they would never admit it. *Strive to be a better person,* she reminded herself. *Be tolerant of your parents' shortcomings. Their entire generation is like that. Blame it on colonialism.*

"I wish that were true," Mark replied. "Not everyone in the U.S. is as tolerant as they should be, I'm afraid."

"But that's true of all cultures and all people," Fayrouz said.

"Yes, of course," Gameela acquiesced, thinking of her father's nickname for her.

"Oh, I'm sure you're exaggerating," Nora smiled. "I've always dreamed of visiting America, you know. Such a fascinating country."

"Well, now you'll get to visit as often as you wish," Fayrouz said, reaching over and patting her mother's knee.

Nora wiped away a tear. "I'm happy for both of you, Rose. I really am. It's hard thinking of you so far away, though."

"Don't be silly, Nora. She's a grown woman. She'll be fine." Ahmed smiled at Fayrouz.

"And we're not going anywhere anytime soon," Mark said. "My contract here doesn't expire for another ten months. And, by then, who knows? Maybe we'll just stay here."

"Would you really consider that?" Gameela asked. "Staying here for good?"

"Sure. I know at least one American journalist who's been living in Cairo for fifteen years. I'll probably stay for as long as the office here will keep me."

"Unless I get accepted into a PhD program in the U.S.," Fayrouz interjected.

"You're applying to PhD programs?" Gameela asked, her voice hoarse.

"Yes."

"That's wonderful, *habibti*! Good for you," Nora said, tearing up again.

"You'd want to leave even if Mark is willing to stay?" Gameela asked.

"This is still all premature, Gameela," Ahmed said. "We're just getting to know Mark today. I'm sure we'll have time to discuss all of that later."

"No. It's not premature. Don't you think it's important to know which continent your daughter will end up living on?" Gameela snapped at her father.

"This is not the time to talk about this, Gameela," Nora said.

"Then what is this the time for? Talk of hunting habits in West Virginia and the tolerance of Americans compared to all the Europeans you don't know?" Gameela could feel her heart racing. *Strive to be a better person,* her inner voice repeated. *Shut up,* she replied. *Just shut the hell up.*

"As the youngest person here by far, you shouldn't tell the rest of us what is an appropriate topic of conversation," Ahmed said.

"I'm not a child! I'm twenty-one! Just because I'm the youngest person here doesn't mean I can't have an opinion."

"We are all perfectly aware of how opinionated you are, *hajjah* Gameela."

Gameela jumped. "Why do you always do that?"

"Do what?" Ahmed seemed puzzled.

"Gameela, seriously. This is my life. I'll decide what I want to do when the time comes," Fayrouz said. Gameela looked at her sister's pursed lips, at her furrowed forehead. "Why can't you just be happy for me?" Fayrouz's voice quivered.

"I'm trying," Gameela replied, her eyes watering. "You have no idea how hard I'm trying."

She hurried to her room, closed the door behind her, leaned against it. *Stop being childish and self-centered*, she reminded herself. *Try to be a better person. Respect your parents. Respect your sister's wishes. Be kind.*

Her face was flushed crimson, emanating a heat that suffocated her. She grabbed her head scarf and tore it away, snatching at it as the pins keeping it in place caught on her hair, pulling it away with such might that it came off with a thin strand of hair attached to it, leaving her with a painfully tingling spot on her scalp. She tossed the scarf on the bed, paced the room, crying. She *had* to do better. She *had* to be happy for her sister, to accept Mark as the Muslim he claimed to be, to celebrate her sister's career. Wasn't it great that she wanted to pursue a PhD? What if America was part of Mark's charm—what was wrong with that? And maybe it wasn't. Maybe Fayrouz did love him regardless of the promise of the American Dream that came entangled with him.

What if her sister chose to immigrate? What if she did it because she wanted to, not because she had to? What was wrong with that? Why couldn't she accept her sister's choices?

How could Fayrouz willingly want to move so far away?

Gameela had been convinced that the previous two years were a mere hiccup in her relationship with her sister; that once enough time had passed, they would have become close again despite their age difference, despite Gameela's head cover and Fayrouz's fondness for tank tops. That one day they would each be married, live a few minutes apart, take their kids to soccer practice together, and meet on weekends for dinner with their parents.

Apparently, that was not going to happen. Never had she imagined that one could so painfully mourn a future that failed to materialize.

She let herself fall facedown on her bed, silently crying.

Why could she not stop thinking of herself and start thinking of her sister's happiness? Why was it so hard to be a better person? Why did she keep failing at it?

How could she call herself religious if she couldn't prefer her sister's happiness to her own?

Outside, she heard the echoes of muffled laughter.

Again, she felt alone. Again, again, and again, all Gameela could feel was how utterly alone she was, how foreign in her own home.

7

They married. Moved to the U.S. just in time for Rose to start her PhD program at Columbia in the fall of 2010. Mark worked in the offices of *The New York Times*, occasionally traveling around the U.S. on writing assignments. They rented a studio in Queens for a year before moving to a one-bedroom in Greenpoint, Brooklyn, where Rose walked to Polish delis for fresh bread, to produce stands for plums and peaches, to Starbucks for coffee, where she could hop on a train and be at the Columbia campus in just over half an hour. She decorated her small apartment with spare, clean-cut furniture—a glass-top breakfast table; a cream loveseat and two beige armchairs in the living room; a bed with an upholstered headboard, also cream, and mismatched nightstands that she bought at a flea market. Rose was happy.

She assumed Mark was, too. Thinking back, she could not remember a single instance when he gave her reason to think otherwise. Not until three years into their marriage, when dinner party chitchat led to a simple question.

"What was the fuss about this morning? Did you have it out with Elinor again?"

The one asking the question was Ted, Mark's friend and coworker and Ingrid's boyfriend. They were all done eating dinner but still sat at the table, the partially carved-out turkey in front of them, the light hanging above creating multiple shadows that disappeared into the glass top.

"Same old stuff. I pitched a story, she said it was great, then she suggested I work on another story that she probably had planned to assign to me before I even stepped into her office. She systematically rejects every second piece I pitch to her."

"That means she agrees to every second one you pitch. That's not bad at all."

"It is, compared to what I was used to in the foreign office."

"You're not in a ten-person office anymore. You're one peg in the massive *New York Times*. Welcome to the machine."

"I hate the machine."

"I know at least eight journalists who would kill to get your job."

"I know. I'm honored and privileged and all that. But that doesn't mean I have to love sitting in a cubicle and scribbling generic pieces that any other journalist could have churned out just as efficiently." Then, after a sigh, "I just wish I were still in Egypt."

"That's new," Rose said. She stole a glance at Ingrid and met her eyes.

"See, Rose? You learn something new every day," Ted said, smiling and patting her on the hand.

Rose pulled her hand back. She got up to carry the turkey to the countertop and, after washing her hands, started pulling pieces of meat off its carcass.

"I'll help," Ingrid said, getting up. "Where do you keep your Tupperware? Or do you prefer a Ziploc bag?"

"A bag is fine. I'll freeze it," Rose said. She pointed with her head to a cabinet a few feet away. "They're up there, all the way to the left."

Ingrid walked up to the cabinet, stretched to reach the box of Ziploc bags. Rose saw Ted look at Ingrid's behind and smile, then he turned toward her and, catching her looking at him, smiled at her, too. She looked away.

"Tell me why you miss Egypt," Ted asked Mark.

Rose scooped up the turkey pieces and put them in the bag Ingrid was holding open for her.

"I'll tell you what I missed in Egypt—I missed a fucking revolution."

"You weren't there in 2011?"

"Nope. We left the previous summer. After a seven-year stint in the Middle East, I missed covering a revolution by five months."

"So why didn't you go back?"

Mark got up and started clearing the table. Rose, finding nothing more to carve off the turkey, picked the carcass up and wrapped it in a shopping bag before throwing it away, then stood at the sink, washing her hands. She waited for Mark to answer Ted's question, but he seemed intent on scraping leftover food from one plate to another.

"We had to stay because I had just started my PhD," Rose finally said. She dried her hands on a kitchen towel and watched as Ingrid put the bag of meat in the freezer.

"Bad timing, huh?" Ted asked. He had stood up to clear some room for Mark, but did not offer to help.

Rose looked at him. "Would you please bring that bowl with the mashed potatoes over here, Ted? I need to wash it."

Her voice was calm, delicate, as it always was. Her mom would have been proud.

Ted carried the bowl over and stood by Rose, watching her rinse it. "You still could have gone back, you know," he said, turning to Mark, leaning next to Rose, one elbow resting on the counter. "Rose would have survived here on her own for a few months."

"That's exactly what I told him then," Rose said. She scrubbed hard, attacking a strip of mashed potatoes that had already dried up and stuck to the bowl.

"Wouldn't that have been dangerous, though?" Ingrid asked, taking the plates from Mark and rinsing them before putting them in the dishwasher. "I remember watching CNN and seeing Anderson Cooper stuck in an apartment while shots were fired outside. It was horrible. He and another reporter were whispering and had the shutters closed; you could tell they were afraid someone would barge in on them."

"I remember that," Rose said as she dried the bowl and put it in the cabinet. "I was so scared he would get hurt. Sounds awful, I know, considering how many Egyptians ended up dying during the revolution, but all I could think of was how bad that would make Egypt look, if Anderson Cooper got killed there."

"But he didn't get killed, did he?" Mark asked.

"No. But he could have. He got harassed on the streets a few days later. Many Western journalists did."

"And they all survived to tell the tale," Mark replied.

They were facing each other now, while Ted and Ingrid both watched them. Mark stood with his arms crossed, his feet apart. Rose knew they were not talking about Anderson Cooper.

"I was afraid you'd get hurt, Mark. I didn't want you to go back because I was afraid you'd get hurt."

"I'm not a child, Rose."

"That's not fair. It's not like I forced you to stay. You agreed to stay."

"Because you wanted me to."

"And because it worked out this way!" Her voice was gaining an edge. Keenly aware of Ted and Ingrid's presence, Rose felt her face warm up, hoped her dark skin would conceal her blushing. She and Mark rarely ever fought. Now they were gliding toward a fight in the presence of witnesses, of Mark's friend and hers. Ted must now believe she was a manipulative wife who ruined her husband's career.

"You had a job offer you would have had to turn down," she went on, both to remind him and to explain to Ted and Ingrid. "No one knew how long the revolution would last. It could all have boiled down to nothing within two or three weeks. It's not like we all knew Egypt would be a great source of journalistic material for the following three years!"

She tossed the towel on the countertop, looked at it as it hit the wall in a messy flop, then slowly picked it up and hung it on the towel ring.

Straightened the towel's edges. Made sure the decorative border was facing the correct way. Breathed.

"That makes perfect sense to me," Ingrid said.

Rose looked up at Ingrid, flashed her the most grateful smile she remembered giving anyone.

"It's easy enough to look back and realize you could have done things differently, but you really couldn't have, at the time and based on what information you had available, could you?" Ingrid went on, addressing Mark using her calm, professorial voice. She lifted a finger and pushed her glasses back in place.

"I love it when you sound all academic, honey," Ted said, winking at her.

"Ah, shush," Ingrid said, smiling.

"I bet you do that at work all the time. Analyze everything and then quote a couple of peer-reviewed articles in support of your argument, too."

Ingrid responded to his chuckle with a straight face. "He's making fun of me for trying to dissuade him from going skydiving."

"What's wrong with skydiving?" Ted asked, raising both hands, the hand holding his wineglass toasting skydivers everywhere.

"What's right with it? Who in his right mind choses to jump out of a plane?"

"You're just too scared to do it."

"I'm too wise."

Ted rolled his eyes, and Ingrid looked at Rose and rolled her eyes. Rose glanced at Mark, who was slowly wiping the table, now cleared of plates, with a wet washcloth, his hand going from side to side, again and again, as if he were caressing the table to sleep.

"Wait till you see what I made for dessert!" Rose said. She headed to the fridge, pulled out a tray carrying bowls of homemade rice pudding sprinkled with crushed hazelnuts, and a tub of vanilla ice cream from the freezer. She walked up to the table and stood in place, tray in hand, and waited as

Mark wiped the table with a dry cloth, now rubbing it in spots, scraping at it with his thumbnail, making sure every crumb was gone, every inch was glistening, until the table looked as if it had been carved out of ice.

ROSE SPENT THE rest of the evening trying to make up for the awkwardness her scuffle with Mark had created. She could feel its effect in the way Mark smiled a bit too widely, in the way Ted told nonstop jokes, in the way Ingrid stretched that story about the time she face-planted in front of a classroom of students. To counter the air of discomfort, Rose had tried so hard to appear okay that, in the middle of an overly exuberant laugh she burst into in response to one of Ted's jokes, the word "chipper" hopped up in front of her. She saw it as a tiny bird that hovered right by Ted's head. For a moment she stared up in the air, imagining the word/bird fluttering hysterically at her artificial laughter and then suddenly turning sideways and freezing in place, wings clasped by its side, exactly like the hieroglyphic symbol for the letter *w*, drawn as a quail chick. After that, she became silent, looking down at her bowl of half-finished rice pudding, trying to sort out her languages: American English versus British English (was "chipper" an American or a British word?), English versus Arabic, Arabic versus the German words Ingrid occasionally slipped in the middle of her sentences, German versus the hieroglyphs the Pharaohs used to depict their spoken language. One form of that ancient language still survived in the Coptic language that Egyptian Orthodox Christians used in their prayers, and Rose understood it. She was very proud of that knowledge, limited though it was. Now, sitting at a dinner table with her American husband and their American and German friends, thinking of a word and imagining a bird floating in the air, Rose was suddenly embarrassed to be here. Uncomfortable. As if she had just spent an hour speaking a foreign language, only to realize that she had been butchering the accent, mispronouncing words, and confidently stringing senseless sentences together.

For the rest of the evening, she remained subdued, speaking only when addressed.

When Ted and Ingrid got up to leave, Ingrid grasped Rose's hand and pulled her aside.

"We'll talk tomorrow at work, okay?" she whispered. "Just relax."

Rose nodded, let Ingrid give her a hug, let Ted do the same. She stood at the top of the stairs while Mark walked them down, watched Ted and Mark share a final few whispers in the lobby and then burst into laughter. She walked back into the apartment before they were done talking.

She picked up the dessert bowls, rinsed them, placed them in the dishwasher. She heard Mark return but waited till she dried her hands before she looked up at him. She had found that this little pause helped, whenever she was upset. A soft breath to calm herself.

"I didn't know you were still upset about Egypt," she told him. She poured herself a glass of iced tea and walked over to the living room, sat on the sofa, lifted her feet up on the coffee table. Mark followed and sat in the closer armchair.

"I wouldn't say I was upset."

"I would. Ted would. Ingrid would, too. I'm sure all three of us would agree you were upset."

"You're exaggerating, Rose."

"I'm not. I'm embarrassed you had to criticize me in front of our guests."

"I wasn't criticizing you. And Ted is practically family."

"I don't care how close you are or how long you've known each other. Even if he's your best friend, he's still a guest. I've known him only since I married you. And I'm not sure I like him, to be honest."

"Why not?"

"He's not right for Ingrid. We introduced them, and I keep fearing she will hate me for it one day. Don't see how they've lasted six months already. He's too sleazy."

"No, he's not. You don't know him."

"Exactly. I don't. Which is why I would rather not discuss private affairs in his presence."

She took a sip of her tea before placing the glass on the side table.

"Look. I'm sorry if I embarrassed you. I don't know what brought all of this out. I had a bad day at work today, this shitty assignment that I'm not enjoying at all, and I got online to check out Egypt's news and saw so much I could have been reporting on. And I just regretted not staying."

"We didn't stay because I got accepted at Columbia! You know how important that was for me. And it's not like you had to flip burgers; you got a good job, too. One bad day at work doesn't mean you don't have a good job."

"I know. I know." He leaned forward, put his hand on her knee, then rested his forehead on his hand. She could feel the weight of his head pushing her leg down. She shifted her other leg, putting her foot on the floor to help steady the leg he was leaning on. Mark looked up but she patted his head, pushed it gently back down, ran her fingers through his hair.

"You don't really regret moving back to the U.S., do you? Moving away from Egypt?"

Her words were soft, and she imagined them landing on his fine blond hair, tiny birds all symbolizing the *w* sound.

"No. I don't. It had to be done. I know." Mark's words sounded muffled.

"Would you go back now, if you had the chance? Maybe you could get your post back."

He lifted his head and sank back in the armchair. "We can't move now. You know that. My contract doesn't expire for another two years. And you're still two years away from finishing your PhD."

"I could stay here and finish it and then catch up with you. And you could get out of that contract, if you wanted to."

Mark shook his head. "Wouldn't want to break a contract prematurely. It wouldn't look good. Word would get around." He looked up at her. "And I don't want to be away from you for two years."

She got up, squeezed next to him in the armchair, tangled her legs in his. Her ankles rested on his, her skin dark, his pale, and, as usual, she watched the two skin tones with admiration, took in the way each tone brought out the other's qualities, a mixture of cream and brown as artistic as the elaborate patterns baristas drew on the surface of her lattes. She rubbed her ankle against his, then looked to the side, where their shared bookcase stood, its middle occupied by souvenirs, reminders of every trip they had made, every vacation they had enjoyed. Three years together, and she had never imagined that Mark found their life any less perfect than she did.

"I'm sorry I never realized you were unhappy."

"Who said I was unhappy? I'm not unhappy. I'm perfectly happy." He kissed her forehead, clutched her closer to him.

"That won't do, Mark. You can't suppress something that you obviously crave. Sacrifices like those are highly overrated. All they do is bury discontentment deeply enough for it to fester with time. I don't want you to look back and have any regrets. Certainly not on my account."

"I won't. Seriously. You're making too big a deal out of this."

She shook her head and sat up straight. "There has to be a way out of this."

"There isn't any." Mark's voice took on a frustrated edge. He got up, stretching. "I told you. I can't just leave in the middle of my contract."

"But you don't really have to abandon your job, do you?" She shot up, her eyes gleaming with excitement. "How about if you just went away for a week or two?"

"What would I do in a week or two? Job hunt?"

"No, no. Write a freelance piece!"

He shook his head.

"Why not?"

"Because you don't go roam the streets in Egypt for two weeks and stumble upon a story. It could end up being a total waste of time. And money."

"Then you start the piece here." She walked up and down the living room, gesticulating as she spoke. "You decide what you would like to write about, do all the research you can do from here, and then go there for whatever needs to be done on site. You know—interviews and stuff."

She saw him look at her, his head tilted.

"You know there is merit to this," she said.

"I don't know. It could end up coming down to nothing."

"At least you would have tried."

"We can't afford this, Rose."

"We can certainly afford one plane ticket! We'll put it on your credit card. We'll get you the cheapest ticket around. Fly you to Egypt via India, if we have to."

He laughed, and his laugh made her smile. She couldn't remember the last time she had heard this particular laugh of his—loud, open.

"And you won't even have to spend any money there. You'll stay with my parents. So room and board are taken care of."

She walked up to him and held him by the arms. "It can be done, Mark."

He nodded, smiling. "Maybe." He pulled her close to him, hugged her. "Maybe."

8

Insert intelligent-sounding prospectus title here
Introduction
Purpose
Importance of problem
Methodology

Six months after that dinner party, Rose sat at her desk, wedged in the corner of the bedroom of their Brooklyn apartment, her laptop open in front of her. She stared at her computer screen, then picked up her notebook and flipped through the notes she had been scribbling for the previous three months. She was more than three years into her PhD and three months into trying to write a presentable prospectus of her thesis. In her mind, her ideas positively teetered on the edge of brilliance, seeming to need only a nudge to fall into the pool of groundbreaking discoveries and cause a glorious splash, its ripples affecting the entire global community of Egyptologists.

In reality, she felt unable to string two coherent sentences together.

"I am a fraud," she said out loud.

Academic sources littered the entire room. Books lay in stacks on top of and under her nightstand, overflowing onto the floor and all the way to the corner of the room, where they formed a stepped tower at least four feet tall before falling again in a trail of shorter stacks tracing the length of the room and reaching the foot of her desk at the opposite corner. A box by her feet held printouts of so many peer-reviewed articles on ancient Egyptian literature of the Middle Kingdom that she was certain she had killed at least two trees and used up four or five cartridges of ink. She didn't even want to calculate how much she had paid for copies at five cents per page. Now her laptop carried three files of brainstorming for possible directions to take her thesis in; her notebooks oozed scribbles, notes, and arrows connecting ideas across pages; and she was certain that all of this would amount to nothing. Her stomach churned so loudly that she groaned.

In the kitchen, she poured herself another cup of coffee, then brewed a new pot. She stood at the window, watching Mrs. Kumiega sit in the backyard under the shade of the magnolia that, in the spring, exploded with some of the most beautiful pink flowers Rose had ever seen. Mrs. Kumiega was taking full advantage of the warm weather that had popped up in the middle of an otherwise cold, dreary week in January. Rose considered taking her coffee cup and joining the landlady, spending her only weekday off under the shade of the large, welcoming tree, basking in sunshine that might not hit the yard again till March. She contemplated taking the laundry to the corner laundromat, telling herself that she would not be abandoning her work, that she could sit there and let the washing machine's hypnotic twirl and hum clear her mind and, she hoped, reset it into a semi-intelligent state. She worried about what she and Mark would have for dinner. The thought of dinner made her stomach growl again, so she opened the fridge, pulled out a cup of fruit yogurt, and ate it standing by the window.

She took her coffee cup back to the desk, sat down, let her head fall forward, and banged her forehead on her open notebook a few times.

She was in the fourth year of her PhD studies. She had survived more than three years. She just needed to survive the remaining two.

She lifted her head, moved the mouse to wake up her computer, stared at the few lines glowing in angry black ink on her screen.

Introduction: Explaining where whatever my dissertation will be about falls within the larger field of Egyptology and why it will be brilliant and groundbreaking.

She called her parents.

"Rose, *habibti!*" her mother's voice greeted her. "What a nice surprise."

"Hey, Mama. How's life?"

"Good, *alhamdu lellah.* How's your thesis going?"

Rose grunted. "It's not going anywhere. It may go to the sewer and take me with it."

Nora laughed. "No, it won't. I have full faith in your ability to pull through this."

"How's Baba?"

"He's right here. Let me put you on the speakerphone."

A moment later, Rose heard her father's voice, a bit distant, echoing. "*Habibti!* You're missing out on my famous marble cake. How come you're not at school?"

"It's Friday. No classes on Friday."

"Working on your thesis?"

Rose eyed the litter of books and papers around her. "Yes," she lied.

"When is Mark flying over?" her mother asked.

"Next week. His flight arrives in Cairo late Thursday night."

"Tell him to send us his flight information so that we can meet him at the airport."

"Has he read about the new constitution being approved? In the referendum, ninety-eight percent voted yes," her father said.

Rose grimaced. "I'm sure he has."

"Make sure he writes about that," her mother added. "Make sure he lets the West know how the people support Al-Sisi and the interim government. How they are restoring order to Egypt. How they saved us all from the extremist Muslim Brotherhood."

"I can't control what he writes, Mama."

"You can guide him."

Rose sighed. Her parents, like almost all liberal, middle-class Egyptians of their generation, she was finding out, were staunch supporters of Colonel General Al-Sisi, the head of the Egyptian armed forces, who overthrew the elected Muslim Brotherhood president, Mohammed Morsi. Almost three years to the day since the Egyptian revolution, and everyone in Egypt was still consumed by politics, everyone firmly planted in either the camp of the military rulers or the camp of the ousted Muslim Brotherhood. There seemed to be no middle ground.

Mark, she knew, was a creature of the middle ground. He thrived in between ideologies, in between extremes, in gray areas populated by the skeptics and the tolerant alike.

"How is Gameela?" Rose asked. She was getting sick of talk of politics, which, for a full three years, had permeated every single conversation she had with her parents.

"She's in her room. I'll go get her," her father said.

She heard his steps walking away, then heard her mother pick the receiver up. Her voice came hushed but clear.

"I've taken you off the speaker. Your sister has been acting weirdly lately. She's on that damned phone the entire time, texting someone. And she goes out for hours at a time, comes back home in the middle of the night."

"She's a grown woman, Mama."

"She's twenty-five!"

"Exactly."

"I don't want her roaming the streets till midnight every night. It started with the revolution and now everything is topsy-turvy. No rules anymore."

"She's probably just spending time with Marwa. She stayed there all the time during the revolution, right?"

"Yes. But the revolution is over, isn't it?"

"She's still friends with Marwa."

"She's coming. If you find anything out, tell me, okay? She won't tell me anything."

"If she won't tell you, she won't tell me, Mama."

"Your sister is here. She wants to talk to you," Nora shouted into the receiver. Rose pulled the phone away from her ear.

"Hey, Rosie," Gameela's voice came.

"Gigi. Miss you, *habibti*."

"Miss you, too. How's America?"

"Beautiful. Cold, usually, but not today. How's Egypt?"

"Beautiful, too."

"I heard you have a working constitution now."

"Wait. I'm taking the phone to my room. Mama is turning the TV on and I can't hear a thing."

Rose got up, walked to the kitchen, and looked out the window. Mrs. Kumiega was still sitting in the sun.

"They're driving me absolutely bonkers," came Gameela's whispered voice.

Rose laughed. "Politics? Or your personal life?"

"Both. But mainly politics. It's like I'm living with Al-Sisi's personal propaganda machine. All I hear all day is how great he is, how he's saved Egypt from the Brotherhood, how he is the hero who responded to the people's call for help and stopped Egypt from turning into another Iran, run by extremist clerics. How he has to run for president because he is Egypt's only hope. The police arrested hundreds of protesters across the country just a few weeks ago, and they don't care!"

"I think it's a generational thing. Marwa's parents are the same, aren't they? They've all lived under military rule since the fifties. They are back in their comfort zone. And it was kind of terrifying, the way the Brotherhood was trying to consolidate all power in their hands. You can't blame them for being relieved that didn't happen."

Gameela sighed. "I'm just so disappointed. You should have seen how beautiful it was, during the revolution. People had such high hopes."

Once, in the midst of a march where hundreds of thousands swarmed Cairo's streets, Gameela had called Rose to let her hear the chants, even though the noise was so deafening there was no way for the sisters to hear each other above the crowds. But Rose still remembered the chants for *Bread, liberty, and social justice*, the calls shouted up to spectators looking down from the balconies of their apartments: *Walk down, Egyptian—your country calls you.* She had watched the live coverage on CNN as millions of people flooded Egypt's various cities on January 25, 2011, and stayed there till Mubarak relinquished his thirty-year rule two weeks later. Gameela had been among those people, and she had given Rose the chance to be there, for a few short minutes, listening to the hope in the people's voices, participating in the Arab Spring via an international phone call. The hairs on Rose's arms stood on end now, remembering all this. Back then, she had cried openly as she held on to her phone, watched CNN on mute, getting the sound live courtesy of her sister.

"Mama has high hopes you will get married soon. I think she suspects you're sneaking out to meet a guy," Rose said, laughing.

On the other end of the line, Gameela grew silent. Rose's laugh died down.

"*Are* you sneaking out to meet a guy?"

"I don't see how that's any of Mama's business." Gameela's voice came sharp and cold. "And I don't see why she can't ask me personally, rather than have you do it."

"I'm asking you personally. I'm not asking on her behalf." Rose would not have told her mother anything her sister wished to withhold, but she wasn't sure Gameela believed that. "I think she's probably just worried you're dating a Muslim Brotherhood guy." Rose attempted a chuckle, croaked out an awkward, unidentifiable noise instead.

"I'm not. Just because I'm the only woman in this family who wears a *hijab* doesn't mean you all should treat me like some sort of religious extremist. I like my *hijab*. It makes me feel peaceful."

"I know, Gigi. I didn't—"

"And just because I'm opposed to the way the interim government is cracking down on activists doesn't mean I'm pro-Brotherhood either, Rose. You, of all people, should know that."

"I know that! Who said I didn't know that?"

"You act like you don't."

"I'm just worried about you."

"Nothing to worry about, thank you very much."

They fell silent. Rose grabbed a fresh mug and walked up to the coffee machine, slammed the mug on the countertop so forcefully she feared she had broken it. She picked it up, turned it around. It was still intact.

"Why is it that every time I talk to you or to Mama and Baba, we have to either talk politics or religion?" She poured herself a cup of coffee, grabbed the cream from the fridge. "Why can't we be like normal people and talk about our lives, for a change?"

"Because now our lives here are about politics. And religion. Every single day. That's what's on the news. That's what people are arguing about. You moved to America just before the revolution, so you haven't lived through this." Then, with a sharp, spitting emphasis: "We're not all American, Rose. Some of us don't have the luxury of a normal life."

Rose pulled her coffee cup away from her mouth, placed it on the countertop, and was on the verge of responding, when she remembered something. Slowly, deliberately, she placed the phone next to the coffee cup, stood straight with her heels together, clasped both hands in front of her chest, then inhaled, deeply, counting to ten. When she was done, she counted one more time. Then she picked the phone up.

"Rose? Are you still there?" Gameela was asking.

"Sorry. Lost you there for a moment. What were you saying?"

"I was asking how your thesis is going."

"Great. It's going great."

Rose picked up her coffee, sipped, let the warm liquid twirl in her mouth. Savored the bitterness.

"I'm sorry I snapped at you, Rose. I'm . . . I've been a bit . . ."

Rose sat down at the breakfast table. The sun, lower now, shone through the window and onto the floor. She extended one socked foot into the path of the sun rays and wiggled her toes.

"I just haven't been feeling too well," Gameela said.

"Anything you want to talk about?"

"Nothing in particular. Work. Life."

"I know."

Rose leaned back in her chair, looked across the backyard and at the neighboring apartment building.

"I'm sorry I called you American, Rose."

"It's not an insult, *habibti*."

"I know it's not. But still."

A sparrow landed on the laundry line that ran out of the kitchen window and all the way to a pulley fastened to the electric pole at the end of the backyard. Rose watched it flick its wings, hop in place, and change direction. When she first arrived in the U.S., she was amazed to find the exact same sparrows here that populated the trees in Cairo. She hadn't expected that. She considered sharing this information with Gameela, but said nothing.

"GAMEELA CALLED ME AN AMERICAN," Rose told Mark on the phone.

"I hate to break this to you, but you are almost an American. You will officially be one by next year."

"I know that." Rose copied her husband's intonation, slow and singsongy. "But she wasn't stating a fact. She was underscoring a difference. Apparently, as an American, I'm not allowed to have opinions about Egypt anymore. And I'm not qualified to empathize with my parents or with her. American, in this context, meant 'Other.' You *know* that."

"And?"

"I breathed and counted till ten. Twice. It worked, surprisingly. Thanks for the tip."

Mark laughed. "If it works with my mom, it should work with your sister."

"I was so pissed, though. Why can't I just talk to her like we used to?"

"Just give it time."

She was back at her desk, trying, again, to work on her thesis. She started doodling in her notebook, drawing spirals that intersected with other spirals, starting at the corner of the page and slowly covering the entire sheet.

"I still can't forgive her for how judgmental she got, when we got married." The spirals grew tighter, closer together. She had to concentrate to spread them apart.

"You need to get over that. She's very religious. Of course she didn't like you marrying an American."

"Well, she wasn't always 'very religious.' And you converted, Mark. You're a Muslim now." *Technically, at least,* she thought but did not say out loud. "Even someone 'very religious' can't find fault with that. And what if I had married someone who was Muslim by birth but was not practicing? Half the people in Egypt are Muslim in name only. Would she have submitted them all to a religious test? And why do religious people have to be so judgmental anyway? Shouldn't religiousness lead people to be more tolerant? Why does it never work that way?" She paused, looked at the doodles.

"How are your parents?" Mark asked.

"They're okay. My mom said to remind you to send her your flight information."

"I will. Tonight. Are you sure they're okay with me staying with them for a full ten days?"

"Sure they are."

"Gameela, too? She'll have to wear her *hijab* at home."

"Her choice. Not your problem." She started doodling an oval face wearing a *hijab*.

"Maybe I should stay with Tony. He's still stationed in Cairo. I'd get to see the cats."

"You're not staying with your friend when my parents have a spare bedroom, Mark. And I'm not telling them you'd rather spend time with the stray cats you rescued than with them. Besides, the food will be better at my mom's. And they're literally a stone's throw away from Tahrir Square. Not that anything is happening there now, but at least you can be near where the Arab Spring happened. You can walk over and inhale the same air the revolutionaries breathed."

She heard him tap his pencil on the desk. "Seriously, honey. They don't care," Rose repeated. Then, after a pause, "Of course, if you end up writing something in support of the Muslim Brotherhood, they may disown me."

"Can't promise you anything."

"Just don't totally take their side, will you?"

"Never tell a writer what to write, Rose."

She sighed, put her own pencil down. Stared at her blank document again.

"How about you tell this struggling writer what to write? I've been working on my prospectus all day. Trying to anyway. So far, I've spoken to my parents, resisted hanging out with Mrs. Kumiega, who's been sitting in the glorious sun all morning, drunk six cups of coffee, and eaten three days worth of calories. At least. Maybe four. And I cleaned the bathroom." She heard him chuckle. "You think I should do the laundry today? Get it out of the way?"

"I think you should do some writing. I'll do the laundry when I get home."

"I think I have writer's block."

"No, you don't. You're just starting. You're just overwhelmed because it's a large project. Just take it one page at a time. One sentence at a time."

She stared at the screen, at the vertical line marking the last word she typed. The line blinked. She pushed her chair back, walked to the fridge, pulled out a box of blueberries, and started picking them straight out of the box, lifting the receiver up so that he didn't hear her munching.

"What are you doing?"

"Eating blueberries," she said, her mouth full.

"Go write your prospectus."

"Eating blueberries is easier."

"Go write, Rose."

She huffed. "We're having Chinese tonight."

"Sounds good."

She hung up and walked back to her desk.

Introduction: Explaining where whatever my dissertation will be about falls within the larger field of Egyptology and why it will be brilliant and groundbreaking.

Rose stared at the screen and thought of her sister. She tried to think back to the time before Gameela fell so deeply into religion, the time when, surprisingly, Rose, the older sister, used to remind Gameela to pray *Ishaa*, the evening prayer, only to see her sister roll in bed, pull the covers over her head, and pretend to sleep. Rose remembered exactly when this started to change, when Gameela, during her first year in college, brought home cassettes with religious lectures on them, handed to her by who knows whom, cassettes carrying sweet, syrupy voices of men telling her that she needed to cover her hair, as God required, asking her why she felt it was okay to deny God such a small request, reminding her of all the rewards waiting for those who obeyed His teachings, of the hell waiting for those who won't.

Even now, Rose felt guilty remembering those words.

Ahmed had had a minor fit when Gameela emerged from her room one morning with her hair covered in a pink floral scarf. He had not liked the idea of his daughter wearing the *hijab* and had not understood why she would want to cover up the abundance of auburn curls that gave him such joy to look at. Nora hadn't liked it either, had openly told Gameela that she looked like a peasant, that such backward traditions were not for people of their class and education.

Gameela had assured them both that her mind was made up. Her face had remained calm, but Rose had seen her mouth twitch, had recognized that look on her sister's face, the one she took on whenever, as a child, she would trip and skin her knee but remain too proud to cry in front of strangers.

Rose had followed Gameela out of the apartment and joined her as she waited for the elevator.

"It looks good, Gameela. It does. You look great," she had said, reaching out and touching her sister's head scarf, straightening its edge.

Gameela had looked at her with moist eyes. "It's not about looking good, Rose. That's not the point. I'm free to do whatever I want to do."

Rose pulled her hand back. "Of course you are, *habibti*."

She had waited with her sister, had not walked back into the apartment until she saw Gameela step into the elevator, the sliding door separating them.

Now, sitting in her apartment in New York, Rose remembered that day and wondered, for the hundredth time, whether it was all a matter of degrees, whether all people of different faiths fell on exactly the same scale but on different parts of it, and whether there was something about religion that caused everyone to wish all the others were exactly as religious as they were, not more, not less.

Rose, too, considered herself religious, but she suspected Gameela did not believe that. Rose still prayed five times a day most days. She still fasted the entire month of Ramadan. Her religiousness, though, was a part of her whole, not the center of her being, and she was happy with that. It was precisely *because* she was religious that she refused to believe that God, the all-merciful, all-knowing God, would hang her by her feet and let every exposed inch of her skin burn in the fires of hell as punishment for her failure to wear the *hijab*, as the man on her sister's cassette had claimed.

In a way, Rose knew she was just like Gameela: she, too, wanted others to be just as religious as she was, not more, not less.

Mark's mom was the same. In her home in West Virginia, she had a painting of a white, blond Jesus smiling down on all who entered the house. She had not taken Mark's conversion well, and Rose still felt the need to apologize to her for that. The poor woman believed she had forever lost her only son, repeatedly reminding Mark that leaving Christianity for Islam would throw him in the same fires of hell that Gameela claimed women forgoing the *hijab* would roast in.

Rose imagined a version of hell that was a composite of all the versions painted by various religious people, and realized that this co-op hell would, eventually, have room for every single person on earth. One large hell to encompass them all, with infinite numbers of small, exclusive heavens that included only those who were exactly as religious as each other, who practiced the same religion with the exact same vehemence, no more, no less.

Even the Pharaohs had similar beliefs, painting the walls of their tombs with scenes where the souls of the dead stood in front of a deity, where the person's heart was weighed against a feather to see if it contained an iota of malice, to judge whether it was pure enough to be granted entry into heaven.

Rose wished everyone would study ancient Egyptian religion, then go on to study Judaism, Christianity, Coptic Christianity—as she did during her MA in Egypt—and Islam, and then go on to read about every major religion practiced on earth, like she had done after meeting Mark. If more people did so, perhaps they would finally recognize their similarities and learn to live with their differences, practicing their beliefs their own way and not expecting others to follow suit. She wished people would travel more, too, like she did when she came to the U.S., like Mark did when he worked in Lebanon and Egypt, like Sinuhe did when he left Egypt for Palestine in the ancient Egyptian tale, lamenting his departure and yearning to go back home, yes, but learning, too, because he must have learned something through travel, mustn't he?

Rose sat up straight in her desk.

Travel. Travel and learning. Religion and expatriation. Immigration.

The words flooded her brain. She could see them, sparks of light shooting colors in all directions at once, a minor show of fireworks exclusively for her.

Sinuhe's tale is one of a failed immigration—he returned to Egypt, found a happy ending in his homeland under the grace of a kind Pharaoh.

Why didn't his immigration work? Why did ancient Egyptians cling so closely to home? Why did they think that those who were buried in foreign soil would not be resurrected? What is the relationship between all of that and between ancient Egyptian religion? The obvious, of course, was a kind of clinging to the way one practiced one's religion, to the exact degree of religiousness, not more, not less.

But was there more to it?

Rose remained very still. She was chasing a thought that was so delicate, so shy, that she feared even the slightest move would send it scurrying away, forever lost.

She had come across a paper published just the previous year about an ethnoarchaeological approach to the tale of Sinuhe, about how it can be used to understand Egypt's relationship to other cultures. She had also read a book that claimed Egypt's culture was centered around death and salvation, that death, in fact, was the center of all cultures.

Couldn't she build on the work of those scholars, compare attitudes toward travel to those toward death, and use that to examine the idea of otherness in ancient Egypt and how this affected ancient Egyptian society? Or something along those lines?

Where was that article? And the book?

She dumped the contents of the box filled with scholarly articles on the floor, crouched next to it, sifting through its contents.

How about communication between the living and the dead? The winged *ba*, a part of the soul flying between the tomb and the world of the living. What does that say about . . . what, exactly? What was she trying to say?

She lifted the articles one by one, scanned their titles, tossed them aside.

So mundane, on the surface, the idea of travel and understanding, of religion and death, so general, what's new about it. Yet there was something there to connect all of that, something that she just *knew* she'd be able to find carved on a wall of an Egyptian tomb or inside a sarcophagus, something that has survived four thousand years and that was, somehow, still relevant.

The thought circled her brain, like the taunting, elusive winged *ba*, the part of the soul that makes the person unique. Vexing, elusive thought. Out of reach yet right there, she knew. *Right there.*

She picked up a handful of articles that she had put aside, took them to her laptop, started typing, chasing those thoughts before they vanished.

The dissertation is about: Immigration in ancient Egypt. Expatriates. Death as expatriation. Religion as a way to negotiate otherness in life. The relationship between the living and the dead as a metaphor for the relationship between the Egyptian and the foreigner and how this is represented in tomb engravings. In the Book of the Dead. *In catacomb engravings. Religion and otherness and how they were reflected in Egyptian society in the Middle Kingdom.*

She went on and on, filling page after page.

The dissertation, she knew, would end up being about none of that. But somehow she also knew she had to go through it all, if she were to find that small thought that seemed to be galloping just out of her reach.

She was not hungry anymore. When, an hour later, her phone rang, she reached over and switched it to silent mode.

She had glimpsed an idea and, God help her, she was not letting it escape.

9

Mark did not realize he had forgotten his keys until he was standing at the door to his in-laws' apartment. He glanced at his watch—1:15 A.M. Both Ahmed and Nora would be asleep by now, for sure. He checked for the keys again, dug his hands deep into his jacket pockets, even though he clearly remembered seeing his keychain on the nightstand in the guest room, remembered telling himself to get the keys, then walking out without picking them up. He stood staring at the door. He might have to wake them.

Or . . . could Gameela still be awake?

He sent her a text message.

At the door and forgot my keys. Help, please?

He heard her slide open the security chain, unlock both padlocks before softly swinging the door open.

"You're an angel, Gameela."

The living room was doused in the soft light of a single floor lamp standing in the corner between the sofa and one of the armchairs. Gameela, in sweatpants, a T-shirt, and a hoodie, went back to sitting in the corner of the sofa, pulling both feet up and covering her lap with a blanket. It was only sixty degrees outside, quite normal for Cairo in January, but Egyptian apartment buildings lacked central heating. Mark let himself fall on the armchair next to her, rubbed his hands to warm them.

Gameela was texting someone. Mark watched her, her hair thick and auburn, falling in curly cascades and covering half of her face as she bent her head down to look at her phone. She looked nothing like Rose, and, at home, looked nothing like the girl he used to see during the years he spent in Egypt. Back then, she never took her head cover off in his presence, not even after he married Rose. He had felt quite uncomfortable, knowing that she had to scramble to her room to grab a scarf and drape it around her head whenever he arrived, knowing that, even after he married her sister, he still did not fall into the category of men she could let see her hair, a category limited to her future husband and her father, uncles, grandparents, and her brothers, if she had any. Per religious classification, he was and would always remain a man foreign to her, a man in front of whom she needed to cover up.

But when he arrived in Egypt this time around, Gameela seemed surprisingly relaxed in his presence. The first time Mark walked into the room and saw her sitting in a corner, barely acknowledging him, nonchalantly raising a strand of hair that had fallen in front of her eyes and tucking it behind her ear, he had not recognized her. That evening, he called Rose and told her how her sister, who still wore the head scarf in public, chose not to wear it at home while he was there, and Rose had been as puzzled by this unexpected development as he had.

"Any luck?" Gameela asked him, putting her phone away.

Mark shook his head. "Nothing. At all. Dragged me all the way to *Masr El-Gedeeda* just to have five members of the Muslim Brotherhood lecture me for three hours on how the Morsi overthrow was an illegitimate coup, even if Al-Sisi had only done so after millions of people demanded it of him in those protests, and even though he is not the president and will not be, unless he decides to run in the elections. Which I'm pretty sure he will do, but that's not the point. I kept telling them I understand their point of view, I do, but that's not the subject matter I am interested in. Noah had promised me I'd meet a young member of the Brotherhood with a story to tell, not a group of older leaders who all want me to join their propaganda machine."

"I told you that you couldn't trust them."

"You told me I couldn't trust the Brotherhood. I don't. I did, however, trust Noah."

"Who is a member of the Brotherhood."

"Whom I've known for seven years."

"Who is a member of the Brotherhood."

Mark sighed, let his head fall back. "This is looking more like a wild-goose chase each day. And I have only five days left in Egypt."

"What, exactly, do you hope to find here?"

Except for a short exchange earlier that morning, when she inquired where he was going that day, Gameela had not spoken to him in private since he arrived. In fact, Mark could not remember having had a one-on-one conversation with Gameela at all, prior to this visit to Egypt, something that Rose chalked up to Gameela's attitude toward their marriage, a resistance through silent treatment. Now, looking at Gameela, Mark was surprised to see that she shared some of Rose's features, even if both her skin and hair were shades lighter. She had Rose's eyes and eyebrows. When asked a question that she needed to reflect upon, she crinkled her nose, a fleeting reaction that Rose also shared. Looking at her, Mark remembered, with a jolt, that this woman was his wife's sister.

"I'm hoping to talk to a couple of people who participated in the revolution and write portraits of their lives," he said. "Simple, personal portraits. Nothing that directly addresses politics, but something that, through the variety of the people interviewed, can still shed some light on the impact of Egypt's politics on its society."

"Then why are you limiting yourself to a Muslim Brotherhood source?"

"I'm not. I've already interviewed two people that a colleague of mine set me up with: an older, middle-class lady who is firmly pro Al-Sisi, and a young revolutionary secular man who identifies as a socialist. And I have one more person I'm supposed to talk to tomorrow, a lawyer who wants to discuss the new constitution, though that's not confirmed yet. But I need someone to represent the Brotherhood, too. I can't honestly portray Egypt's society while totally ignoring the Islamists. I'm writing for an American audience, and the profiles should work together to form a story. The whole purpose is to show Egypt's political diversity. If I write about the seculars only, I would not be presenting an honest portrait. And if I write about the Islamists only, I would be reinforcing the stereotype that all Arabs are religious fanatics. But if I can get people back home to sympathize with multiple, seemingly conflicting members of Egypt's society—"

"Then you would have presented a complex, honest portrait and challenged the stereotype," she continued his sentence, nodding.

He leaned back in his chair, crossing his arms. She was still looking down at her lap. She picked her phone up, seemed about to look for something, then put it back down. Mark wondered whom she was texting at such a late hour.

"Many people here don't like American journalists," she said. "If they do speak to you, they will expect you to defend their political views, whatever they are. Take sides."

"I won't."

"But isn't writing inherently subjective? You'll have to take a side, even if you don't intend to."

"Then I'll take the side of decency and humanity."

Gameela laughed. Mark, only slightly embarrassed, smiled.

"Rose always said you were an idealist."

"Is this a bad thing?"

She shrugged, smiling. Then she crossed her arms, dug deep into the back of the sofa, her legs folded under her, and looked up at the ceiling. In the evening light, the yellow lamp illuminated her hair, casting tangled shadows on the sofa's dark brown upholstery.

The colors reminded Mark of Rose. Perhaps because of the late hour, or because of having spent his day roaming crowded streets and interviewing strangers, Mark watched Gameela and realized that her exact current pose seemed to replicate the palette of colors that, in his mind, portrayed Rose: Gameela's auburn hair had the same golden sheen that emanated from Rose's skin after a day in the sun; the black of the throw covering Gameela's legs was the color of Rose's hair; Gameela's face and hands, both slightly more tanned than the rest of her, because they were the only parts of her body that experienced direct sunrays, seemed the exact shade of Rose's palms or of the soles of her feet. Mark could see a tan line at Gameela's wrists, her hands gloved in darker skin. He had traveled a lot since he married Rose, but never alone to Egypt, to be surrounded by Rose's family, sleeping next door to her childhood bed. He wished she could have come with him.

Now, watching Gameela rest her head on the back of the sofa, Mark decided he might be able to like her. Perhaps Rose's anger with her had, in fact, reflected her disappointment in a younger sister who failed to dote on her, just as much as it was the result of Gameela's opposition to their marriage. But Gameela was not the doting kind. That much Mark could tell.

"You're not going to bed?" he asked her.

Gameela nodded. "Yes. Soon."

"How can you all stay up so late all the time?" He glanced at his watch. "It's almost two A.M. I bet you the streets are just as busy now as they were two or three hours ago."

"It's a big city," Gameela said. "Rose says New York is the same."

"True."

"And we stay up late because most of us sleep at work. Did you know there was a study that claimed Egyptians work, on average, twenty-eight minutes per day?"

Mark laughed. He had barely ever heard Gameela joke before, and now her smile infused her face with a new, relaxed air.

"How's Rose doing?" she asked.

"She's fine." He glanced at his phone. "I'm about to call her, if you want to talk to her. It's early evening back home."

Gameela looked down, hesitated. "It's okay. I need to go to bed."

She got up, folded the blanket, carried it on her arm. "I'll call her tomorrow," she said, more to herself than to Mark.

A few steps into heading to her room, she paused.

"Listen, Mark." Gameela turned around, facing him again. "I think I may be able to help you."

He searched her face and thought that, for a fleeting moment, he may have seen a glimmer in her eyes, a spark resembling the one that lights up Rose's face whenever she tells him a story of ancient Egypt, a particularly exciting one that she feels everyone should know because it is so relevant, still.

He sat straight up, his grip holding the chair's arm. He waited for her to elaborate.

THE MAN'S NAME WAS SAABER. He was twenty-one, Gameela told Mark, and had participated both in the revolution and in several of the subsequent demonstrations. Gameela did not know him personally, but she knew of him through a friend called Fouad, who was now sitting in the front passenger seat of the cab driving all three of them from Zamalek, where Mark's in-laws lived, to Boolak, just across the Nile.

Fifteen minutes into the three-mile drive, the cab was stuck in traffic on top of the 6th of October Bridge. Mark was used to the old Lada cabs zooming through the cars lined up six rows wide in four-lane highways, to the fact that no one wore seat belts. He didn't even flinch when he saw the truck right next to them, so close that, had he extended his arm just to the elbow out of his window, he would have been able to hold on to its side railing. The truck was loaded with such a tall stack of boxes of tomatoes that it seemed ready to tilt over at any second and douse them all in fresh tomato sauce. Mark semi-enjoyed all of this, the thrill of riding in a taxicab through Cairo's busy streets akin to the one he experienced on roller coasters. He looked to the front and noted that the cab's side-view mirror on the driver's side was missing, doubtless shorn off after a too-close pass by another vehicle.

"He doesn't speak English," Fouad said of Saaber, "but I'll be happy to interpret. He is a shy kid, but he's been through a lot. I think we can get him to open up to you."

Fouad sat with his arm around the back of the cabdriver's seat. He spoke English with an unmistakable British accent, not the fake imitation of how British royalty are perceived to talk that Mark occasionally came across when dealing with Egypt's upper classes, but an earthy, worn-out accent, something that Mark could have sworn had traces of the Scottish rolled *r* in it. Fouad's left hand held on to the cabdriver's headrest just inches away from Mark's face. Mark examined the watch on Fouad's wrist.

"Nice watch. You think it's safe to wear a Rolex where we're going?"

Fouad pulled his arm away, rubbed a thumb around the edge of the silver face of the vintage watch. "This watch is forty years old. Can't imagine it's worth much now. I wouldn't wear it—I hate such signs of elitism—but it belonged to my father."

"Fouad is a socialist," Gameela said, smiling at Fouad's back.

"I hate labels, too," Fouad replied.

"He is a socialist who hates labels," Gameela said.

Fouad looked at Gameela through the side-view mirror then smiled and shook his head. Gameela, apparently catching his eye, smiled, too, then looked out the window. They were crossing the Nile, the river wide and calm, running through a city that seems to grow by the minute, the river acting as a natural barrier where the expansions had no choice but to stop. The three and a half years that Mark had spent away seemed to have added a million or so people to Cairo's population. Mark knew this could not be true, but because they were caught in traffic in the middle of the day with no estimated time of arrival in sight, Mark allowed the city to draw him in, to envelop him in the world he was part of for years and that he was now trying to pretend he was permanently back in, not only visiting for a short trip. Even the dusty, warm, polluted air blowing through the cab's open window rejuvenated him. He could not think of a reasonable, logical explanation for how much he loved this country. How at home he felt in it. He breathed in, closing his eyes.

"Not carsick, are you?" Gameela asked.

"No. Just enjoying the ride." Mark opened his eyes.

Fouad chuckled. "Glad you find this congestion enjoyable."

"I like being in Egypt."

"How long are you staying?" Fouad asked.

"Just three more days."

"Pity you're not here longer. I could have taken you out to the farm."

"Fouad lives on a farm in Rasheed, on Egypt's northern coast."

"Rosetta!" Fouad said, turning to face Mark. "That's what the British called it."

"Where they found the Rosetta stone." Mark nodded. "Did you grow up there?"

"No. My dad did. I grew up in Cairo but moved there to take care of the farm shortly before he died. Was supposed to spend a couple of weeks and then come back. That was over thirty years ago." Fouad laughed.

"What kind of farm is it?"

"Citrus, mostly. But we also have hundreds of palm trees. We grow some of the best dates in Egypt."

"Says the farm owner," Gameela said.

"They're good dates! You know that!" Fouad said, turning to face Gameela.

"Yes. Just teasing you."

Now Fouad looked straight at her, and Mark marveled at how much younger he seemed, when smiling. He must have been in his fifties, at least, but now he glowed with youth, despite the gray hair.

"How do you two know each other?" Mark asked.

Gameela, who had been returning Fouad's smile, looked toward Mark, her smile vanishing, her face adopting its usual serenity again. "Fouad is Marwa's cousin."

Mark remembered Marwa, who had attended his wedding years before: short and plump, with long, thick hair and a piercing laugh. Rose had told him how Marwa was Gameela's best friend since childhood, but she had never mentioned a cousin. That was another thing Mark loved about Egypt: how friends and families merged and intersected, how people never seemed to be lonely. Almost like an exaggerated version of West Virginia, where his mother used to sell cupcakes for his basketball team's baked-goods sales. On game days, she used to run the concession stand with other mothers, and by the time he'd graduated from high school, she was either a friend of or at least a good acquaintance of half of Charleston, including the mothers of players on competing teams. Over a decade of living in New York, seven years right after college and four now, and he still didn't feel that sense of community there, not like he felt it in Charleston, where every grocery store run brought him into the path of a childhood acquaintance, and not like he felt it in Egypt, where even people who barely knew each other hugged on first meeting.

"The boy was one of the electricians working on my apartment a couple of months ago," Fouad said. "When Gameela told me you were looking for someone to interview, I thought he'd be perfect. His brother was apparently some kind of fundamentalist who ended up getting killed during one of the bloody protests last year. The boy witnessed it all but, according to his boss, wants nothing to do with politics, which is quite typical of most common people here. I think the underlying logic is that the country has survived for seven thousand years under the rule of every race and power you can think of—Greek, Roman, Arab, Ottoman, British—you name it. People just adapt and go on with their lives. They've seen power change hands so many times that it almost becomes secondary. The rulers will change, but the people will stay, so the people win by default."

"So the boy is not politically active?"

"Not really, or at least not anymore. Everyone became politically active during the eighteen days of the revolution, but few people still are. Even back then, I doubt he would have participated, were it not for his brother, who seemed to have been deeply involved in politics. I think Saaber was hanging along for the excitement of it."

"How do you know so much about him?" Gameela asked.

"People will gladly tell you their life stories, if you only listen. They worked on my bathroom and kitchen for two weeks. I had a long time to listen."

Mark nodded. Fouad's remark reminded him of an observation an older reporter had made to him years earlier, back when he started writing profiles: that most ordinary people become excellent storytellers, when the story is their own. All he needed to do was learn to ask the right questions and listen to the story being told—and, of course, infer what is being left out. Very few people can see the whole story when they are at its center.

"Almost there," Fouad said.

They had finally made it through the bridge's traffic and were now driving north alongside the Nile toward the Fairmont Hotel, a five-star luxury complex flanked on each side by two identical high-rises, the Nile City Towers, each boasting thirty-four floors of premium office space. Mark bent down to look through the windshield, taking in what he could of the row of high-rises overlooking the Nile. When the cab made it close to the hotel, Fouad signaled to the driver to pull into the drop-off lane.

"We'll get off here and walk."

Fouad insisted on paying the fare, and Mark knew better than to argue. He stood at the hotel's door, peeking through the glass façade into the lobby. The entire place glimmered in shades of gold, the sun hitting the four metallic columns supporting the large awning and mirroring blinding light everywhere. Inside, slabs of marble covered the floors, and a large fountain reflected the dizzying lights of the atrium, decked out in tones of beige, brown, and gold, not earthy tones but glimmering ones, signs of wealth. Mark had attended a wedding at the hotel, years earlier—the daughter of the editor in chief of one of Egypt's government-owned newspapers. The man was rumored to make close to 20 million pounds a month, but Mark didn't know if that figure was believable. The bride had walked into the reception hall wearing a trailing gown of white lace embroidered with what must have been thousands of Swarovski crystals threaded with wires of actual gold (if her father was to be believed). Now Mark walked closer to the glass panels, to peer inside the hotel. In the glass, he saw the reflection of the three security guards in their navy suits and earpieces as they turned around, watching him. A bellman in a gray uniform and cap trotted his way.

"Checking in?" the bellman asked in English.

Mark shook his head and looked back to find Gameela right behind him. "He's with us," she said, pulling him by the arm. "Let's go."

They walked down the ramp of the drop-off lane, Fouad in the lead. When they reached the corner at the end of the block, Fouad turned right, away from the Nile, and continued walking around the hotel complex until they reached the wide road behind it. There, Fouad stopped at the corner, pointed toward the neighborhood that was visible behind a meager row of trees: "Ramela Boolak. This is where Saaber lives."

Mark had been to similar neighborhoods before. Colloquially, they were referred to as "the Randoms" because of the way they spring up, room by small room, multiplying one next to the other with no building permits, no urban planning, no utilities, no running water or sewer system, the roads between them never wide enough or straight enough to allow for the passage of an ambulance, let alone a fire truck. Mark glanced behind him and made sure Gameela was still in tow before following Fouad down the row of trees and then along a dirt road barely six feet wide, overshadowed by the clay-and-brick rooms built on either side of it. Some of these neighborhoods boasted concrete buildings four or even five stories high, but here the fragile rooms rarely extended higher than three stories, never enough to block the view of the Nile City Towers looming over the neighborhood, drowning it in their shadow. Mark peeked, as inconspicuously as possible, through the single windows here and there, the doors left ajar. In one open doorway, a stout, middle-aged woman in a bright red floral dress, her head tied in a scarf, stood watching them pass, her hands crossed. Mark made eye contact with her and looked away before she did, her curiosity more unapologetic than his. He was a rare sight, he knew, a foreigner who must seem to her to have taken a wrong turn from the set tracks tourists were supposed to walk: the Nile, the Egyptian Museum, the pyramids, El-Moez Street, the heart of Cairo's historic Islamic district with its street cafés that oblige by conforming to the way Cairo is often still depicted in American movies, offering delicately worn-out wooden chairs and rickety tables, hookahs that fill the air with the smoky smell of apples and tobacco, small, quaint bazaars selling overpriced miniature statues of Tut Ankh Amun and Nefertiti. This was the Cairo that tourists were meant to see. The Cairo he now walked was a sight restricted to the locals, a degree of poverty no one wanted foreigners to witness. The poor, Mark learned early on during his days in Egypt, held on to their pride with fervent tenacity.

"It's estimated that over half of Cairo's fifteen million inhabitants live in neighborhoods like this one," Fouad said, falling behind to walk next to Mark. Both were keeping their eyes down, watching their step on the treacherously uneven ground. "Many of them were born and raised here, but some immigrate from all over Egypt in search of what they think will be a better life. You'll find experienced farmers here wasting their talents driving cabs or working construction jobs, building high-rises they will never be allowed to enter once they are finished. I hope you don't mind me dragging you here; Saaber wanted to meet you elsewhere—he was embarrassed to have a journalist see the extent of poverty he lives in, I know—but I thought you needed to see this. I thought it might help you understand."

"I've seen similar neighborhoods before, but, yes, I prefer to interview people in their own homes or on their job sites, if possible. Puts everything in context."

"I told you he'd appreciate coming here," Fouad turned to address Gameela. "It's like a backstage pass," he laughed. "Should be mandatory viewing for everyone, if you ask me. Just a glimpse into one's own backyard."

Gameela did not reply to Fouad's remarks but seemed surprisingly comfortable, dressed in sneakers, jeans, and a tunic that extended to her knees, holding on to her messenger bag as she walked, head bent down. Mark wondered if she had ever been in one of these neighborhoods before, or if Rose ever had. The thought of Rose led to other thoughts of home, and he suddenly found himself flooded with nostalgia, not for New York and the apartment he shares with Rose, but for West Virginia, where he grew up and where his parents still lived, and where neighborhoods crammed with five-thousand-square-foot homes were a five-minute drive away from roads edging shallow creeks, where trailers stood, some decaying, some surrounded by wire fences that kept barking dogs in place, and occasionally, some kept immaculately clean, their windows proudly displaying flower boxes bursting with colors. He remembered his school bus passing through one of these roads every morning, remembered the trailer where that one boy lived—what was his name? For a moment, he panicked, thinking he had forgotten, but then it came back to him: Dillon. His name was Dillon. He still felt a kind of survivor's guilt whenever he thought of Dillon. He felt that same guilt here, walking in his memory-foam-lined Skechers and avoiding the sight of the bare, calloused feet of a man sitting on a plastic chair in front of an open door. Mark looked through another door as he passed by a room at the corner of the narrow alley, and he saw a young boy staring back at him from the corner. For a second, Mark, disoriented, could have sworn the boy looked exactly like Dillon, his face wearing Dillon's same expression as he stepped into a bus filled with rich, indifferent kids and stared defiantly at them.

"It's that room there." Fouad pointed. "Let me walk in first and make sure he's home."

Mark stopped in the middle of a patio surrounded by two- and three-story buildings on all sides, all constructed in unpainted gray brick, two of them with second stories made from exposed wood paneling. As Fouad walked into one of the buildings, Gameela waited by Mark. He itched to take his camera out and snap some photos, but he didn't want to do that before interviewing Saaber. The place, he had to admit, was remarkable. Every building they'd passed by looked like it was about to collapse; every corner housed a pile of garbage. The patio they now stood in was an accurate representative of the entire neighborhood. One corner of the patio was covered in rubble that seemed to have come from the fallen wall of one of the rooms above, which now stood gaping. The rubble must have been there for some time, and, on top of it, people had started piling up other discarded items: two broken chairs; a mangle of gray, smashed wood that might once have been a table. Across from all of that, extending from one window on the right-hand side to another on the opposite side, ran a clothesline where two rows of bright red, yellow, and blue garments hung to dry. In one corner of the patio stood a worn-out three-seater, its wood gilded with gold leaf—an out-of-place item that doubtless once belonged to some middle-class family's living-room set, another piece of the French furniture that never failed to appear in Egypt's homes. On the sofa sat an old man in gray pants, a light blue shirt, and flip-flops; next to him sat a woman, leaning back in the sofa, wearing a black floral dress and a white head scarf. The man and woman were both watching Mark and Gameela, as was another, younger woman, bareheaded and in a red T-shirt, who looked out of the window of one of the buildings. The sun, blinding, shone all around but seemed absorbed by the prevalent grayness, its rays sucked in but not reflected, emitting instead a suffocating, dull warmth.

"*Assalamu alaikum ya Hajjah,*" Gameela said, greeting the seated old woman.

"*Wa-alaikum assalam,*" the woman replied in a deep, husky voice. "*Ay khedmah?*"

Mark understood the question—*Any way we can be of service?*—a traditional way to politely ask what they were doing there.

"*Alf shokr,*" Gameela thanked her. "We are just waiting for our colleague."

The old man was still openly staring at Mark.

"Ask them if they know the boy we're here to meet," Mark whispered to Gameela.

"I'm sure they do, but if we start talking to them then they'll want to know who we are and what we're doing here, and I don't want to get into that. They may give him a hard time after we leave. They'll say an American journalist was here talking to him and then he'll be accused of being a spy or something."

Mark rolled his eyes. "What is it with you people and fear of journalists? What exactly would I be interested in learning from him? How to invade Cairo through its poorest neighborhoods?"

"That's not funny, Mark. The boy can seriously get in trouble."

"Then maybe you should have mentioned that earlier?" Mark didn't try to hide his irritation. "A bit too late now, don't you think?"

"I did mention it earlier. Fouad didn't listen. I thought it would be a lot safer to talk to Saaber somewhere else, where people didn't know him. Somewhere where he can maintain his anonymity. Here—this is making me uncomfortable. You haven't been in Egypt for years. Things are different now. Security is tighter."

"I would think you would have discussed that with me, not just with Fouad."

"I assumed you'd know that."

Mark did know, of course. Every time someone spoke to him, they were at some degree of risk, especially if they were perceived to be criticizing the government. But he didn't think a simple profile could have any negative repercussions. "I'm not going to talk politics to him. I'm not interested in that. Why would he come to any harm?"

Fouad emerged before Gameela could reply. "He's here and waiting for you," Fouad waved them in.

Gameela walked into the building, and Mark followed her, glancing back. The old man was still staring at him.

THE BOY HAD a piercing gaze. Mark was almost distracted by the round, dark eyes that stared at him since he had walked into the room. Even when addressing Fouad, Saaber only glanced at him before focusing on Mark again.

"He says he would rather we sit down somewhere else," Fouad said. "I told him you wanted to conduct the interview here, at his home, but he seems to have other plans." Fouad turned to talk to Saaber again, and Mark looked around.

He could see why the boy would not want them to stay here. The room was cramped and stuffy, with one bench pushed against the wall and no other furniture. It opened up to a hallway that housed a stove in the corner and that Mark suspected functioned as the dwelling's kitchen. That hallway led to another room where a number of younger kids—four or five, Mark couldn't tell—hovered around the doorway. Behind them, sitting on a bed, was a slim woman clad in black, a loose scarf draped around her head. She, too, looked straight at Mark. When one of the younger children ventured one bare foot out of the doorway and toward the front room, the woman barked a word at him and he shrank back.

"*Salam ya Hajjah,*" Gameela greeted her.

The woman nodded.

Saaber and Fouad were still standing in the center of the room, which was lit only through a small window opening to the patio. They were talking rapidly in Arabic, and Mark tried to follow what they were saying, caught some words and missed others.

"He says it's too dark in here, and he wants to show you another place anyway," Fouad said. "I think he is just embarrassed. Doesn't want an American to see how poor he is. They always feel guilty, these people, as if their poverty is somehow their fault. I tried to explain to him that no one will help them if they don't see how they live, that exposing such circumstances—"

"Maybe you should let Mark decide what he wants to do?" Gameela interrupted him. "This is, after all, his article."

Fouad took a deep breath in, then exhaled, looking at Gameela.

"What would you like to do, Mark?" he finally asked, only now turning to face Mark.

Saaber stood a foot or two away from Mark. Mark stepped toward him, extended his hand to shake the boy's. Saaber hesitated and then reached out and let Mark grab his hand. He wore a clean, striped shirt and gray slacks, a thin, trimmed beard framing his face. No mustache. From afar, he may have looked older, but this close, he looked barely twenty. The gaze he had focused on Mark for so long now shifted away, looking down.

"Let him take us wherever he wants to," Mark told Fouad. "Tell him I'm here to see all he wants to show me."

"Did you really need to drag Gameela there with you?" Rose asked Mark on the phone later that evening.

"Honey, Gameela is the one who did the dragging. She and that friend of hers. I would gladly have gone alone, with one of the interpreters from the office. They wouldn't let me."

He was slouching on the guest room's bed, too excited to fall asleep.

"You should have seen that place, though. And the boy. There is something very sinister about him, I think, but I can't put my finger on it."

"Which friend?"

"Some older guy. A cousin of that other friend of hers. The one who came to our wedding."

"That's not very specific. Half a dozen of Gameela's friends came to our wedding."

Mark grabbed his camera from the nightstand, started scrolling through the photos he took earlier. "That boy, though. Very interesting perspective. Exactly what I needed. Totally different from the other three profiles I have."

"You didn't tell my parents you took Gameela there with you, did you?"

Mark put the camera back. "Seriously, Rose. What's the big deal? She's not a child. She can go anywhere she wants to."

"Except to interview a Muslim Brotherhood guy. Pretty sure my parents wouldn't appreciate that. Consorting with the enemy and whatnot."

Mark laughed. "He's not officially Muslim Brotherhood, just a sympathizer. But I won't say anything if you don't. She might, though."

"She won't. She didn't even tell me she set that whole thing up for you. Maybe she thinks her American sister won't approve."

"You're too hard on her, Rose. She's been very kind to me. Maybe she no longer disapproves of your American husband. People occasionally change their attitudes, you know."

"I wish I could change my attitude toward this never-ending thesis. I spent my entire week working on one chapter and I still can't get it remotely close to where it needs to be."

"Less than two more years and you'll have your PhD and it will all have been worth it."

"If I survive, that is."

"You will."

Mark picked his camera up again, scrolled to one photo of Saaber's face, round, dark eyes staring straight at the camera, the tall Nile City Towers looming distorted in the background, out of focus.

"You come from a very interesting country, Rose."

"So do you, honey. So do you."

10

Gameela assured herself that, technically speaking, this was not a break-in. Standing with her back against the closed front door, she gave her racing heart a few moments to calm down and allowed her eyes to adjust to the dimly lit room. All the wooden shutters were closed. The resulting effect was one of a place that stubbornly refused to give in to the glaring sun blinding everyone out on the streets, a place that resisted light.

No wonder Fouad could not remain here for long stretches of time.

Gradually, Gameela's eyes adjusted to the darkness. She could clearly make out a sofa and three armchairs ahead, a coffee table, a tall floor lamp. Gameela knew the apartment's layout by heart; it was a replica of Marwa's, only one story below. Slowly, she made her way to the lamp, fiddled around for its switch, let its yellow light seep through the surrounding darkness. The entry room she had walked into had only one window overlooking the street below, and this window was hidden behind heavy curtains. She could turn on a dozen search lights here, and no one would notice.

She placed the key she used to let herself in back into the zippered compartment of her purse, sat down on the nearest armchair, then immediately stood back up. Now that she was here, she wasn't sure what to do next. Walk around the rooms? Take a quick glance then rush back out? She took a step toward the nearest room—the one where Marwa's dining room would be—then stopped, her heart pounding again, looking at her feet. She had not worn shoes appropriate to break-ins. The block heels of her ankle boots clucked on the wooden floor, and she imagined Marwa's parents looking up, wondering who was in their nephew's apartment while he was gone, walking up to investigate, or worse, calling the police. The thought of being found in the apartment of a bachelor, even one who was currently four hours away, was so mortifying that Gameela's face burned, beads of sweat forming on her forehead. She listened. No steps rushed up the stairs outside; no commotion below. Slowly, she slipped her boots off and walked around in her socks.

She covered the entire apartment in minutes. The dining room mirrored the one below, but, apart from that, the apartment seemed shuffled. Where Marwa's bedroom stood, she found a formal living room, with access to a balcony identical to the one she and Marwa liked to hang out on and watch passersby. The layout of the kitchen matched the one below, but the cabinets were dark cherry instead of white. The darker colors would have made it look smaller, were it not for its clutter-free countertops, bare save for a canister of sugar and a dish rack still holding an upturned teapot and one cup. Gameela walked in, picked up the teacup: delicate china, cream with yellow butterflies dancing on its rim. Not what she would expect Fouad to be drinking from when home alone; then again, Fouad did not conform to expectations.

Minutes later, she walked out of the kitchen with that same teacup in hand, filled with steaming black tea. On the saucer, she placed two cookies out of a pack she found in one of the cabinets. She carried the cup to the dining room, sat down at the head of the table, placing the cup in front of her, watching the steam rise. The room was as dark as the rest of the apartment. Despite the street noise seeping in, Gameela felt a sudden discomfort, as if Fouad's mother were resurrected and sitting across from her at the opposite end of the table, silently questioning why she thought she had the right to be here. Gameela put her hands on the tabletop, spreading her fingers. She waited for her heartbeat to slow down again, then carried the cup out of the room and straight into Fouad's bedroom.

He clearly kept his childhood room, forsaking the master bedroom, which was apparently unchanged since his mother's death, down to the doilies on the nightstands, the toiletries on the dresser, and the crocheted cream bedspread. Gameela walked over to the bed, placed the teacup on the nightstand, sat down amid the unmade, crumpled bed linens. Resting her back against the headboard, she looked at Fouad's things scattered around the room. Here, as well as in the kitchen and bathroom, were his possessions, all patiently awaiting his return. She decided there was ample proof that he would, in fact, return, that this trip to his farm in Rasheed was going to last a few days only, as he'd promised, that he was not gone for good, as Marwa and her mother had both implied. "He does that all the time—comes to Cairo, makes us all believe he will settle down here, then disappears without notice," Aunt Ameera had said. "He has already stayed here longer than usual—three years now, since the revolution—so his return to Rasheed is long overdue. He can never remain in the city. He always runs back to his farm. It may be years before we see him again." But he would not have left his cologne in the bathroom, his jeans on the armchair in the bedroom, his sneakers under the bed, milk in the fridge. She hoped that even Fouad was not that disorganized.

Gameela picked up the cup, took a sip of hot tea, let it swirl in her mouth. The room—messy, dusty, in desperate need of a good airing—felt like a warm hug. She leaned her head back, closed her eyes, and took a deep breath in. In the layers between the musty smell of unwashed sheets and stale air she could clearly distinguish it: Fouad's scent. This was his room, his bed, and she was here. She smiled.

AN HOUR LATER, Gameela was back in the Tawfiks' apartment below, sitting on Marwa's bed.

"My mom is worried about you," Marwa said.

Gameela shifted in place. She knew what was coming.

"She says that Fouad is way too old for you. She gave him a lecture the other day, the night before he left. She thinks that was perhaps why he went back to Rasheed." Marwa was whispering, though they were behind closed doors.

"There is nothing for her to worry about."

"That's what Fouad kept saying."

Gameela looked out the French doors leading to the balcony. Amazing how much light those shutters kept out, when closed.

"You know you can trust me, don't you? I'm always here for you."

Gameela nodded.

"She is only concerned because he is so much older than you are."

"I really don't know what the fuss is about. It's not like we're dating or anything."

"You're not?"

"No!" Gameela's reply came out louder than she intended, tinged with frustration both at being wrongly accused of something and at being denied the guilt she wished were true. If only Fouad did say something. If only he did speak out, confess—what? His love? Infatuation? Aimless flirtation? Whatever it was, she wished he would speak up and spell it out. "There is nothing going on." She tried to keep the disappointment out of her voice.

Marwa tilted her head to the side.

"Seriously!" Gameela insisted. "Nothing going on."

"It's not that I wouldn't love for you to officially be part of the family. But I just don't get it. He's old enough to be your dad."

Gameela focused on the building across the street, started counting the balusters decorating its balconies, then tried to sync her breath to the counting: *one—breathe in; two—breathe out; three—breathe in*. Her efforts failed. Before she knew it, her eyes watered. She jumped up and walked out on the balcony, grateful to Marwa for not following her. Across the street, a young boy walked out on one of the balconies of the opposing building, one story higher than where Gameela stood. Gameela watched him wrap one arm around each of the thick balusters and look down at her. She waved at him, but he did not wave back.

Before leaving, Gameela sneaked into the kitchen and slipped the key to Fouad's apartment back where she had stolen it from: in the second drawer from the left, where Aunt Ameera kept it, where she often saw her pull it out and give it to the maid who walked up to clean the apartment from time to time. No one saw Gameela return the key, just as no one had seen her take it or use it to get in and out of the apartment above. On the walk back home, Gameela marveled at this new piece of information: how easy it was to do things behind people's backs. How exciting.

Was that how it felt to keep secrets?

It had been so effortless. All she had to do was walk into that kitchen, open the drawer, and take the key. Then she told Marwa that she had to run to the post office to drop off a letter her mom had asked her to mail—a simple excuse, nothing too elaborate or suspicious. She walked out of the apartment and, instead of leaving, walked up one floor, let herself into Fouad's apartment, spent an hour there, then walked back down to Marwa's. For the first few minutes, she had sat in silence, expecting to be discovered, anticipating a comment revealing that everyone knew exactly where she had been and what she had been doing. None of that happened. Her minor adventure had gone unnoticed, leaving no trace except for a lingering adrenaline rush. And, now that she was halfway home, a creeping guilt.

No, this had not been a break-in. She had taken nothing, disturbed nothing, and had been very careful to leave everything just as she had found it, down to the angle of the washed cup resting on the dish rack. Morally speaking, she had done nothing wrong, because her intentions were not reprimandable. All she had wanted was to satisfy her curiosity, to ease her crippling anxiety, to find out if Fouad truly was coming back, as he'd promised, or if she should train herself to live, again, without the expectation of seeing him.

He had done this before—disappeared without saying goodbye. One year after they first met, Gameela found out during her usual visit to Marwa's that Fouad had gone back to his farm in Rasheed on Egypt's northern coast, and had not left word on when (or if) he was coming back. That day, she had sunk into the sofa in Marwa's living room, trying her best to hide her disappointment. She had refrained from contacting him for an entire twenty-four hours, then she had sent a simple text: Coming back to Cairo soon?

His response, hours later: Not sure.

He did come back, but not until a full month had passed. His arrival, just like his disappearance, came unannounced—she had walked into Marwa's apartment and found him sitting in his usual armchair, as if he had never left. The surprise had rooted her in place long enough for Marwa to pull her into the apartment and start on a tirade about her workday, doubtless to cover up for her friend's revealing reaction. Everyone knew Gameela and Fouad were attracted to each other. No one approved of it. Every time Gameela visited her friend, she wondered whether that would be the day Aunt Ameera finally took her aside and addressed her relationship with Fouad directly, or worse, phoned her mother and warned her of her daughter's inadvisable romantic misadventure. But Aunt Ameera never did, resorting instead to a steady stream of passive-aggressiveness directed at her nephew: sideways glances, muttered, generalized insults whenever he changed his seat to get closer to Gameela (*some people have all the nerve!*) and the occasional plate of food shoved in front of him with such force that the sauce splattered like a minuscule erupting volcano. All Fouad did in response was smile at his aunt, wink at her, one time even pulling her into his lap and giving her a hug, to which Ameera reacted with a shove that almost sent him tumbling down from his seat. Gameela watched all of this with feigned indifference, laughing at Fouad's reactions as if all she were witnessing was the loving bickering between family members. As if the assumption that she would fall in love with a man twice her age was so absurd that it never crossed her mind.

Gameela herself would not have thought it possible, that first day when she met him, back when he arrived in Cairo three days after the start of the 2011 revolution. Her memories of him were now forever tinged with the excitement of the Arab Spring, with the promise of positive change, of miracles materializing for the asking. In the span of a handful of days, he had gone from a stranger sitting in the living room of her best friend to a man who marched beside her, who chanted the slogans demanding *Bread, liberty, and social justice* with a fervor that matched hers.

Then he became the man who gave her things.

She had accepted the first items out of sheer bewilderment: What was she supposed to do when offered a pencil stub? An apple? A box of bubble gum? Three paper clips strung together? A paper airplane made out of a magazine cutting that, when unfolded, revealed a yellowed 1979 feature about Umm Kulthum, the famous Egyptian singer? Had the gifts been expensive or suggestive of anything inappropriate or romantic (the categories being, because of their age difference, interchangeable), Gameela would have firmly refused the first one, just as she had refused the beautiful Qur'an housed in a small silver box that a college friend had offered her with terrifying reverence. But that first pencil stub—he had simply held it in front of her, and she, reflexively, had accepted it, only to watch him turn around and go back to his seat, never offering an explanation. The whole thing had seemed so natural that, for a moment, she suspected she had been asked to do something that needed a pencil to be accomplished—to jot down a phone number or an address—and that she had been too absentminded to notice the request. But the moment had passed and no one seemed to have noticed—the entire Tawfik family had been in the room with them—and she was left holding a short, yellow-and-black pencil in her hand. She had stared at it. Then, for reasons she could never explain, she had tucked it in her purse. She could have put it down on the coffee table, among the pile of books, magazines, art supplies, and half-filled tea-cups that inevitably covered all of the Tawfiks' living-room surfaces. She could have given it back to Fouad, treating it as the jest it probably was. She could have inquired why exactly he thought she needed a pencil. But she had done no such thing. She had accepted his gift, had held on to it, and had tucked it in her purse in a manner both conspiratorial and promising. In short, she had accepted whatever he was offering her without even understanding what the offer was. Which, once he disappeared, seemed like an apt analogy for their relationship.

She had kept those items, tucked them reverently into a box that she hid in her armoire for months, until he left for Rasheed with no promise of return. Even then, she had waited a good three weeks before getting up in the middle of the night, pulling the box out, and spreading the items on her bed. She placed the smaller ones in the center, looping them in concentric circles: the clips and pins, the wooden clothespin, the guitar pick, four different buttons given to her on four different occasions, the tube of paint, the twig. She formed three circles before she started placing the larger items around them: a stapler, a small clay planter (empty but previously used, its inside tinted a suspicious greenish brown), a folded table runner (crocheted, currently a faded ecru but probably a deep rose in its earlier life). By the time she was done, her entire bed was covered.

Gameela stood looking at Fouad's offerings. At some point—perhaps after the tenth or twentieth item—she had started trying to decipher a pattern to his gifts, a connection among them that would, perhaps, imply that what he was really giving her was not just the individual items but rather the sum of all their small pieces, an encoded message. Every time he handed her something, she would accept it with the excitement of a child getting one more clue in a scavenger hunt. She had spent nights sorting the items in groups, had even started keeping a log of when he gave her each piece, trying to discern a pattern of repetition or a connection that would finally spell out the secret that she knew he was hiding and that she believed he was trying to relay to her, bit by bit. Now, looking at those items, it occurred to her that they revealed the simplest of messages: she was at the center of a juvenile infatuation with an older man still trapped in teenage land, a man who would not open up to her, a man who offered her nothing but a bedload of junk. Slowly, deliberately, she had picked all the items up, stuffed them into a shopping bag, walked to the kitchen, and tucked the bag deep into the trash can.

When he reappeared a week later, she was still too angry with him to regret having thrown his gifts away. She would have stayed angry, would certainly have fulfilled her vow never to let him manipulate her again, had the man who returned after that month's absence not been so utterly different from the one who had left.

On the day of his return, he had stood up when she was ready to leave, announcing that he was going to walk her home.

"I don't need a chaperone, thank you," she had said, loud enough for Marwa and her parents to hear.

"I know. I would still like to walk you home. Please. I need to talk to you."

She had not known how to respond. Never had he so clearly singled her out, and the bewildered, alarmed look in Aunt Ameera's eyes confirmed that. Gameela should have refused. She should have demanded that he leave her alone.

She did not.

That day, they walked around the city for hours. He spoke to her of his family, of his British mother and doctor father—Aunt Ameera's older brother—of his life on the farm, of his resistance to living in Cairo, of how his last trip to Rasheed had not provided the refuge he usually found there. Instead, it had shown him that he needed to come back to the city. He told her he was here to stay.

That had been two years ago. Since then, the walk back home had turned into a routine; the late-night texting and midday phone calls discussing nothing had become the norm. Gradually, their conversations gained intimacy, their mutual need becoming unquestionable. Yet he never spelled out any plans for the future. Gameela had savored the bits and pieces of himself that he revealed to her at an excruciatingly slow pace, but after two years of this, she was becoming restless. What were they anyway? Friends? Lovers? Soul mates destined to stay apart because society deemed their match inappropriate? For months, Gameela had mulled the options as she waited for signs that he was finally ready to spell his feelings out, to commit to her and disregard their age difference, challenge anyone who was going to oppose them, including her family. Instead, he had scurried away to Rasheed unannounced. That was not the sign she was hoping for. Of course she feared that he was not coming back.

She vowed not to contact him, even if she had to wait for weeks or months. But she had not had to. He had called her the evening of his departure, apologizing for leaving without a warning, saying that urgent business had called him back to his farm (what kind of excuse was that?) and promising to come back soon.

She waited three days before deciding she still did not trust his promise. His trips to the farm were usually planned days in advance, and most urgent decisions were easily discussed on the phone with his estate manager. The idea of an emergency that needed him to hurry back without prior notice was hardly believable. To add to her suspicions, Fouad had been in a solemn mood for days before he left. The last time she met him, a week after Mark had returned to the U.S. with four finished profiles tucked contentedly on his hard drive, Fouad had been uneasy with worry. His excitement in the days leading to Saaber's interview had been replaced by a handful of what-ifs: What if the boy got in trouble because of that interview? What if they had both helped an American journalist portray an Islamist in a good light? Fouad had brought Mark to Saaber because he believed in championing the poor and downtrodden, but what if Mark focused on Saaber's ties to the Muslim Brotherhood, an organization that Fouad believed took advantage of the poor, one that he detested for being opportunistic and hypocritical? Fouad had wanted to help Mark depict a true picture of Egypt, but what if Mark's truth ended up being different from Fouad's?

Despite her own apprehensions—she shared some of his fears—Gameela had assuaged Fouad as much as she could, but his uneasiness made his subsequent disappearance seem suspicious. Maybe he did have to go to the farm on urgent business, and maybe he was running away again, just as he had done before. Running away from her. Was his withdrawal a sign that their relationship was ending? She had to find out. His apartment, she told herself, might provide her with an answer.

Now, walking home, she assured herself that his apartment had indicated his imminent return, even though she was not sure how much of what she saw was wishful thinking. His clothes still strewn all around his bedroom? He may not need them. The food in the fridge? Easy enough to ask Aunt Ameera to have her maid clean that out. His laptop lying on the sofa in his living room? He may have bought a new one. He may still be gone for good.

Arriving at her parents' apartment building, Gameela paused, stepping up to the parapet overlooking the Nile, looking out on the running water. She would go up to her parents and tell them nothing of her minor adventure. She no longer felt guilt or excitement, merely disappointment. Ever since she could remember, Gameela had taken pride in her morality, in her honesty, in her ability to distinguish right from wrong and then tread the right path with utter certainty, regardless of how difficult that path was. Now she felt as if her morality so far was not the result of her excellent character and religious observation, but rather a coincidental by-product of never having been tested. All she had to do was fall in love—yes, she was in love with Fouad, had been for three years now, was going to stay in love with him forever, even if he never reciprocated her feelings. All she had to do was fall in love, and there went her moral aptitude. Now she was as good as a common criminal, breaking into apartments, justifying her transgression. Sipping Fouad's tea while he was away. Eating his cookies. She sighed, then laughed. On the scale of transgressions, this was not too bad. On the scale of morality, the size of the transgression did not matter; what mattered was that something was done that contradicted the moral code she had always preached. Something that could be hard to explain to God. She blushed. Then again, God would certainly understand.

In the pocket of her jeans, her phone buzzed, shocking her out of her reveries. She pulled it out, saw that the message was from Fouad.

Coming back tomorrow.

She smiled ear to ear.

Have you seen this?

She clicked on the link he sent her, waited as her phone loaded *The New York Times*' page, Mark's byline under the title. He had been gone for only ten days—she had not expected the article to be published already. Flipping the phone sideways and zooming in, she began to read.

EGYPT AFTER THE REVOLUTION: PROFILE 4
PIGEONS

By Mark Hatfield

Cairo—Saaber wants to raise pigeons. Amid dozens of scattered dwellings stands a pigeon house his father built years earlier. Each morning, Saaber climbs the wooden ladder and refills the water bowls and grain dishes. "There is good money in pigeons," he says. "Also, they are loyal. They know me. All of them."

He crouches in the center of the clearing surrounded by the wooden cages, which are lined up along the perimeter of a rectangular platform that stands on top of wooden scaffolding and juts higher than the two- and three-story buildings around it. The cages are painted sky blue and have sliding doors that, during the day, are left open, allowing the birds to roam free. Pigeons pick grain out of Saaber's opened palm, and when one of them catches skin in its beak, he winces and draws his hand back. "Sometimes they bite," he says, rubbing his palm on his thigh.

From the pigeon house, the neighborhood is visible, sprawling and stretching until it is abruptly interrupted by a wall of new high-rises, marking the border of the upscale neighborhood of Zamalek. Here, in Ramela Boolak, buildings spawn free of any planning, infrastructure, or zoning regulations. This is one of Cairo's multiple slums dubbed as Ashwaeyat—the Randoms—home to the city's poorest residents. "We cannot afford apartments, so we build our own. But the government doesn't like that," Saaber says.

Five years earlier, Saaber's father was jailed after getting in a fight with a neighbor and striking him dead. He and the neighbor had fought over a piece of land that Saaber's father had constructed a dwelling on, the same dwelling Saaber still occupies with his mother and four younger siblings. Saaber's father, a diabetic, died while serving his prison sentence.

When the revolution erupted in January 2011, Saaber and his older brother, Houda, glimpsed hope. "There were chants of 'Bread, liberty, and social justice.' For the first time in my life, I saw a possibility for change."

But change did not come, at least not in the form Saaber had hoped for. Now, three years after the revolution, the most prominent change affecting Saaber is the absence of Houda, who, together with Saaber, had been the main source of the family's income since their father's imprisonment and subsequent death.

Houda was killed during a protest in 2013, two years after the revolution. Even now Saaber still has trouble speaking of his brother's death. His eyes grow dark, wider than they already are under his thick, bushy eyebrows, and his gaze wanders. "I was there. I was standing right next to him, and I couldn't do anything."

No one could prove who was responsible for Houda's death. The police inquiry closed with no conclusion because the bullet could not be traced to a specific weapon. Saaber insists Houda was shot by a sniper working for the antiriot forces that were openly attacking protesters, but the judge argued that some of the protesters were armed, too, and that the bullet could have come from anywhere. Saaber points at the center of his own forehead, indicating where his brother was shot. He doesn't believe such perfect aim could have been the result of a random shot accidentally fired by one of the protesters.

Since then, Saaber has stopped participating in protests. Growing up hopping from one apprenticeship to the next, Saaber has settled in the same job for the last year, working for the local electrician. His job takes him into the apartment buildings of Cairo's middle- and upper-class residents, and Saaber describes with awe an apartment they are working on now: gilded ceiling trims, multicolored solid wood parquet floors, and marble everywhere—countertops, vanities, even bathroom floors. He plans on one day having his own electrician's shop, but knows that such a plan requires an initial investment that he may never be able to raise. A pigeon trade, on the other hand, can start cheaply and be quite lucrative. Even if it isn't, at least it's a reliable source of food. Nowadays, feeding his younger siblings is becoming more and more challenging. His mother earns some money sewing for neighborhood women, but the bulk of the responsibility falls on Saaber's shoulders. At twenty-one, he is the family's main provider.

"This is one thing I miss about the Brotherhood. They used to fill my mother's pantry—oil, rice, sugar. They even provided my father with his diabetes medication. Now they are gone and no one has filled that void." The Muslim Brotherhood's support was the main reason Saaber and Houda felt compelled to join the protests after the Brotherhood's president, Mohammed Morsi, was forcibly removed from office one year after his election. "They are good people. Religious people. They helped us out for years. And they always said they stood for God and what He wants, so we had to support them."

Saaber grows a narrow, neatly trimmed beard, and no mustache. Under Egypt's religious classification, that implies he is a supporter of the Salafis—not the Muslim Brotherhood—a different group of Islamists who adhere to the fundamentals of Islam but who are not as politically organized as the Muslim Brotherhood was. For Saaber, however, such distinctions seem trivial, and he claims he doesn't know the difference between both ideologies. "Houda used to grow his beard like this, so I copied him. He was the one who knew all about politics. I merely followed him around."

Like many young men of his generation, Saaber is only superficially versed in Egypt's modern political Islam. He claims he belongs to the Islamists, but when asked about details of their ideologies—the role of women in society, for example, or their attitude toward freedom of expression— he has only the broadest of answers. As far as he is concerned, any organization that says it is there to implement God's will is better than any secular organization. Criticizing such an organization, or denying it support, is, to him, blasphemous. He believes in simple classifications: you are either with God or against him, and being with God is always better.

Equally simple is Saaber's dream of renovating his pigeon house. The scaffolding is strong, but the cages are built on a narrow platform that could easily be expanded to include at least fifty more. He is trying to educate himself in the business—pigeons are grown not just for food, but for collectors as well, who pay upward of three hundred pounds for the right pigeon. He points to a larger, freestanding pigeon house in the distance, one of several similar wooden structures dotting the neighborhood. That pigeon house, which is a good twenty feet higher than Saaber's and at least twice as large, belongs to a friend of his father's who, now that sunset is approaching, can be seen standing on top of the structure and waving a large flag to call his flock home. "One day, I will have a pigeon house just like his," Saaber says. "Wait and see."

11

S aaber stared at his own face, glowing back at him through the computer screen. The article was in English, but the Egyptian newspaper that covered it had translated it, and Saaber read it multiple times over before clicking on the link again and visiting the original. The English version's photo had better resolution than the one the Egyptian newspaper included, and when Saaber zoomed in, he could see his own eyes staring at him with admirable, intense resolve. He looked like a man with purpose.

AM LOTFY OWNED A TV SET. He was a friend of Saaber's father's and lived on the adjacent street. When the TV anchor pulled up the Egyptian newspaper with the translated article and held it up for the camera to see, Am Lotfy sent his youngest son, Soliman, to fetch Saaber.

Saaber ran all the way to Am Lotfy's rooms. He stood in the entryway, watching the TV, a crowd of neighbors gathering around him. The anchor was discussing the story with a guest, arguing about how the West chooses to cover the revolution.

"They focus only on the bad stuff. A boy like that, a kid—why feature him? The others, I may understand—the young revolutionary and the older woman and the lawyer. But why this boy? All they want is to highlight his dead brother, then start to talk about human rights issues, all to destabilize Egypt. Turn our country into another Syria or Iraq," the anchor was shouting.

Soliman stood next to Saaber, tugging on his sleeve. "You're on TV!" he kept repeating. "You're on TV."

"I know," Saaber said.

Behind him, he could hear the murmurs.

"What's going on?"

"Saaber is on TV. A famous newspaper in America interviewed him."

Saaber pretended not to hear them. The anchor put the newspaper down, and Saaber was a tad disappointed. For a moment, he had hoped that the man would raise money for him to construct a larger pigeon house. This anchor was famous for stunts like that. Standing there, seeing his own face on TV, Saaber had even imagined the anchor inviting him in as a guest on his show, telling him of the money he raised, featuring his finished, new pigeon house. But the man had been interested only in Houda's story. Still, Saaber had been featured on TV. Soliman still held on to Saaber's sleeve, even after the anchor switched to another story.

"You're getting famous, *wala ya* Saaber!" *Am* Lotfy said, accenting his words with a loud, guttural laugh.

Saaber chuckled. Behind him, he could hear his name resonate again and again, as if someone had whispered it in an echo chamber.

THE NEIGHBORS PEEKED OUT of their windows when he walked by. Neighborhood kids trailed him, chanting "Saaber was in the newspapers. Saaber was in the newspapers." The grocer, who had had multiple disagreements with Saaber's father and therefore never liked Saaber, looked at him when he walked by and nodded.

Saaber's mother watched all this and clicked her tongue.

At work, Master Zahi, the electrician Saaber apprenticed for, disapproved. "Why mess with journalists, boy? And Americans, too? Who do you think you are? Nothing good will come out of this." Master Zahi was the closest person to a father Saaber had since his own father passed away.

His disapproval almost made Saaber regret giving the interview. But the other apprentices made room for him to join them when they sat down for tea. One of them even started offering Saaber cigarettes. Saaber sat with them and accepted the cigarettes, even though he did not smoke. Master Zahi will come around, he told himself.

SAABER'S MOTHER FRETTED about his newfound fame.

"Why did you talk to this journalist to start with?" she asked him, standing in front of the tabletop stove shoved in the alcove between the front room and the bedroom. She emptied a bag of pasta into a pot of boiling water, stirred it with a metal spoon. In the bedroom, two of Saaber's younger siblings sat on the bed, fighting over a scrap of cloth. The other two had run out of the dwelling a few minutes earlier and could be heard playing outside.

"Why not? Why shouldn't I tell my story, if the American finds it interesting? Why shouldn't I tell them about Houda?"

His mother tossed the metal spoon to the side. It landed with a clang. He knew she still could not bear to hear his brother's name, but he thought she might approve of the article more if she viewed it as vindication for his brother's death, not only an article focusing on Saaber and his dreams.

"What good will it do, to talk about your brother? Will it bring him back?" she yelled at Saaber. "Is it not enough that I lost one son? You had to go put yourself in harm's way, too? You need to stay low if you want to survive, Saaber. You bring yourself up in the light like that, you take risks. No one likes a loudmouth."

The two kids in the bedroom screamed simultaneously, and Samah, the older girl, started to cry. Saaber's mother turned to the bedroom and yelled at them to stop. They didn't. "What am I supposed to do if you end up in trouble?" his mother turned to face him again. "How will I feed those hungry mouths?" She pointed at his siblings.

Saaber looked at the two girls, their continuous screams deafening. His father died before the youngest of his siblings turned two, and now Saaber was expected to feed all the mouths his parents brought into this world. He wanted to ask his mother how come she was more worried about losing the income he provided than she was about losing him, but when he turned to look at her, he did not feel like speaking anymore. He walked out of the room.

SAABER CLIMBED THE PIGEON house's scaffolding without looking down. Once he reached the top, he slowly walked onto the platform surrounded by the birdcages, their doors now open for the day.

There were dozens of them, flying in groups in and out of the house, pecking at the seeds scattered on the floor around their cages and at the saucers of water Saaber judiciously filled for them every morning. Saaber fell to his knees, scooped up some seeds off the floor, and held his hand out for the pigeons, who immediately accepted his offering. He felt their sharp claws dig into his arm, his shoulders, even his legs as soon as he made himself comfortable, extending them straight in front. The pigeons' beaks picked at his palm, occasionally pinching him. He grimaced but tried to remain still to avoid startling them. When the food in his right hand diminished, he scooped up more with his left and scattered it across his open palm to renew the offering.

When he was much younger, Saaber believed he could communicate with the pigeons. He used to imagine he'd lock eyes with one and it would pause, look at him thoroughly, not just in passing as everyone else did, and then it would understand him. It would become his companion, hopping up to his shoulder and never leaving his side, perhaps even following him once he walked back home, building its nest on top of his parents' dwelling, waiting up on the parapet for the first sight of him, and then, once it spotted him walking out of the door to go to the carpentry shop where he had worked as a child or to run an errand for his mother, the pigeon would follow him around, flying from building to building, drawing an aerial map that mirrored his steps. He had not thought of this childhood fantasy for years, but now it didn't seem so foolish. Saaber looked around, trying to find the right pigeon. On his right stood a single bird, its feathers tipped with metallic blue and green, its neck puffed with soft down. He extended his hand to it, stared, waiting for it to look his way. For a moment, he thought it was going to. But then the bird, hopping toward him, flapped its wings once and lifted just high enough to land on his palm, its claws digging into the mound below his thumb, its beak already pecking too hard at the food, catching skin and muscle, hurting him. Saaber jumped, flicking the bird away and, once he was upright, kicking at the rest of the birds gathered around him for good measure.

He examined his palm, squeezed out a drop of blood, then wiped it on his pants. He was getting too hot, standing in the afternoon sun, so he stepped around the cages and onto the shady part of the platform that ran around the wooden birdhouses, its narrow edge traced with a low parapet. Standing up there, he could see all the way to the horizon, an endless city of high-rises surrounding his neighborhood. Closer, two- and three-story buildings stood crowded together, most of them unfinished, columns jutting up their roofs, their outer shells content with exposing their structure of red brick. Here and there someone was apparently better off than the rest and had shown his wealth by finishing up his apartment per his taste, the uniformity of the red brick occasionally interrupted by baby-blue balconies, walls painted in green and white diamonds, or yellow plaster that coated a single third-story apartment but not the rest of the building. Behind him, the tall twin buildings flanking the Fairmont Hotel cast their shadow on Saaber, and he turned to examine the windows stretching up to the sky, wondering how it would feel to look down from one of them onto his pigeon house.

Once, after an argument with his mother (over money, again), his father had dragged Saaber by the arm and pulled him up the ladders to this same spot. Perched up on top of the entire neighborhood, his father had pointed far away to the tall buildings on the other side of the Nile.

"Look at these people, living like kings in their million-pound apartments. Do we have a chance of ever getting even a bit of what they have?" Silent, Saaber looked at his father. "No. We don't. Ever. This is a country where the poor are gnawed at, their bones sucked dry of all meat and juices before they are tossed to the dogs. *Yakloona lahm we yermoona adm.* They eat our meat and throw the bones away."

Saaber had narrowed his eyes, peering into the barely visible balconies, imagining piles of bones under each of these buildings, herds of dogs circling them in anticipation of more.

"Your mother thinks that if I could just work hard enough we'd be able to live like those people do." Saaber's father snickered. "Women are such idiots, boy. Remember that. You know what she never understands? That it doesn't matter how hard I work. Those people," he pointed again at the buildings, "they don't like to share. They know that our work only helps them increase *their* money. They don't work like we do, from morning till night. They *give orders.* All they know is how to tell poor people like us what to do. Well, you know what? I'm not playing that game."

His father had reacted to the view from the pigeon house by stubbornly committing to resist all that society—with its rich people, its religious people, its moral people—told him to do.

"It's called civil disobedience," he whispered into Saaber's ear. "Only I'm doing it on my own. So it's not really civil disobedience—it's Mansour disobedience." His father's laughter rang so loudly a dozen birds flew off in a single flutter.

After that, Saaber started noticing how everything his father did was, in fact, a refusal to do something else. Mansour refused to work longer than the minimum necessary to procure his daily joints of hashish and his *arak,* the homemade alcoholic beverage that was rumored to turn people blind. "Not that it would make a huge difference if I did turn blind," his father had chuckled. He refused to shave, until people started identifying beards with religiousness, at which point he refused to let his beard grow. Years earlier, Mansour had started his uninterrupted run of refusals by refusing to pray and fast, so the beard had seemed hypocritical.

"I don't do pretend," he told Saaber. "This," he said, pounding his chest, "is white. Pure white."

He refused to use titles when addressing people, scandalizing his family by calling even the elderly by their given names, forgoing the customary "Aunt," "Uncle," or "Mother." Later, he even refused to use people's names, stamping nearby shopkeepers with nicknames of his invention that he blared at them whenever he passed the open gates of their stores, the stores' contents as out of his reach as any prospect of a pocket full of money was. So the butcher became "Assassin," the grocer "Thief," the dressmaker "Zipper," and the barber "Baldy," even though the latter had a full head of hair. "Hey, Thief, how's business today?" he would yell at the grocer as he passed by, his smile revealing decayed teeth, his wave dismissive of the glare the grocer threw his way, as all the insulted invariably did.

"*Yallah ya haramy,*" he'd murmur as he passed by. "*Haramy we gabaan.*" A thief and a coward.

Only two people were exempt from Mansour's name-calling. The first was Saaber.

"I called you Saaber in the hope that you'd learn to withstand this life better than I did."

Saaber nodded, letting his name envelop him: The Patient One. The waiting one. The one, like Job, who can withstand life's trials.

The other exception befell the local preacher and Imam; him Mansour always called "*Ya Sheikhna*"—our elder, our preacher. Even Mansour never insulted a man of religion, acknowledging the boundary drawn by a turban and a brown *galabeyya* falling to the ankles. He could refuse to pray, yes— but he would not, publicly, reject a man of God.

Later, Mansour had refused to acknowledge the deed his neighbor showed him, proving that Mansour's brother had sold his half of the building to the neighbor only weeks before he died. "How could he have sold him something we don't own? These are the Randoms, Saaber! No one has a deed to these buildings. My brother sold this fool the street tram!" Mansour laughed, repeating the popular saying. The neighbor threatened to sue him if he did not return the money his brother stole, but Mansour refused to pay him back one penny. "I don't have your money!" he told the neighbor. "Go to the cemetery and ask my brother where he spent it."

When the neighbor showed up at Mansour's doorstep, armed with a piece of pipe, and tried to break in to claim the money he was certain Mansour was hiding, Mansour had struck him on the head with a brick. The man fell to the floor, dead. "I was defending myself!" Mansour had yelled at the police, refusing to admit any fault. He had even tried to refuse going to jail, which the police jotted down as "resisted arrest and assaulted an officer while performing his duty," a note that was later used to prolong his prison sentence by two years.

"*It's not fair!*" he had yelled as he was being dragged away.

"Life is not fair," Saaber's mother always barked at him whenever he would repeat what his father had said. "Deal with it."

Sitting in the pigeon house, Saaber remembered his father's words. He knew there was truth in them: it was not fair that he had to drop out of school after sixth grade to work to help support his family when other kids went on to college, benefiting from the free education; it was not fair that he worked so many hours and earned so little money; it was not fair that people walked into that hotel a stone's throw away and spent as much on one dinner as he earned during an entire year; it was not fair that his father had to die in prison because they neglected to give him his medication; it was not fair that he had been imprisoned in the first place for defending his family; it was not fair that his father, the rebel, had had to spend the last years of his life in jail, doing what he was told, having his refusal shoved down his throat and his lips held shut until he was forced to swallow; it was not fair that others Saaber's age were already courting young women when he had no way of procuring a place of his own to live in and therefore no way to marry any woman, not even the poorest one; it was not fair that he was already twenty-one and still stuck taking orders from his mother; it was not fair that his mother expected him to support his siblings, and not fair that his siblings will grow up to a fate no better than his.

It was not fair that his mother begrudged him that article, the one time someone paid attention to him, the one instance of recognition he got, the one chance to talk and have someone listen.

Saaber looked around him at the pigeon house. Was it too much to ask for, to want a bigger one? To dream of making a trade out of this? He wondered what his father would have thought of his plans and of the article the American wrote. He was quite certain Mansour would have rejoiced in the sight of his son's face gracing the American newspaper.

Dusk was already falling, and Saaber stretched, looking around him. Soon he would wave his pigeons back home. For a few more minutes, he stood in the shade, all the way on top of the neighborhood, and took in the surrounding buildings. He wondered how many people had seen the article or watched the TV anchor mention him. Even if the anchor didn't understand the story Saaber was trying to tell, it was still exciting to have him give Saaber such attention. Saaber scanned the buildings, looked through the open windows, and wondered if anyone was watching him, too.

He looked down at the yard in front of his mother's dwelling and saw that someone was watching him.

Am Ismail, his elderly neighbor, the father of the man Mansour had killed, was standing in the middle of the yard, his arms crossed, and looking straight up at Saaber. Even when Saaber locked eyes with him, *Am* Ismail did not budge.

Saaber stepped back around the pigeon cages and onto the center of the platform, shielded by the cages on all sides. He hated both *Am* Ismail and his wife, who always sat on that weird sofa in the yard, watching him, his mother, and his siblings come and go, never saying a word. Blaming them for their son's death, even though their son was the reason Mansour went to jail and died there. Saaber stayed in the center of the platform, occasionally peeking between the cages, until he saw *Am* Ismail shuffle back to his own dwelling.

Around him, the pigeons flapped their wings, flying in and out of their cages. Saaber grabbed the flag he kept by the cages, stepped out onto the platform, leaned against the parapet, and let the flag unfold in the breeze, waving it from side to side, calling his pigeons home.

12

"Are you out of your mind?" Ted whispered the moment he and Mark stepped out of the editor's office.

"Is that a rhetorical question?"

"You seriously told her you didn't want to do that story?"

"I still don't want to do it."

"You don't have a choice, do you?"

They walked together to their adjacent cubicles, Mark entering his, falling on his seat and tossing the sheets of paper he had in his hand on the desk. From his own cubicle, Ted leaned on top of the divider, his head reaching over Mark's desktop screen as he mouthed his judgment again. "You are out of your mind."

"I heard you the first time."

"What's wrong with the assignment she gave you? I'd trade you for it any day." Ted kept his voice low and leaned closer to make sure those in the neighboring cubicles didn't hear them. "She did you a favor. She's letting you cover a national political scandal, not some petty neighborhood dispute on the Upper East Side like me."

"I was there to pitch a story, not to be assigned one," Mark huffed, tossing his pencil on the desk. It slid, hitting his metal paperweight with a clank. The paperweight was a souvenir from Egypt, brass and decorated with carvings of the winged Nut, the ancient Egyptian goddess of the sky. Mark reached over and adjusted it so that Nut was facing him but looking to the side still, as all ancient Egyptian engravings did. They never looked one directly in the eyes, Mark thought.

"You got spoiled, that's what happened. You know you were lucky to get away with what you did. You know Elinor. She let it slide, but she was bound to respond."

"I know." Mark looked down at his keyboard, nodding.

Ted was right. Assigning him a story was an obvious power play, but Elinor could have done much worse. She could have assigned him some crappy report that was bound to be condensed to three hundred words and buried deep in the newspaper's online edition. Instead, she assigned him a piece on the Christie Bridgegate scandal, which was still today's hot news, even months after the intentional traffic jams took place. The message was clear: *I know you're a good reporter, but you're still* my *good reporter, and you will do as I say.* Of course she would feel the need to make a statement after the stunt he pulled: going to Egypt on a so-called vacation, then returning with four written profiles and presenting them to her, pitching stories that did not fall under his jurisdiction as a metro-area political reporter. Elinor had read them, nonetheless. She could have refused to pass them on to his old Middle East editor, reminding him that he was no longer a foreign correspondent and that whatever happened in Egypt was not his professional concern anymore. But she had not. She had shared them with her colleague, who loved the profiles and published them. Nothing Elinor did was spontaneous, no word uncalculated. With the *yes* she had granted his pieces came a *however*. Now it was time to execute the however. For all he knew, she could be assigning him pieces for the next three months, just to prove a point. He remembered how he used to complain about her refusing every second story he pitched. He would take a 50 percent rate of story approval with open arms now.

"I really don't want to be second string on Bridgegate."

"You don't have a choice."

"I know."

Ted sat back down, shaking his head. "You're nothing but trouble, man," Ted said across the cubicle wall.

In front of Mark, Nut's wings spread wide, keeping guard of the night sky. Mark turned the paperweight around so that the short edge of the oblong weight faced him. On each side, brass feathers flared away from the weight, as if Nut were trying to take off, held back only by the heaviness of the brass.

MARK LEFT EARLY to meet with a source who promised insider information on the Bridge report, but instead of heading straight to Battery Park, where they were to meet, he got off at West Fourth Street, stood in front of the Cage, and watched basketball players shove and tackle each other in the cramped, undersize court. The sounds soothed him: the players' shuffling feet, the dribbling ball, New Yorkers walking out of the subway station, tourists watching the ongoing game. He associated these familiar sounds both with his life in West Virginia, where he was on his high school basketball team, and with his years in New York when he first moved here, before the various Middle East positions. Sounds, scents, and places could all shift his mood, bringing one of the many versions of him to the forefront and silencing the others: The smell of falafel awakened Mark the foreign correspondent walking Egypt's streets; the vibration of the subway under his feet summoned Mark the New Yorker; the *azhan*—the call for prayer—evoked Mark the Muslim, just as the texture of black leather binders joyfully reminded him of his days singing in the choir of the Episcopal church as a teenager. He was all of these people combined, was usually happy to let them all coexist, but in the three weeks since he'd returned from Egypt, he felt his different selves clash, as if they were all suddenly resisting their confinement in one body. He needed to focus on this Mark, the New York Mark who had a New York piece to write, and to silence the Egypt Mark, the one who was (rightfully) still excited about the profiles he had just published, the one whose consciousness still lingered half the world away. For the first time, Mark felt his different selves competing for his attention, and the resulting strain distracted him. He needed to focus.

Leaning against one of the trees by the metal fence bordering the court, Mark watched the players, his arms crossed. A women's tournament; one team in blue, the other in white, all jumping, passing, wiping away sweat, dribbling, cursing. Any one of those girls would doubtless beat him in a one on one. The thought made him smile. He looked around, imagined the man standing by the far end of the court to be the father of one of the girls, imagined that the man's beaming face reflected his pride. Already Mark had a backstory forming: the man was poor, a janitor at a local school. For years he had been taking his daughter to basketball courts every afternoon, spending hours honing the skills that he knew would put her through college. She was to become a doctor, maybe, or an accountant, or a teacher at the very school the man worked at. Or maybe it was the other way around: the man might be a doctor or an accountant, toiling at a job he hated day after day just so his daughter could play basketball, just so she could become whatever she wanted to be—an athlete, an artist, a mother. Mark was good at imagining how others felt, a useful talent for a writer. That was the reason those profiles had turned out so well: he knew how to put himself in the shoes of others, and he knew how to make readers see what he saw—how Saaber yearned for a good life raising pigeons; how the elderly mother wished for her kids' safe future and saw that future in the stability the army rule provided; how ardently the agnostic revolutionary advocated for the separation of religion and state; how the lawyer focused on the new constitution, believing that the country's future lay in a strong legal foundation. He had poured his soul into those profiles, and draining though they were, they had left him, surprisingly, thirsty for more. More pieces on social justice; more intimate, personal profiles; and, above all, more of Egypt.

He pulled out his phone, sent Rose a text—Your day going ok?—then put the phone back in his pocket, not expecting an immediate reply. He watched a man in a suit scurry past, checking his watch once and then again seconds later as he waited for the light to turn so that he could cross the street. Being in a rush was such a New York state of mind, one that usually affected Mark, who normally would have been rushing to meet his source. Instead, he was tempted to stay here for as long as he possibly could, forcing himself to break his self-imposed rule never to waste time in the middle of a workday. Ever since he came back from Egypt, he had felt the futility of stressing over minutes. *Human history spans such a long time,* Rose liked to remind him whenever they discussed Egypt's slow pace compared to New York's. Egyptians, she explained, are habitually laid back, making appointments not by naming an hour but by referring to an intentionally vague time of day: *I'll see you in the afternoon. We'll talk in the evening. I'm going there after dinner.* She laughed at his incomprehension. *What are a few minutes here or there in a country that's been around for seven thousand years? What difference will half an hour make in the grand scheme of things?*

She liked that expression: the grand scheme of things. He liked the way she articulated the English language—with authority but care, as if it were one of the artifacts she handled with white gloves and cleaned with a horsehair brush. People always complimented her on her English, and, from the way her face beamed, he knew she was proud of her talent with languages. Still, she didn't sound American—her expressions too formal, her sentence structure too complex for day-to-day talk. He never revealed that to her. He didn't want her to feel self-conscious or, worse, try to change in order to fit in.

When they first arrived together in the U.S., he had explained that fitting in was a matter of place, not of people. Trying to ease her transition, he had introduced her not only to his friends but to New York's various nooks and corners: the spot in Brooklyn Heights where the city's silhouette looked best at night; the bench overlooking the pond at Central Park where he often sat during his first months in New York; the Polish deli in

Greenpoint that sold the best freshly baked bread; the Indian grocery stores that carried her favorite fruit—mangoes. Places, he explained, opened up to newcomers before people did. Places did not care how long you've lived here or where you were born; they welcomed you the moment you set foot in them. That, he told her, was the key to fitting in. She had to make New York her own.

He, too, had made Egypt his own, spending four glorious years there, never once considering the disadvantage of having so much fun in a place where he did not belong or dwelling over the inevitable time when he would have to leave it all behind. The effect was similar to splitting one's soul into pieces and scattering them around the globe. Every new place he loved eventually became a place he was destined to miss. Now, the taste of Egypt so fresh on his lips, he missed it more than ever, even more than he had when he decided to go back for those profiles. Rose's assumption that going back to write a few pieces would somehow flush the country out of his system was dead wrong. After spending a mere ten days there, he was struggling to fit back into New York's rhythm, more so than he did upon his initial return after his four-year tenure in Egypt.

His phone buzzed in his pocket. Rose had texted him back: Just got out of class. Meet me for lunch?

Can't do lunch. Meeting with a source.

New story?

Yes. Will tell you about it later.

Ok. Thai for dinner?

Sure. I'll pick it up on the way home.

He put the phone back in his pocket just as a girl on the blue team took a shot from beyond the three-point line. The ball curved up then fell straight through the hoop, and the entire blue team seemed to lift off simultaneously, jumping in joy. The girl, too, jumped, and the moment she landed, she turned and looked at the man Mark had been watching, who was still standing in the opposite corner. The man lifted his hands and clapped high above his head. Mark could not see the girl's face, but he knew she must have smiled.

"THAT SOUNDS LIKE an important issue to write about," Rose said. They were sitting at their kitchen table, eating Pad Thai noodles out of plastic containers. Mark used chopsticks; Rose, as usual, tried to use them but quickly gave up and picked up a fork instead.

"It's a very important issue. I still can't bring myself to care about it."

"Why not?"

He looped a few noodles around his chopsticks, lifted them a couple of inches above the container, and held them there, examining them. "I just can't focus."

"Maybe you're still tired after the trip to Egypt. That was a lot to do in ten days."

"But I've been back for two weeks. I can't stay tired forever."

"Then what is it?"

He took a bite of his noodles. "I want to keep on writing about social issues. I just can't get my head into politics."

"Politics affect social issues. That's exactly what your Egypt pieces show."

"Yes. But I still feel like I can make more of a difference if I write something more personal. If I shine a light on something that can be changed, rather than report on an issue that happened already and that I'm just trying to expose."

"You expose something precisely because you want to bring about change."

"But it's not the same kind of change. It doesn't affect people personally, at least not right away. It's not as intimate as . . ." He trailed off. Rose waited, watching him. "I just keep thinking of Saaber. I keep imagining that, perhaps, someone will read my profile of him and donate a new pigeon house or give him a job somewhere." Rose smiled, and Mark laughed. "Silly, I know."

"Not silly. A tad too optimistic, perhaps, but not silly."

"You don't think it can happen?"

"It could. Anything can happen." She did not lift her eyes from her noodles, stabbing them with the fork, turning it to wrap them around its prongs.

"You don't sound convinced."

"I can't be convinced of a prediction." She let her fork drop. "I'm not hungry anymore."

"What's wrong?"

"I spoke to my parents and Gameela today. My mom and dad are furious that you came through as supportive of a Brotherhood sympathizer, even though that was just one of four profiles. They wanted you to focus solely on how the army saved the country from the Islamists." Rose rolled her eyes.

"Your parents have no right to—"

"Trust me, I know. I'm just explaining my mood. And then Gameela sounded all negative, too. She was worried that the boy may get in trouble for talking to you."

Mark leaned back in his seat, crossing his arms. "Your sister started saying the exact thing to me *after* we got to Saaber's home and right before I interviewed him. If she was so worried about him, then maybe she shouldn't have led me to him."

"That's exactly what I told her. And now she's mad at me."

"She's just being paranoid."

"The entire country is paranoid. You know that."

Mark nodded. He heard evidence of her claim firsthand while in Egypt: conspiracy theories running amok, the most prevalent of them claiming that any event that could destabilize the country (an attack on a church; a recurrence of protests) was, in fact, orchestrated by the West in an organized effort to bring down Egypt's military and throw the country into the clutches of war, just like Iraq and Syria. All part of the West's alleged war on Islam. George W. Bush's "crusade" announcement remained fresh in people's minds a decade and a half after its utterance.

"Listen," Rose said, leaning closer across the table. "You wrote an insightful, compassionate series of profiles. You should be proud of them for painting a more honest picture of Egypt than many Americans get to see. If something good comes out of them, then great. If not, don't be disappointed. You know how Egypt is. It's not that easy to change things there."

"It's not easy to change things anywhere. But that doesn't mean we can't try, does it?"

She got up, walked around the table, and gave him a hug. "Of course not."

He patted her arm. He understood her reluctance to be optimistic, especially considering what had happened in Egypt in recent years, after a revolution that promised positive change ended up opening the doors to chaos. Rose was still more Egyptian than American, and her attitude was tinged with Egypt's millennia-long history of disappointments and bolstered by the Arab Spring's legacy of cynicism. His attitude was different. Such negativity was almost un-American. Wasn't working toward achieving positive change part of the fabric of his country? Wasn't that part of the West's promise and responsibility—to succeed and help others achieve similar success? Wasn't that the main allure of his job? He wasn't naive; he knew that the West's interventions were not always well intentioned or successful (the Iraq War fiasco provided ample, painful proof), but that didn't mean the underlying principle was necessarily false. The privileged were still morally obliged to help the less fortunate.

"I still hope something good will come out of those profiles," he addressed Rose's back as she washed her hands at the sink.

"It's possible. You never know."

He thought she didn't sound sincere, but without seeing her face, he couldn't be sure.

13

When the police arrived, Saaber was up in the pigeon house again. He heard the commotion and looked down to see three orderlies at the door to his mother's dwelling, on foot, their van parked at the end of the narrow alley. They were shouting at his mother, and his mother was shouting back, her curses directed at the police orderlies and the officer sitting in the van, who didn't seem moved by her clearly expressed prayer that they all burn in hell; that they all be shut out of Allah's mercy for eternity; that they get struck in what they hold dearest, in their children and wives and health; all while a small crowd gathered in front of the decrepit shack, idly chatting with the orderlies and throwing inquisitive glances at the lone police officer who waited in the van. Saaber watched from the pigeon house. He knew they were there for him.

They would have found him eventually, of course, even if *Am* Ismail had not led them to him. Saaber looked down at the man, his finger pointed upward, and watched the faces of the crowd collectively turn toward him. He remained perfectly still.

"Get down, boy," one of the orderlies called to him.

"What do you want?" A foolish question, Saaber knew.

"I said get down!" the same orderly shouted.

Saaber retreated, stepping back to the center of the pigeon house, surrounded by dozens of cages. He did not know what to do. His instinct was to flee, but he did not know where to go or what he was fleeing from. Stories of cramped, filthy cells packed with dozens of detainees flooded his head, stories of abuse, of torture. His father had died in jail. Saaber had never been arrested before.

"Don't make us come get you!" he heard someone shout from below.

Around him, pigeons were flocking in and out of their cages. Would they know to come back at dusk without him there? He told himself they must know. Walking around the cages, he started checking their doors, making sure none of the birds was trapped inside. He imagined birds dying of hunger, of thirst. Around he walked, opening cage doors, closing some by mistake then opening them again, always looking inside for a pigeon he'd missed. What else was he looking for? A sense of urgency came over him, a conviction that he was forgetting something important.

"I told you not to make us come get you."

Saaber turned. The oldest of the orderlies, a fat, sweaty man, was standing at the edge of the platform, panting as he spoke. Saaber stepped back until he hit the row of cages behind him.

"I didn't do anything."

"Not my job, boy. I just need to bring you in."

"What for?"

"Not my job to know." The orderly stepped closer, wiping sweat off his brow. Behind him, another one emerged, atop the wooden ladder.

"Man, this is high," he said, looking down as he hopped onto the platform.

"Now you need to come with us, boy. The officer is waiting in the van. Making him wait is only going to make him angry."

"I didn't do anything," Saaber repeated.

The sweaty orderly grabbed Saaber by the arm. The sun shone straight behind the man, making it hard for Saaber to see his face. He winced, looked at the other, younger orderly, and saw him standing by a row of cages.

"You think we can grab a couple of these for dinner?" the young orderly asked his colleague, snickering.

"Stop messing around. Let's get this over with," the older man said, dragging Saaber behind him. "It's too damn hot for February. My sweater is suffocating me."

The younger orderly reached into a cage and grabbed a pigeon, holding it up to look at it. "Would sure love to taste some stuffed pigeons," he said.

"Leave them alone," Saaber yelled.

The orderly turned to look at him.

"Stop messing around," the older orderly repeated. "Let's go." He walked up to the ladder, pulling Saaber toward it. "We have people waiting for you below, so don't try anything foolish."

Saaber stepped toward the ladder, his eyes still on the younger orderly, who was staring straight at him. Slowly, without looking away, the orderly lifted his other hand to the pigeon, wrapped his palm around its head, and started a slow, exaggerated motion of twisting its neck.

Saaber lunged at him, both hands outstretched, trying to grab the pigeon and set it free. Instead, he slammed straight into the orderly, who slammed into the cages behind him, which instantly gave under his weight. For a second, it seemed that the orderly was suspended in midair at an impossible angle, his feet on the platform, his arms in the air, a look of bewilderment on his face. He let go of the pigeon, which flew away with a flutter. Then he fell.

THE OLDER ORDERLY testified that Saaber dove at the younger orderly, sending him flying off the pigeon house and onto the roof of the adjacent building.

Am Lofty testified that he saw the man trip and fall on his own.

Saaber's mother testified that she saw the orderlies beat her son up as they tried to arrest him.

And *Am* Ismail, whose son had died in a scuffle with Saaber's father, testified that he clearly saw Saaber hold the man up and push him off the ledge, laughing out loud as he watched him fall.

Am Ismail, it turned out, was also the one who called the police in on Saaber, claiming that he had been in constant contact with foreigners, that he had been visited by multiple journalists, and that he was openly criticizing the government and trying to destabilize the nation by spreading lies about how his brother died. *Am* Ismail produced the newspaper article as proof, Saaber's face large and blurry in the online printout.

"We were just going to question you, boy," the police officer who took Saaber's statement said. "Why did you have to resist arrest?"

"I didn't do anything," Saaber repeated.

"You almost killed an orderly while he was performing his duties. You're lucky the man only ended up with a broken hip. You could have been facing a murder charge."

"He almost killed one of my pigeons."

The police officer chuckled. "Seriously? That's your defense?"

Saaber blinked. The police officer sighed, shook his head, and leaned back in his chair, fingers laced behind his head, looking out the barred window. Saaber looked out, too. Outside, a flock of birds could be seen in the distance, too far for him to determine if they were pigeons.

Part Three

14

Whenever Rose visits West Virginia, she marvels at the state's untamed connection to nature, a quality so different from Cairo or New York that she feels she is visiting an ancient, independent country. In the rental car during the nine-hour drive to Charleston, she and Mark rarely speak. He plays music—country, Garth Brooks and Tim McGraw—an indulgence he never reveals in front of their New York friends. *Hillbilly music*, he tells Rose, laughing, and she smiles, feeling a minor pang of pride at being privy to seeing the West Virginia Mark as well as the New York one—the two mutually exclusive in front of everyone else. "It's called a multiple personality disorder," she had once commented on the many versions of him that exist. "It's called a well-rounded personality," Mark had retorted. "Very few people are comfortable in as many skins as I am."

In the car, Rose reclines the passenger seat and alternates between sleeping and pretending to sleep. Her visit to Egypt was so short that she should not have felt jet-lagged when she returned to the U.S., and yet, for the previous two weeks, her sleep schedule has been a total mess. She wakes up in the middle of the night and tosses and turns for hours, insomniac and exhausted, and during the day, she craves sleep with an insatiable appetite. Never in her life has she obsessed about sleep as much as she has in the month since her sister died. Often, she wakes up from dreamless nights feeling like she just climbed out of a pitch-black abyss and hungry to jump straight back in. When she opens her eyes, sweaty and anxious, her mind struggling to escape a recent nightmare, she longs to go back to sleep, imagining that only a deep slumber can erase the memory of bad dreams. Sleep, it seems, is her only sanctuary.

Whenever she wakes up from napping during the car ride, Rose stays still and listens to the music. When she first arrived in the U.S., she had been surprised to learn that country music was considered an inferior art, as far as their New York friends were concerned. She had grown up listening to Olivia Newton-John (a remnant of her mother's infatuation with *Grease*) and had not known that she was classified as a country singer. This, to her, had been American music. Now she knows the term "American" refers to so many different, often contradictory things, that it is naive to use it and expect the listener to imagine any one, concrete attribute.

In the background, a man croons about how short life is, how he would have been a better person and shown more love if he had realized that in his youth.

"Not very subtle, country music, is it?" Rose asks.

"I didn't realize you were awake." Mark scrolls through his phone and changes the song.

"You don't have to change it. I like it."

"Wait. I've got a good one for you."

Now he plays a song about a man who, in response to his preacher's advice to pray more often, prays that his ex-lover meets with a colorful array of calamities. Rose laughs softly with every new curse disguised as a prayer.

"Never subtle, no. But that's part of the charm," Mark says, smiling.

Rose turns in her seat and faces him. "How come you don't listen to country music in New York?"

Mark shrugs. "I don't know. Doesn't seem to suit the place."

"I listen to Egyptian music there all the time."

"That's different."

"No, it's not."

They have been driving for close to four hours and still she does not see the familiar West Virginia mountains, their crests forming a wavy horizon.

"Where are we?"

"We just entered Maryland. About halfway there."

"You know the distance from New York to Charleston is about the same as the distance from Cairo to Aswan? I looked it up."

"So I'm basically driving all the way across Egypt today?"

"More or less."

"I hope my mom appreciates that."

"I'm sure she will."

To celebrate Mark's parents' fiftieth wedding anniversary, Mark's older sister, Emily, has planned a surprise visit by all three kids, each one driving from his or her current city of residence: Emily from Columbus; April from Pittsburgh; and Mark and Rose from New York. Emily has been planning the weekend with the care and attention usually reserved to weddings: sending her siblings save-the-date texts months in advance, ordering a cake from their favorite Charleston bakery, setting up a catered meal to be delivered to her parents' home the evening following their arrival. In a series of texts to the group chat she created to keep her siblings updated, she has suggested that they all bring "something appropriate" to wear to that dinner, even though it was to be held at home and no one was going to attend it except them. *I want them to feel special on their special day,* she said of her parents. Rose doubted her mother-in-law would feel the need to have a black-tie event, but just in case, she had brought her only semiformal dress, which was now hanging in a garment bag off the handle of the backseat window behind Mark. Rose glances at it. The bag, a translucent white, reveals the bodice of the peach-colored dress—sleeveless, with a delicate trail of fabric flowers in cream and peach decorating one shoulder strap and weaving its way down the bodice to the empire waist. She hopes the dress is appropriate—a happy medium between casual and dressy. Still, she is uncomfortable picturing herself wearing this to a dinner at home. The prospect makes her feel as if she were suddenly transported to a British manor populated with maids in black dresses and white aprons and a stern-chinned butler oozing superiority.

"Emily is taking this to the max, isn't she?"

"I think she is projecting her insecurities about her own marriage onto this entire thing."

Rose turns to face Mark, folding one arm under her head. "She's having marriage trouble?"

"Has been since she got married, according to Mom. She's probably persevering on the force of sheer stubbornness." He glances her way. "Don't tell Mom I told you that."

"Like your mom and I ever have intimate conversations." Rose looks out the window again. Way ahead, a mass of black clouds looms, promising a drenching.

"Emily is very grateful to you for coming with me. She would have understood if you had stayed home. I'm sure my parents would have, too."

Rose nods. Of course she had not liked the idea of dressing up and joining the festivities a mere four weeks after Gameela's death. But while staying home was certainly tempting, she didn't feel courageous enough to do so. There was a risk that Mark would bow out at the last moment, use her as an excuse to avoid attending the celebration. She knew how busy he was, how difficult it has been for him to carve out a four-day weekend. If he had not attended, though, his family would have assumed he had skipped to stay home with her. The last thing she needed right now was one more nail in the coffin of her relationship with her mother-in-law.

"It's going to rain," she says.

"Rain makes me feel at home. It always rains in West Virginia."

"It never rains in Cairo."

Rose pulls the back of her seat farther up, sitting straight, then puts her feet on the dashboard, trying to find a comfortable position. She ends up sitting diagonally, her back closer to Mark, her feet on the corner of the dashboard, her white socks taking in the bit of sun still shining at their car, despite the impending rain. On the side of the highway, the trees are splattered with leaves that have started to turn, glowing in yellow, orange, and red hues that remind Rose of fire.

Rose loves the trees. She loves all trees, mainly because Egypt has so few of them. Not that this is something she complains about: the sprawling desert is, after all, the main reason the temples and tombs of the Pharaohs remained intact, the dry climate of southern Egypt preserving them over millennia. All the palaces, towns, and living quarters that once dotted the humid Nile Delta in the north are eroded now, as her exasperated colleagues working on the new delta excavation projects keep lamenting. But *these* trees—the West Virginia trees she is taking in as she stands on Mark's parents' deck—are different from any other trees Rose has seen: wild, spreading endlessly in waves that hug the curves of the mountains ahead, claiming ownership of the land. The trees belong here with an authority that the Central Park trees can never boast. Rose reaches over and touches the rounded, lobbed leaves of an ancient white oak, its branches extending to within inches of the deck. During her first visit here, Mark dug up a massive folder containing a tree identification project he completed in seventh grade. Flipping through the pages, he acquainted her with trees that had stood in place since his childhood: the white oak to the left; the two sugar maples ahead; the row of thuja trees forming a privacy screen to her right. The backyard sloped down in a neat lawn that eventually gave way to an untamed forest of maples, oaks, and beech trees, among others, many of them overgrown with climbing vines and weeds that rivaled the trees in height. Sometimes, Mark told her, you could see a family of deer strolling out of the forest and onto the lawn. Every time Rose was here, she looked out for deer, almost squealing in delight whenever she saw one. They, too, belonged here in a way that Rose envied.

She leans against the deck's railing, watching a pair of squirrels chase each other across the lawn. Now more than ever does she believe Mark's claim that belonging starts with an identification with the place, not the people. "The natives may take you in, or they may refuse to do so, regardless of how long you've lived among them," he had once told her as they strolled along the Nile. "But places are always more welcoming. Places don't care where you were born or how long you've lived in them. If you like them and make the effort to know them, they make you feel like you belong there. It's their gift to you. Their way of liking you back."

Throughout his travels, Mark had made it a priority to know the place that was to become his home. In his first years in New York and, later, in Lebanon and Egypt, he had kept journals with folded-up maps nestled within their pages, had scribbled descriptions of the most random of spots—the corner of Thirty-sixth and Broadway, where he tried honey-roasted nuts for the first time; the brick-paved stretch of Hamra Street in Beirut, where he often stood under the same palm tree and watched the stores light up at dusk; the row of shops bordering the Zamalek Sporting Club in Cairo; the first bench on the right-hand side as one walks off the Qasr El-Nil Bridge; the coffee shop a few steps below the sidewalk on El-Moez Street. The more of these random nooks he could claim an intimate knowledge of, the more he felt at home.

Now, looking at the forest beyond the deck, Rose understands. She closes her eyes and thinks of her own nooks, the places where she feels the happiest: her desk at the Met; the stoop in front of Mrs. Kumiega's apartment building, where she keeps her geraniums in the spring; the table by the tennis courts in the Gezira Club, where she used to eat breakfast and go over her course work during her college years in Egypt; the hall at the Egyptian Museum where she often sat, cross-legged, and sketched in front of the statue of Akhenaten, the Pharaoh who called for the worship of one god only and angered the priests. Her places, collected, are as unique and individual as Mark's. Her places make her who she is. And now, strangely, she realizes that this spot on her in-laws' deck is one of her places, too.

"Beautiful out here, isn't it?" Her mother-in-law steps up next to her, her hand extended with a cup filled with steaming coffee. "Cream, no sugar. Just the way you like it."

Rose takes the cup, holds it in both hands, and rests her elbows on the railing. "Thank you, Laura. I needed this."

"I figured you did."

They stand in silence, looking out on the forest ahead. The sky is streaked pink and purple, the setting sun already out of sight.

"Thank you for coming, Rose. I know it's not easy for you. But seeing you all here was the best surprise I've had in a long time."

Following Emily's plan, the three siblings had met in the empty parking lot of a nearby elementary school, Mark and Rose arriving there second, after Emily, and then waiting for forty-five minutes for April to get there, Biscuit, her golden retriever, riding in the passenger seat. They had driven to their parents' home together, a convoy of offspring, and had rung the bell together. Emily's two girls stood in the front and held a bouquet of flowers as tall as the five-year-old and taller than her three-year-old sister, Biscuit barking happily behind them. When Laura answered the door, she stood in place, one hand on her mouth, and teared up. Rose had never seen her mother-in-law show that much emotion before.

"We're happy to be here," Rose says. "But Emily gets all the credit. She is the one who organized this."

"I thought she did. But you had a legitimate excuse not to show up. I just want you to know I appreciate your coming. And your drive here was the longest, you and my New Yorker son." Laura is looking out at the trees, holding on to the railing with both hands. Slowly, she closes her eyes, lets her head drop back, and takes a deep breath in. "I love this place," she says. "Never could understand why anyone would want to live anywhere else."

"My sister would have said the same thing about Egypt," Rose says, immediately regretting mentioning Gameela. She doesn't want to talk about her sister to anyone, let alone to her mother-in-law. The pain she sees in the eyes of those trying to console her often enhances her sense of loss, and their inevitable questions underscore her vexing ignorance. *So you don't know what happened? It couldn't have been a coincidence, could it? Wasn't that the same boy Mark interviewed? Do you think she was there to meet him?* Better avoid the topic altogether, rather than mumble a string of excuses for her unsisterly lack of information.

"What I mean is that I know what you're talking about. It must be hard to imagine anyone choosing to leave a place you love so much. But I think people who move away usually think more about the destination than they do about the place they leave behind. It's like chasing a dream. You just don't look back until much later. At least that's how it was with me." She takes a sip of her coffee, stops short of explaining how she had been so excited about the move to the U.S. that she had barely given a thought to the ocean that would separate her from her family. On the phone with her parents during her first months in the U.S., she had shed silent tears, marveling at how someone's voice could be so deceptively close when they were on the other side of the globe. "But it must be nice to grow old in the same town where you were born, so close to your family."

"It is. I grew up two miles away from here, on Loudon Heights Road." Laura points to the right. Rose can see only more trees in that direction. "My kids went to the same elementary school I went to—a private Catholic school. One of the best in town. Good education, of course, but my parents sent me there for the religious instruction, and I did the same with my kids, even though we're technically Episcopalian, not Catholic. Now one of my kids is a Muslim, the other an agnostic, and the third is religious but otherwise a mess," Laura laughs. "So much for planning."

Rose doesn't know how to respond. She focuses on her coffee, gulps it all down a bit too quickly, then holds on to the empty mug. She can feel Laura's eyes on her but does not look her way.

"How are your parents holding up?" Laura asks.

"Surviving. One day at a time."

"You talk to them often?"

"I call them every day."

Laura nods. "Good."

She is still looking at Rose, and now Rose looks back, examines her mother-in-law: tall, skinny, her hair a short, silver bob, her eyes a piercing blue. She must have been a remarkable beauty in her youth—even now, in her seventies, she looks more put together in her knee-length floral dress than Rose ever does. Rose is irked by how much Laura intimidates her. Much of it is her appearance, which Rose knows is petty, but some of it is Laura's confidence, the way she fills up the space she takes in the world with the same authority as those trees do, an authority that has given her perfect posture and the impression of a radiating aura, as if her cells exude light. Rose forces herself to hold Laura's gaze, tries to absorb some of that confidence and reflect it back on her, pulls her shoulders back and reminds herself to stand up straight.

Behind them, they hear a bang. Through the windows overlooking the deck, Rose sees Mark sitting at the kitchen table with his father. They are both laughing out loud while Emily kneels to pick something up from the floor. Mark moves to help her, bending down and emerging with pieces of a broken mug in his hands—a victim of his father's renowned gesturing, apparently. Laura watches them and shakes her head.

"He is a walking hazard," she says of her husband. "I'm surprised he hasn't accidentally caused any of us physical harm yet. I can easily imagine him waving a knife around and impaling someone. I bet he'd find even that funny."

"He does see humor in everything, doesn't he? I would love to have that attitude."

"You wouldn't love to live with that attitude for fifty years."

Rose looks at Laura, surprised.

"I probably shouldn't have said that. Now I've ruined your mental image of a perfect marriage." She smiles at Rose. "I didn't mean that I don't appreciate his sense of humor, of course. It was probably the reason I fell in love with him in high school. I just meant that it's hard to live with someone who has such a different disposition than I do. But I guess all marriages are like that."

Laura's words remind Rose of the first time she met her in-laws—in Egypt, when they arrived to attend her wedding. Jarred, all smiles and ringing laughter, squeezing Rose in a hug so tight it made her ribs hurt; Laura, giving her a firm handshake, looking at her with unabashed curiosity, with fixed, narrowed eyes that as much as spelled out her thoughts—*So this is the woman who made my son leave his religion.* Of course, Rose may have been imagining things, her guilt about Mark's conversion mixed with his description of his religious upbringing imposing thoughts on her mother-in-law that she may not have entertained. Then again, Laura had not taken Mark's conversion lightly, and Rose still does not blame her.

"So what's your secret to a successful marriage?" Rose asks her mother-in-law.

"If I knew the answer to this question, I'd have put it in a book and become rich and famous."

Rose glances back at Mark. He is seated at the table again, listening to his father talk, a broad smile on his face.

"Did Mark ever tell you about our dog Mandy?" Laura asks.

"No."

Laura turns and points to a large oak standing at the end of the lawn. "She is buried under that tree. She was a rescue, a cute puppy that grew into a fairly obnoxious beast. Never friendly, hiding from everyone, scared of her own shadow. She fell ill one day when she was about seven years old and died a few days later. We buried her there, held a ceremony and everything. Emily and April both cried their eyes out, but Mark just stood to the side, totally silent. I didn't think much of it—he rarely ever played with that dog anyway, and he was what—twelve, maybe?" She glances at her son, smiling. "That evening, I woke up in the middle of the night thinking I heard a sound. I stayed in bed for a while but couldn't go back to sleep, so I walked around the house checking on the kids and saw that Mark was not in his bed." In the kitchen, Biscuit barks, and Rose looks at her husband, who is holding a treat up high, teasing the dog before feeding him and petting him on the head. "I woke Jarred up and we searched the entire house—nothing. I was about ready to call the police, when Jarred stepped outside and found Mark in his sleeping bag, next to the dog's grave, fast asleep. In the middle of the night, out in the backyard." Laura pauses and looks at the oak again. Rose watches it, too, tries to imagine a young Mark lying down by its trunk.

"Now, I'm as much of a country girl as anyone, but I still have great respect for the wildlife," Laura continues. "We have everything here: bears, raccoons, even coyotes, sometimes. Naturally, I freaked out and ran outside and wanted to wake him up and take him indoors, but Jarred stopped me. Guess what he did?" She looks at Rose but does not wait for a reply. "He went to the garage, got his camping tent and his own sleeping bag, set up the tent around Mark as he slept—just a cover, of course, no ground cloth or anything—got in there with him, and they both slept through the night together by the dog's grave."

Now Laura is watching her husband. He seems to be in the middle of telling a story, too, but his story has him agitated, his hands waving in the air until he drops one hand and pounds three times on the tabletop. Mark, Emily, and April, who is now standing next to her father, erupt in laughter again.

"He does have the most contagious laugh I ever heard," Laura says, smiling.

Rose watches Mark. All that laughter has relaxed his face in a way she has not witnessed in a long time, and he now looks so much like the Mark she first saw in Egypt, all wide-eyed and joyful, that the association makes her nostalgic. Mark, perhaps sensing Rose's prolonged examination of him, turns toward her. For a moment, he, Rose, and Laura silently observe one another, until Laura moves closer to Rose and wraps an arm around her shoulders, pulling her in, squeezing her tight.

Laura's embrace is as assertive as everything else about her. Rose feels she is fixed in place, anchored, contained with such protective force that before she can see it coming or stop herself, she starts to cry. Mark walks up to her. Only when he has wrapped his arm around her, too, does Laura let go of Rose's shoulders. With two quick taps on Rose's back, Laura walks inside, leaving Mark and Rose alone on the deck.

Rose does not wear the peach dress. Instead, she chooses black slacks and a light gray top with minuscule blue flowers, form-fitting but not too tight, something she feels comfortable in. From her jewelry box, she pulls out the necklace Gameela gave her for her birthday years ago. The turquoise stone falls perfectly in the center of her V-neck. Rose watches it. She wonders if she ever told her in-laws the meaning of her original name—Fayrouz—but she can't remember. For a few weeks now, she has been suffering from an onset of regret, often wishing she had not officially changed her name—she could have kept Fayrouz but gone by Rose—then reminding herself how much this would have complicated things, from her byline on her published research papers to her relationships with colleagues. She lifts her hand and adjusts the pendant. The gold wires wrapped around it remind her of Laura's hug of the evening before.

They are all gathered in the living room—all except Emily, who is on the phone with the caterer, giving him directions, pacing the narrow walkway cutting through the front lawn as she waits for the food delivery. Rose watches her through the living-room bay window. Yesterday's rain has drenched the lawn, but the walkway is dry. Emily stands at the end of the footpath and looks out to her left, one hand holding the cell phone up to her ear, the other shielding her eyes from the sun.

"Her nerves are so tightly strung, I think I can hear them vibrate all the way from here," April whispers as she moves closer to Rose.

"She just wants to make sure everything is perfect."

"Nothing is ever perfect, and there isn't anything she can do about it. She just can't accept that."

"Maybe she needs you to talk to her. If she is stressed and not dealing well with her stress."

"She will never accept anything I say."

Rose shifts in place. She wants to say that she lies awake at night thinking of the endless ways she has not helped Gameela, regretting all the times she almost picked up the phone but got too wrapped up in the hustle of life and postponed the call. For weeks, she has imagined the things Gameela might have told her, if they had spoken more often: revealing why she quit her job; explaining how she managed to keep this a secret from their parents; whispering one detail that Rose may have responded to and somehow changed the course of fate. *No, don't do that. Don't do that.* But don't do what? Which single misstep on the trail that led to Gameela's death could Rose have prevented over the phone? She may never know. She considers explaining all of this to April, urging her to become more involved in Emily's life, to throw fears of intrusion to the wind and just *help your sister*, but she doesn't want to compare Emily to Gameela, and she certainly doesn't want to preach to April, who, along with Jarred, was the first to make her feel like a welcomed member of the family. She glances behind her at her father-in-law, sitting in an armchair, looking up at Bill, Emily's husband, who, drink in hand, has been talking nonstop since Rose entered the room. Jarred catches Rose's eye and winks at her, and Rose smiles. From the dining room, she can hear Laura talking to Mark as they both set the table. Rose suspects they are talking about her, which usually would have irritated her but now doesn't. She had gone to bed early the night before and woken up with a newfound warmth toward her mother-in-law, the result of their encounter on the deck. The feeling is so new and fragile that Rose has tiptoed around Laura all day, afraid to do anything that could sever this brand-new tie.

"Come," April says, pulling her by the elbow.

Rose follows April out the door. They walk up to Emily, who has hung up but who is still standing at the end of the walkway, looking out for the caterer.

"Are they almost here?" April asks.

"He's been 'almost here' for the past fifteen minutes," Emily says. She has her arms wrapped around her chest, her cell phone still clutched in one hand. "The man is an incompetent idiot."

"It's not even two yet. Relax. There's no rush."

Emily exhales loudly, letting her arms fall to her side. She glances at the house where Bill is still talking to Jarred, both visible through the bay window.

"He's going to bore Dad to death," she says.

"No, he's not. You know Dad doesn't mind," April responds.

"He should be watching the girls. I told him to keep an eye on them."

"They were in your bedroom when I walked down just a few minutes ago," Rose says. "Do you want me to go check on them?"

"Would you, please?" Emily asks.

Before Rose turns around to walk back into the house, Emily grabs her forearm and squeezes it. Rose pats Emily's hand, wondering why everyone is suddenly touching her, how un-American it seems, this constant patting and hugging by other women, something that happens all the time in Egypt but that seems surprising here. Must be a side effect of bereavement, she thinks. Emily's grip relaxes, and Rose heads back inside.

The girls, both wearing puffy dresses, have set up a fort between the bed and the dresser, drawing a perimeter using every pillow in the room plus, Rose suspects, quite a few pillows from other rooms as well. They are sitting in the center of the pillow fort, two coloring books abandoned by their sides, playing instead with a long strip of fabric that seems to be made from several sashes and belts tied together, their ends then joined by the leather shoulder strap of Emily's Coach purse. The five-year-old is trying to get her younger sister to hold one end of the sash in place while she wraps it around the pillows, but the younger girl is totally absorbed in picking at the flowers adorning her Mary Janes.

"Where did you get those belts from, Maggie?" Rose asks the older girl.

"Mommy's suitcase."

Out the window, Rose sees Emily and April talking. She knows she should be cleaning up this mess, carrying the pillows back to their rooms, carefully untangling the mass of belts, putting the strap of Emily's purse back on before she discovers the vandalism and suffers another twist to her already frail nerves. In a few minutes, she will do all that and then walk the girls down to join the family. For now, she stays by the window, listening to the two young sisters chatter, watching the two older sisters talk, their heads close together, keeping her arms wrapped around herself, trying to think of nothing.

ON THEIR LAST DAY in West Virginia, Mark takes Rose on a hike. He drives her to Bridge Road, parks in the lot serving the small, upscale strip mall, then guides her a block down a curving street, where they step off the high-traffic road and onto the hiking path and, within minutes, are so fully enclosed in the tree-studded trail that Rose cannot believe they are still in the heart of one of Charleston's busiest residential neighborhoods.

"My aunt brought me here the first time when I was a kid. Back then, she told me a story about how this trail was built by a wealthy man for his wife, who liked to ride in a horse-drawn carriage. I believed that for decades, always associating the trail with some kind of Victorian romance," Mark laughs. "Then I looked it up and it turns out the trail was built by some governor in the early twentieth century so that workers could transport bricks to a house that he was building up the hill. He eventually used it for his carriage, and I'm sure his wife did as well, but the whole brick transport thing ruined the romantic story. I still like the trail, though."

The path winds down, wide and well maintained, unlike the narrow trails strewn with fallen branches that Mark has taken Rose to before. Curving and turning, it alternates between spots totally enclosed in trees and others with a clear view of the river below and the city on the other bank. One such spot has been fitted with a stone bench. Mark takes Rose by the hand and guides her there. They sit down in silence, watching the city, its handful of high-rises sprouting between the river on one side and the forest-covered mountains on the other.

"I have something for you," Mark says.

From his pocket, he takes out a red-and-white-checkered kerchief, unfolds it, and pulls something from its center, placing the object in Rose's palm. For a moment, Rose mistakes it for a stone, but then she recognizes the rough object.

"Is this an arrowhead?"

Mark nods. "I found it on a hike when I was in high school. I tried to look it up back then and was told it may be Early Archaic—as old as the Pharaohs—but of course, this may not be true. You might be able to find out."

The arrowhead is a reddish granite, smooth with a still-sharp point. Rose places it in one palm and runs her fingers around its ridge and down to the base where it was once attached to a wooden shaft.

"That's a perfect gift to give an archaeologist, isn't it?" she smiles. "I feel spoiled, like we're courting all over again."

"I'd like to spoil you a bit. You need it." He pauses, extending one foot and ruffling some leaves that have fallen on the ground before them. "I need it," he adds after a while. "I've been kind of afraid I was losing you." His short, nervous laugh sounds like a hiccup.

Rose says nothing. She wraps her palm around the arrow, feels its sharp edges dig into her skin.

"Am I losing you?" Mark's voice has lost its artificial humor.

Rose opens her palm and looks at the lines the arrow's head has drawn on it, imprints that will soon vanish. She has always taken pride in how transparent her relationship with Mark is, how she never lies to him, never holds anything back. Now it occurs to her that she has taken pride in something that was more coincidental than a product of her character: she has held nothing back because she has had nothing to hide. She thinks of the nights in the previous weeks when she lay in bed, insomniac, thinking of Gameela and of Egypt. She would fall asleep only after playing a trick on her mind: imagining that she was back home, living with her parents again, taking care of them, embracing Egypt the way she should have embraced it back when she lived there but did not, loving the country that she has made into a career but that she has failed to feel attached to the way Gameela had, the country that she has so willingly deserted. She is almost certain that Mark would go back with her to Egypt now, if she wanted to—wasn't that what he had craved? To report on the developing world from the heat of its overcrowded streets? But for the previous weeks, she hasn't been sure she wanted him there with her, and to complicate things, she isn't sure she truly wants to go back herself. Still, the dream of being back home—alone—was the only way for her to fall asleep, and that is something she cannot share with him.

"Of course you're not losing me," she finally says. She considers adding that she feels she is losing herself, that she has been shredded into parts that have been scattered, like Osiris's body, all over the place, but that unlike him, her scattering is not restricted to Egypt, but is global: her arms in Egypt at her parents', wrapped around them in a tight hug; her head in New York, studying and producing enviable scholarly work; her legs in West Virginia, hiking its many trails; her heart buried with Gameela. She imagines Mark in parts, too, and when she looks up at him, she sees not the West Virginia Mark that she is expecting, all at ease and at home, but the eyes of the young Mark she never knew, the one who spent the night out in the cold next to his dead dog, the one who glimpsed something shimmering and reached for it, holding on to his prized arrowhead for decades only to share it with her now, just because he knows she would like it.

"You just need to give me some time," she says.

He nods, reaches over and holds her hand in his. His hand is moist with sweat. Rose has rarely felt his hands sweat before, not even in Cairo, where the temperatures routinely rise to over a hundred degrees in the summer. She wonders if Cairo was too dry to cause his hands to sweat, if this is a product of West Virginia's humid heat, or if this is another manifestation of his stress, a sign to add to the ones she has noticed since Gameela's death: the sudden jerks in the middle of the night; the detached air that sometimes envelops him as he sits in his armchair in the evening, appearing to gaze into a book but obviously far off; that time she passed by the bathroom and saw him standing with his hands on the vanity, his head bowed down, visibly shaking. She had imagined such signs were indications of Gameela's ghost brushing against him. In her darker moods, she had found Mark's suffering gratifying, a well-deserved retribution. Now, with her hand in his, she cannot rejoice in his pain anymore. She squeezes his hand, and he squeezes hers back.

The arrowhead is still nestled in her other palm. Rose examines the stone's uneven surface, the many facets that someone carved thousands of years ago.

"I can't believe you actually found this."

"I've always been lucky."

"Did you look for it? Or did you find it by accident?"

"I looked for an arrowhead every time I went hiking for my entire childhood. The hills here are rumored to be strewn with them, but it's quite hard to find one. It only took me about eight or nine years." He laughs. "Still lucky, though."

"Maybe you're confusing luck with hard work."

He shrugs. "Maybe it's lucky to be able to work hard at something and actually get it."

"Now you're being too philosophical." She reaches over for the kerchief Mark has put on the bench between them, wraps the arrowhead back in it, and places it in her pocket. They stay in place, her hand in his, watching the trees around them and the city ahead, until Rose feels that perhaps those trees, too, have taken her in, and that she can now count this spot as her own.

15

I don't understand," Ingrid says.

Rose sighs. "Why? What don't you understand?"

"Why do you need to collect her things? What do you expect they will tell you?"

"What all things tell us—how she lived, what mattered to her, what she believed in. It's our field, Ingrid. I thought you of all people would understand."

Ingrid runs her tongue between her teeth and her lips, tilts her head to the side, and stares at a point in space right over Rose's shoulder. They are sitting at a coffee shop two blocks away from work. Ingrid just finished her lunch. (A pastry. She said she was in the mood for refined sugar.) Rose, who has not been in the mood for food in general lately, is on her second extra-large cup of coffee. She has been back from West Virginia for only two days, and already she feels as if she has been in New York forever, the massive city actively erasing the memory of all that precedes it. Rose, resistant, insists on wearing the turquoise stone at all times, and now carries the arrowhead in her backpack everywhere she goes.

"It's a basic archaeological approach. Examine artifacts to come to a better understanding of the people who used them. All I need is to catalog all the things I brought with me, find a pattern, a thesis, some general thread that links them all, and then I'll understand her better. It's just killing me, how we hadn't really spoken for so long. And then, if I do that, maybe I'll find out why she happened to be near that boy when he blew himself up. I just can't believe that was a coincidence." She pauses, contemplates adding that driving all this is her suspicion that her own life had influenced her sister in a way that led to her death. But she knows Ingrid will deny that thesis, and she doesn't want to say something designed to produce a reassuring response from her friend.

"I don't see how her basic possessions can reveal anything about how she died, Rose."

"They've already revealed one thing I didn't know: that she had quit her job. I found proof of it among her things, and it's blown my mind, that she could have kept such a thing to herself. Makes me see all the other aspects of her personality in a new light."

Ingrid puts her coffee down, looks at her mug. Behind her, three people sitting at the next table burst out laughing. Rose is tempted to yell at them to be quiet.

"There is one fundamental flaw to this approach," Ingrid starts, speaking slowly. "Yes, we collect artifacts to find out about people, but we do so because artifacts are the only things that survive over hundreds or thousands of years." She looks at Rose, her eyes apologetic. "Artifacts are not the best way to find out about people; they are the *only* way to find out about people who lived a very long time ago. This is the difference. Even now, you still have better access to your sister than whatever those things will tell you. You have her friends. Your parents. Her colleagues at work. All of them knew her. You should be talking to them, not staring at her old T-shirts and scarves and hoping they tell you something. Do you think if we could interview Rameses's priest or even one of his servants we would have spent years staring at wall engravings? Do you think if we could call up the residents of a settlement and ask them what day it was we would have spent a fortune carbon-dating shards of clay?" Ingrid reaches over and clasps Rose's hand. "You need to talk to your parents. They will tell you much more than what your sister's things can reveal."

Rose pulls back, sits straight in her chair. She counts to ten in her head before she speaks. "I am done with interviews. I don't want to think of them, conduct them, or come anywhere near talking to someone I don't know, so that rules out her friends and colleagues. And I can't talk to my parents. Not in any detail. I don't think they're ready to talk about her."

"Is it possible you don't want them to know that you felt so distant from Gameela? That she may have confided in them but not in you?"

Rose looks out of the window to her side. Someone is smoking, a young man in a suit and tie. Rose wonders if he finds the tie constricting. She follows the rising smoke, tries to make out shapes.

"Rose?"

She ventures a look back at Ingrid, whose face is spelling out compassion so openly that Rose inhales deeply to prevent herself from crying.

"I can't go to my parents. Not yet."

Ingrid nods. "Okay. How about her friends? Her colleagues at work? You can't rule them out just because you don't like interviews."

"What am I supposed to say? *Hello, I'm Gameela's sister, and I wonder if you could tell me why she quit her job and didn't let us know and where she was traveling to every time she claimed she was away at work? And, while you're at it, could you let me know if any of this had anything to do with how she died?*"

Ingrid purses her lips. "That does sound ridiculous. Maybe a subtler approach?"

"A lie?"

"A discreet inquiry," Ingrid corrects her. "Something like: *I was wondering if Gameela cashed her last check?* People will always believe that the relatives are after money. They will suspect you of being a bloodhound but not of being a fool who doesn't know anything about her own sister. Then you can try to find out if they know why she quit."

A man and a woman make their way to the table next to Rose's. They squeeze between Ingrid's chair and the table behind her, and Ingrid scoots forward to let them pass. The woman thanks her, a bit too loudly, and Ingrid nods. Both she and Rose watch them settle down. The man pulls his chair closer to his companion, laughing at something she said. They are new to each other, Rose can tell, still all excitement and little familiarity. She looks at Ingrid and catches her watching them, too.

"What does Mark think of your archive?" Ingrid asks.

Rose takes a long sip of her coffee. A gulp. Empties her cup, and looks at its bottom in disappointment. "You think a third extra-large coffee would be too much?"

"Go ahead. The shakes suit you."

Rose raises an eyebrow at Ingrid, who smiles. "So what does he think? Of your quest to catalog your sister's life?"

"I wouldn't quite put it this way. Cataloging her life. I like to think of it more as a memorial. Something to honor her by."

Ingrid's face is blank now. Then inquisitive. A mixture of surprise and doubt. "You didn't tell him, did you?"

Rose glances at the couple next to them, then looks away. "No. I didn't."

"Why not?"

"First, I was afraid he'd lecture me if he found out I took her stuff without asking my parents' permission. Then I thought he wouldn't understand, that he'd treat it all as part of my grieving process. Then I told myself it's none of his business anyway, what goes on between my sister and me." Rose pauses, contemplates this last sentence, ignores how perplexing it sounds. "He just doesn't need to know."

"But don't *you* need him to know? He's your husband, Rose. He'll help you out. Grieving is hard enough. Don't make it harder by shutting out your loved ones."

Rose looks out the window. The man who was smoking earlier is gone. She searches for someone else to focus on and ends up contemplating a fire hydrant.

"You know what I think?" Ingrid starts again. "You're still angry with Mark. That's what all of this boils down to."

Rose considers the possibility. "Yes," she says, slowly. "I'm still angry."

For the first time in five weeks, thinking of Mark's involvement in Gameela's death evokes more sorrow than rage. During the dinner party in West Virginia, Rose had watched April wrap an arm around Mark as he sat next to her and pull him closer, giving him a hug. Nothing had happened to lead to this—no warm comment between siblings, no burst of nostalgia following a childhood story—and yet there it was, a single, fleeting moment of tenderness that left Rose breathless. For minutes afterward, she busied herself with her food, unable to look up. She could not put her finger on the source of the swell of emotion overcoming her. Was it the sight of sibling love reminding her of her loss? Was it Mark's smile, directed at April and filled with such gratitude that Rose wanted to jump and hug him, too, to reassure him that she, too, loved him, that she always will, that she, too, was his family? She still could not tell. All she knew was that now, when thinking of being angry with Mark, her anger was subdued, smothered under a layer of guilt and longing.

"It wasn't his fault, Rose."

Rose nods, still looking away. "I know."

"You need to tell him about Gameela's things. It will be good for both of you to have a way to talk about this."

Rose pretends to look out the window again. In her peripheral vision, she can see the young couple. The woman is talking, gesticulating as she speaks, laughing, while her companion watches her in silence, arms crossed, eyes fixed on her, smiling, listening.

BACK IN THE OFFICE, Rose combs through the ever-increasing mountain of books on her desk, looking for one text that she remembered seeing the day before. Dr. Winkenstein is due back in three weeks, and Rose wants to present a compelling case to him in hopes of persuading him to include ancient Egyptian attitudes toward communication with the dead as part of the upcoming exhibit. She knows she should be working on other aspects of ancient Egyptian daily life. Exploring the influence of the annual inundation of the Nile alone would take her weeks to prepare for—how they used it to set their calendar; how they believed the river's flooding waters were the tears of Isis, mourning the death of Osiris. Rose sits back in her chair, looks at the stack of books ahead of her. She remembers her dissertation, how skeptical she was of Dr. Assmann's theory that all culture in general and ancient Egyptian culture in particular revolved around attitudes toward death. Now she is not so skeptical anymore.

Again she thinks of Isis, the sister who avenged the death of Osiris, her beloved brother. She likes to think of herself as Isis, though she knows the comparison is flawed—Osiris was also Isis's husband, which makes her love for him more complicated than simple sibling loyalty. Still, the ancient Egyptian trinity has been haunting Rose's dreams—Isis, Osiris, and their son, Horus, all working together to restore order, to reinstate balance in the wake of the chaos that is death.

Rose picks up two photocopies that she made the previous day. The first is from the Great Hymn to Osiris:

His sister was his guard,
She who drives off the foes,
Who stops the deeds of the disturber
By the power of her utterance.
The clever-tongued whose speech fails not,
Effective in the word of command,
Mighty Isis who protected her brother,
Who sought him without wearying.
Who roamed the land lamenting,
Not resting till she found him,
Who made a shade with her plumage,
Created breath with her wings.

The second is from the Coffin Texts, spoken by Horus, who is addressing his father, Osiris—the son in the land of the living, the father in the land of the dead:

I am here in this land to assume your throne,
To hold together your despondent ones, to raise your orphans,
To secure your gate, to keep your name alive
On earth in the mouth of the living.
Have patience, have patience,
O you who are divine in that illustrious land where you are!
I am here in this land of the living,
To construct your altars, to establish your mortuary offerings
In your house of eternity on the Isle of Flame!
You are content in that land
as my supporter in the tribunal of the god!
I, however, am here as an advocate in the tribunal of men,
Setting up your boundary stone, holding together your despondent ones,
And serving as your image on earth,
While your gateway is secured by means of that which I do.

Rose puts both hymns in front of her. When she sought them out yesterday, she told herself she was advancing her ongoing research into material for the exhibit. Now she wonders if she had known even then that her work was simply a pretext. The first excerpt is from a stela that is currently housed in the Louvre—impossible to procure for the exhibit—and she wasn't even sure which coffin the second one was inscribed on, but was certain that this one, too, was out of reach. Furthermore, neither pertained directly to ordinary ancient Egyptians.

Both, however, pertained to her. She read both texts once more.

The power of Isis's utterance—her words, designed to avenge her dead brother. Horus, keeping his father's name alive, being his advocate, explaining why he, the son, must remain among the living and not join the dead father in the afterworld. When she chose the works, she had thought only of underscoring the mutually dependent relationship between the living and the dead, an attitude prominent in the lives of ancient Egyptians. Now, however, she thinks of the power of spoken words, of keeping the name of the deceased alive, of being his advocate on earth.

She glances over at Ingrid, her face buried under the halo of hair that flopped down whenever she stood, as she does now, peering down at something. Maybe Ingrid was right. Maybe Rose does need to speak to people, to keep Gameela's name alive.

On her phone, Rose scrolls through the text messages she has exchanged with Marwa over the last month. Their ongoing conversation is a series of mundane *How are you*'s and *Thinking of you*'s splattered with heart and hug emojis. They never mention Gameela, and yet there she is, behind every click between Rose and her sister's best friend, each needing to share her pain with the other but neither willing to increase the other's suffering, a dance of subdued, mutual grieving. Rose would call Marwa, but not now. It's still too soon. She needs someone more detached. Someone who will not burst out crying the moment she hears Rose's voice over the phone.

Rose fumbles through the pockets of her jacket, finds the severance letter still there, reads the name above the signature line: Maha Elattar. Spreading the letter on top of the copies of the ancient Egyptian poems, Rose folds the three sheets, pushing down on the creases with her fingernail, then puts them back in her pocket.

THE NEXT MORNING, Rose waits until Mark leaves before she calls the number she found on the letterhead in Gameela's correspondence. It takes her three separate phone calls to find the person she is looking for, each phone call answered by a disgruntled employee who refers her to another number. By the time she reaches Maha Elattar, it's after 8:00 A.M. Rose knows she will be late for work, but she can't postpone the phone call. It's 2:00 P.M. in Egypt now, and if she waits any longer, all employees will have left the offices of the National Contractors. Rose would rather be late to work than wait another twenty-four hours before speaking to the woman who signed her sister's severance letter.

"I am very sorry about your sister, Madam Fayrouz," Maha Elattar's voice says from across the ocean. Rose imagines her as an older woman, plump, covered up, sitting at a desk shoved against the wall somewhere. "I couldn't sleep for days after hearing what happened." Rose imagines kind eyes watering.

"I was wondering if Gameela ever picked up her last check? I'm helping my parents sort through her stuff, and I wanted to make sure I didn't misplace that last check before we settle all her accounts," Rose lies.

"Oh yes, she picked it up. Came and did it in person just two weeks after she stopped working here. It does take some time for these checks to clear, and I did tell her I could mail it to her, but she said she would rather stop by and take it in person. I don't know if she ever deposited it, but I would be happy to find out for you, if you wish."

"No need, thank you. I'll just have to go through her papers one more time. I probably misplaced it."

"I would think she would have deposited it, though. She was very organized." Rose lifts both eyebrows. "Everyone was very sorry to see her quit. We were all happy for her, of course, but we still wished it weren't so."

"You were happy to see her quit?"

"No, of course not," the woman blurts out. "Happy to know she was getting married. It's a shame her husband didn't want her to work, though, don't you think? He seemed like such a nice guy. A bit too old for her, I thought, but I guess older men often make better husbands."

Rose takes two steps back and lets herself fall on the sofa.

"We were all a bit disappointed she didn't have a big wedding. We would have loved to attend. But it is foolish to spend so much money on one night,

I agree. My sister spent thirty thousand pounds on her daughter's wedding this past summer, and I told her she could have had a small affair at home and given that money to her daughter instead, but you know how people are sometimes." The voice coming across the ocean pauses. "Hello? Are you still there?"

"Yes. Thank you very much. You've been very helpful," Rose hears herself say.

"I'm very happy to help. And please call me if you can't find—"

Rose hangs up.

From her bedroom, she pulls out the bin with her sister's stuff, walks over to the living room, pushes the coffee table to the side, then stands in the middle of the clear space, dumps the stuff out of the bin all around her as she twirls, forming a circle of debris with her at the center. She tosses the bin out of her way, drops to her knees, and starts searching.

عقد زواج عرفي

انه في يوم الخميس الموافق ٧ ابريل ٢٠١٦ تحريراً بين كل من :

الطرف الأول : السيد/ فؤاد سالم صدقي ، مسلم ، المولود في ٥ يناير ١٩٥٩ (الزوج)

الطرف الثاني : الآنسة / جميلة جبران ، سلمة ، المولودة في ١٢ مايو ١٩٨٨ (الزوجة)

بعد أن أقر الطرفان أهليتها للتعاقد و خلوهما من الموانع الشرعية للزواج ،

إتفهم الطرفان في حضور الشهود الموقعون أدناه على ما يلي :

يقر الطرف الأول بعد إيجاب و قبول صريحين بأنه قد قبل الزواج

من الطرف الثاني زواجاً شرعياً على كتاب الله وسنة رسوله صلى الله عليه وسلم

تقر الطرف الثاني بأنها قبلت الزواج برضا تام وفقاً لأحكام الشريعة

الإسلامية .

تحرر هذا العقد من نسختين بيد كل طرف للعمل بها لحين إمكانية

إصدار عقد موثق .

الطرف الثاني (الزوجة)   الطرف الأول (الزوج)

جميلة جبران

الشاهد الثاني   الشاهد الأول
أ/ مصطفى بيومي   أ/ أحمد الشناوي

مصطفى بيومي   أحمد الشناوي

A Traditional Marriage Certificate

It is on the day of Thursday, 7 April 2016, that this contract was written between:

First: *Mr. Fouad Salem Sedky*, of the Muslim faith, born on 5 January 1959 (the husband)

Second: *Ms. Gameela Gubran*, of the Muslim faith, born on 12 May 1988 (the wife)

After both parties have declared their eligibility to marry and denied the existence of any religious prohibitions against this marriage, they agreed, in presence of the two witnesses signing below, on the following:

The first party declares that he has offered and accepted the marriage with the second party, a religiously sound marriage as proclaimed by God's book and the tradition of His prophet, peace be upon his soul.

The second party declares that she has accepted the marriage with the first party, of her free will, and in accordance to the traditions of Islamic law.

Issued in two copies, to be kept by both parties until a legal contract can be obtained.

Signed by:

The first party   The second party

The first witness   The second witness

16

Mark is sitting at his desk, staring at his computer screen, which glares with the blinding white of a half-empty document, but he cannot think of a single word to write. All he has done for the previous hour is stare at his monitor and turn his wedding band around and around on his finger until the silver is polished to a sparkling sheen.

He pulls the ring out to the first knuckle, examines it for scratches, but does not take it completely off. He has not taken it off once since he put it on his right ring finger, seven years earlier, when he and Rose got engaged, and then had Rose move it to his left ring finger as part of their wedding ceremony, as Egyptian custom dictated, sliding the ring from one finger to the other as Mark kept the tops of his fingers touching, so that the ring literally never left his hands. He keeps it on even when polishing it, using a soft cloth to wipe away the dark stains that tarnish the silver.

He lifts his hand, looks at the wide band. He would have preferred a gold one, but Muslim men are not supposed to wear gold, and the silver ring was the first signifier to Rose's family that he had truly converted and was eager to practice the religion. That he had not, as Gameela insisted, converted on paper only just so he could marry Rose. The silver ring was Rose's idea. He was certain she had asked for it only to placate her sister, but at the time, he had not minded.

He slouches forward, lets his head fall between his knees, laces his fingers behind his neck, and takes ten deep breaths, and then ten more. Every time he thinks of Gameela he comes close to getting an anxiety attack, his heart racing uncontrollably, the room swaying around him. He is unsure how to deal with these attacks, which he never used to experience, not even after he found himself in the middle of that street riot in Lebanon years earlier. Considering that it's been only five weeks since Gameela died, he hopes that the attacks are temporary and will eventually go away on their own. He tries not to think of Gameela to stave them off. Still, her image pops into his head uninvited, at least several times each day: the way he saw her last, sitting across from him in her parents' apartment, walking around Cairo with him on that last visit to Egypt two years ago, finally accepting him, it seemed, as the brother he had longed to be.

They had not stayed in touch once he returned from Egypt, but still he had felt a newfound connection between them, a sense of acceptance that had lingered, infusing his days with a surprising degree of peace. The repercussions of his marriage had been unsettling. For a long time, he felt cut off from his family and not fully embraced by Rose's. Finding peace with Gameela had been a promise of hope, an indication that he would soon feel at ease again with both families.

He had dreaded that visit to West Virginia but is now glad he went. His mom seemed more like herself again—friendlier and more sociable than she'd ever been around Rose. He tells himself that Laura may have finally forgiven him his conversion, that Rose's loss may have touched a nerve, driving Laura to see past her disappointment, though he is not sure that is true. His conversion had crushed her.

On his mother's deck one evening soon after he was married and had returned to the States, sitting on a pair of patio chairs with the tree-covered mountains extending beyond them, he had tried to explain his attitude toward religion.

"Muslims still believe in Jesus Christ, Ma. There is an entire chapter in the Qur'an about the Virgin Mary. It's not like I've abandoned Christianity; I'm just open to trying a different approach to worshipping the same god."

His mother, sitting still in her chair, had watched as he spoke, silently weeping, which was the most unnerving thing he had ever seen—Laura never, ever wept. As his lengthy explanation of the similarities between Islam and Christianity wound down, she had had only one response: "Obviously, I have failed in the one thing that mattered."

Now, sitting with his head between his knees, he wished he had found a way to explain to her how the path he had taken in life was not whimsy or coincidental. He had been on a mission to carve a different kind of existence for himself since that day in high school when he sat in the bleachers, listening to the school counselor address the entire student body and try to explain the death of one of their schoolmates. The boy was Mark's age, had shared some of Mark's classes and had been on his bus route, but he and Mark rarely spoke. He had died of alcohol poisoning, found facedown in a stream behind his parents' trailer the night before. Mark had hardly listened to a word the counselor said, instead remembering all the minor interactions he'd had with the boy, the first person he had known who was now so irrevocably gone. He was still mulling this over on his way out of the gym, when he stepped aside to get a water bottle from the vending machine and heard one teacher addressing another. *All that mumbo jumbo about healing and loss. You know what I would have told them, if I was talking to those kids? I would have said this is exactly what you get when you raid your parents' cheap booze. The boy had it coming, is what I would have said. You could see it on his face—no interest in learning, no ambition. No chance he would have ended up any way other than facedown in a ditch.*

Mark had looked up at the teacher—an older man, who had repeatedly made snide remarks about the dead boy, a poor boy, one who, Mark now saw, was totally out of place in a school of middle-class kids, one who, in the previous year, had started to walk to school rather than take the bus. Sometimes, the bus would pass by him and the boy would not look up. Back then, Mark had not given a thought to the reason behind the boy's choice to spend half an hour walking rather than ride with all the other kids. Mark saw the boy's home: a trailer in a decrepit nook of the city. He saw the boy's hunched-up walk, his downward gaze. Mark saw the boy—Dillon—distinctly, as if he were still alive and standing right in front of him, and then he lunged at the teacher.

He never told his parents what happened that day, when they got called to the principal's office to discuss their son's uncharacteristic behavior. *It's simply a response to shock and grief,* the school counselor had insisted, negotiating a more lenient penalty than usual, citing Mark's spotless record so far, eventually persuading the teacher and principal to turn Mark's suspension into a detention.

Throughout all of this, Mark had remained silent, stubbornly refusing to defend himself. He had needed the silence to sort through a new revelation: the idea of a fixed narrative, the lie that is a predetermined destiny, the notion that a person's fate was merely the result of an accident of birth—such a simplistic view of the complex mess that is life, a view that conveniently relieves everyone of responsibility. If those who made bad choices did so because they were destined to do so, society could sit back at ease, smugly satisfied with its own guiltless success. Dillon could have been helped, Mark told himself. Every person who falls does so with the blessing of a society that chooses not to care about him.

For days afterward, Mark walked around mulling this new thought. By the end of the school year, he had made a vow never to let society pull him into a cozy corner of compliance. He would make a difference, and he would make his own life different. No one was ever going to dictate a predetermined narrative and expect him to follow it.

Much later, after the move to New York, the various journalism jobs, and the subsequent posts in the Middle East, after meeting Rose and contemplating pushing his vow to the extreme by changing his religion (why not?), Mark had imagined he was not only challenging the narrative that separated people in different social classes, races, religions, and ethnicities, but building his own narrative, finding a theory akin to Stephen Hawking's elusive Theory of Everything: a narrative that, in its universality, could be embraced by all, one that did not abide by rules of a certain religion or culture but that rather followed a higher moral code that applied to everyone equally.

He happily inhabited that narrative for years, letting his moral code guide him, believing that good intentions led to good outcomes—a variation of the Golden Rule of every religion, whether people chose to call it *karma* or *Do unto others*. Yes, he let that moral code guide his writing. That was what Rose referred to during that fight about the hot dog vendor when she accused him of judging people. He had been offended then, but now he thinks that maybe she was right. Rose was often right.

The first time he saw her, he was visiting the excavation site to write about the new pyramid discovery. Standing in the sun, a solitary petite woman with a mass of black hair pulled up in a messy bun, her arms crossed and feet planted firmly apart, she had listened to a male colleague talk to her for minutes before calmly raising one palm and holding it up in front of his face until he stopped talking and looked at her palm with puzzlement, as if she had pulled a salamander out of her pocket and held it up for him to examine. Then she had spoken, a few sentences that Mark stood too far away to hear, and her colleague had turned in place and walked away, his face flushed, muttering as he retreated. Mark had been transfixed by Rose's unexpected show of authority, had thought up that article on gender relations partly to explore this aspect of Egyptian culture and partly, he had to admit, as a pretext to meet her. The article had been the reason he met her, married her, followed her back to the U.S. when she got accepted to Columbia.

Ironic, how he writes in the hope of initiating change only to see his articles steer his own life into unforeseen directions. Kind of terrifying, how the outcome of his writing is often so different from what he intended.

He sits up, taps a pencil on his desk, and stares at the computer screen, the Word document still dutifully pulled up, a paragraph already typed. He reads through his paragraph again, rests his hands on the keyboard, ready to continue his work. He tries to focus on his topic: how the upcoming elections will affect the future of coal in West Virginia.

Nothing.

He waits, fingers still poised, and does not move until his phone beeps, signaling a text message.

> Hey, Mark. It's Ingrid. Is Rose okay? She hasn't
> shown up for work and is not picking up her phone.

Rose answers neither his calls nor his texts. On his phone, he has an app installed that promises to trace her location via GPS, a safety measure she insisted they both obtain after it took her parents two days to find Gameela. *Just in case,* she had said, not elaborating.

He clicks on the app that he has never used before, signs in, and hopes it works. It tells him that Rose is at home—or, at least, that her phone is. After one last failed attempt at contacting her, he heads out of the office.

HE FINDS HER sitting on the floor in the middle of their living room, her back against the sofa, the area around her covered with junk, as if she had taken the contents of their desk and scattered them all over the room.

"For goodness' sake, Rose. Why aren't you answering your phone?"

She looks up at him, revealing puffy, bloodshot eyes. "Sorry. Ingrid kept calling so I put the phone on silent."

A crumpled piece of paper juts out of her clenched fist, its edge splayed out like a Chinese fan.

"Rose?" He sits on the floor across from her. "What's wrong, honey? What's all this?" On second inspection, he realizes that the items on the floor are not familiar: books, notebooks, letters, even pieces of clothing and jewelry, none he remembers seeing before.

Rose holds the piece of paper up in the air between them. "I excavated and found treasure," she says dramatically, giggling and then immediately sniffling. Reaching over to the box on the side table, Mark grabs a tissue and hands it to her. She exchanges papers with him, giving him the crumpled sheet. After she blows her nose, she carefully adds the tissue to a small mound by her side, pushing the tissues together to form a mass resembling a pyramid.

Mark eases out the creases. It's a sheet torn out of a notebook and covered with writing, with spaces for four different signatures at the bottom. He labors to read the title—a marriage certificate?—then tries to translate the first line, but his Arabic is rusty and he is too impatient to decipher the mangled handwriting. He looks up at Rose.

"It's a marriage contract. Gameela's marriage contract. *Orfi.*" A marriage per custom and Islamic tradition: one that is not officially notarized and therefore bears no legal weight. Mark remembers reading about it while he was in Egypt: how, in one year, eighty-eight thousand of Egypt's youth had written such contracts, which are supposed to fulfill the Islamic requirements for marriage—the intention to stay married; the publicizing of this intention (hence the two witnesses)—without going through government channels. It is what adults do when they want to get married in secret; what college kids do when they want to have religiously sanctioned sex behind their parents' backs.

"Gameela was married?" Mark asks.

Rose nods, an outstretched palm indicating the paper in his hand.

"Why would Gameela need to keep her marriage a secret?"

Rose shrugs. "I don't know. Maybe he was already married and didn't want his first wife to find out. All I know is that he is almost thirty years older than she was and that his name is Fouad Salem Sedky." Rose points to the spot on the paper where the man's name is scribbled.

Mark's heart starts racing. Staring at the paper in his hand, he tries to find the name that Rose just mentioned, hopes, for a second, that she is wrong, that he will not have to tell her that he has met the man, has spent a day with him and Gameela, that his life, again, has crossed paths with Gameela's in an unforeseen way.

"What was the man's name again?"

Rose looks up at him. "Fouad." He knows this glance—inquisitive, suspicious.

He doesn't want to be tangled up in Gameela's life any more than he already is. He contemplates staying quiet, not telling Rose that Gameela introduced him to Fouad two years ago. He looks again at the marriage certificate in his hand, takes his time before he speaks, and tries to maintain a calm tone.

"I may be wrong, Rose, but I think I met him." He hands her the marriage certificate. "I think that's the man Gameela brought with her when we went to interview Saaber."

Rose knots her brows. "Are you sure?"

"The age certainly fits. And that's not a common name in Egypt, is it?"

Rose shakes her head. "No. It's not."

He waits for this information to sink in before he adds, "I have photos of him on my laptop."

HE BRINGS HIS laptop over and sits next to her on the floor, their backs against the sofa. Not until he starts searching through his folder does he realize it would have been better if he had pulled a few photos out before sitting so close to her. The folder containing all his photos from that last trip to Egypt is a mangle of snapshots that include many of both Gameela and Saaber. Rose leans in closer, peers at the photos flashing on his screen one after the other.

"I can find a few photos and just pull those out, if you prefer," he suggests. "You don't need to look at all of them."

"No. It's okay."

Her voice is calm, and she has stopped crying. Mark scrolls down through the photos, starts clicking on some of the ones he took while he, Saaber, and Fouad were up in the pigeon house. Each photo pops up, one after the other, layers of his recorded history. He finds one that clearly shows Fouad's face and enlarges it. For a few moments, he and Rose sit quietly looking at the face filling the laptop's screen: a dark-skinned man, the shade Egyptians refer to as wheat colored, with curly salt-and-pepper hair. He is not smiling in the photo, his clean-shaven face set in concentration, looking somewhere to the left of the photo's frame. Mark tries to remember what Fouad was looking at, but he cannot.

"Did she tell you anything about him?"

Mark shakes his head. "Just whatever I told you back then: that he was the cousin of a friend of hers." He flips through more photos, finds one of Saaber that shows Fouad in the background, minimizes it. "That short, chubby one that came to our wedding—what was her name?"

"Marwa?"

"Yes, Marwa."

Rose gets up, walks up to the bookcase, and pulls their wedding album out. She starts flipping through the pages on her way back, finds the photo she is looking for, and sits down, album in lap, pointing to it.

"This one?"

Mark looks at the photo of him and Rose surrounded by Gameela and six of her friends.

"Yes. That's the one."

"Are you sure?"

He nods. "Unless I got the name wrong back then, but I don't think I did. I distinctly remember thinking how little he looked like her. Not that cousins need to look alike, of course."

He goes back to scrolling through the photos, looking for another clear snapshot of Fouad, trying to avoid looking at both Saaber and Gameela. "Why would she get married in secret?" he murmurs.

Rose does not answer. She is flipping through the album in her lap.

Mark peeks at the photos documenting his wedding day, most of them populated with Rose's family, a few showing his own, his parents and sisters by his side, his mother a bit flustered by the elaborate wedding ceremony, the loud, pounding music, Rose's puffy dress and long train. He had never liked weddings, but seeing photos of his own, he finds himself playing with his wedding band again. Rose has paused at a page showing one of their official wedding portraits—he, facing her, his hands on her waist, while she looks up at him, still a good ten inches shorter even in her high heels. Her face is beaming with a smile he has not seen in a long time. When he looks at her, he sees a faint trace of that smile curling her lips. For a moment, she looks like the Rose he fell in love with, not the Rose currently sitting next to him, the two incarnations of his wife distinctly different.

He goes back to scrolling through the photos on his laptop. The last few are ones he took after they climbed down from the pigeon house, and he opens one taken in the courtyard in front of Saaber's dwelling. In the photo, Gameela, on the right, is looking up at Fouad, who is standing in the center, his hands in his pockets as he glances behind him at the dwelling's door. On the left of the photo stands Saaber, who is looking at Gameela, though neither she nor Fouad seem aware of his presence. Mark studies the three faces: Gameela's discreet smile, Fouad's frown as he looks at the dwelling, and Saaber's intent gaze.

Next to him, Rose has placed the album on the sofa and has moved closer, holding on to his arm. "I can't believe she got married without telling anyone," she whispers. "My poor mom would die if she found out. How could she keep something like this a secret?"

"She was an adult, Rose. She had the right to do anything she wanted to."

"It's out of character. She took pride in how straightforward she was. She never did anything behind anyone's back."

"Maybe she did but was good at hiding it."

Mark glances at the wedding album on the sofa. It's a visual record of part of his own life, just like the photos on his laptop seem to have captured more of Gameela's life than he thought possible. All around him are things, artifacts, as Rose would call them, bearing witness to someone's life, many of them to his own. He starts turning his wedding band around again, rubs it with his thumb, and for a moment he closes his eyes and imagines himself free of all these things, free of any reminders of a past life, living only in the present moment, not encumbered by the weight of memories.

Rose places her head on his shoulder, and he opens his eyes again. On the laptop's screen, the three faces are still frozen in time, unaware that two of them will die a mere two years later. He looks at the third face, at the man glancing sideways, his brows knotted. He wonders if he ever wore a wedding band.

Part Four

17

At Fouad's farm, the peasants called Gameela *el-sett*—"the woman." She relished the definitive "the" that implied her uniqueness, like Sherlock Holmes's one and only woman—the highest of her kind. Secretly, she thought of herself as Mrs. Sherlock Holmes. She rarely asked her sister for anything, but she did request a T-shirt with "I AM SHERLOCKED" printed on it, claiming she was infatuated with Benedict Cumberbatch (not a total lie). Sometimes, while doodling, she practiced signing her name as *Irene*.

It took her two months to start leaving some of her things at the farm. A few items at a time, her presence at the farmhouse became visible: a couple of her T-shirts in the dresser drawers Fouad emptied for her; a day dress and some head scarves in his closet; her nightgowns and underwear, the lacey ones she bought and kept wrapped up in tissue paper at home lest her mother find them and become suspicious.

A spare toothbrush on his sink. An extra pair of slippers under his bed.

In the mornings, they ate breakfast together on the balcony overlooking the guava trees and hidden from the main road. Today, Gameela was indulging in *feteer meshaltet*, the freshly baked flaky pastry one of the peasants' wives had carried to the house this morning, the pastry round and flat, buttery to the touch. Gameela tore a piece, dipped it in the pool of honey covering a small plate set between her and Fouad. The plate was part of Fouad's mother's fine china set, pale cream decorated with faded yellow butterflies. The pool of honey reached the edge and made it look as if the butterflies, too, were sampling the sweet syrupy treat. Gameela liked this set of fine china, the intimacy of knowing she is privy to his mother's things. She chewed on the pastry, licking her honey-covered fingers.

Fouad ate the same breakfast every day: two hard-boiled eggs and a piece of *feteer* with some feta cheese on the side. He cut his eggs in quarters before eating them, just like Gameela's father used to cut them for her when she was young. Ahmed called the egg pieces *felookah*—fishing boats—and sailed them across the plate for his giggling daughter, and, by association, Gameela now watched her husband eat his cut-up eggs and saw him as the child she once was, not as a man closer to her father in age than he was to her. He looked up at her and smiled, and his face lit up with youth.

"Let's go fishing today," she said.

He nodded. "Sure. I'll have Mahmoud fetch us some bait."

"Do you have a lot of work to do?"

"Nothing that can't wait."

He sat back in his chair and lit a cigarette, but when the light breeze carried the smoke her way, he got up, walked to the corner of the balcony, and leaned out, looking onto the fields. Gameela bit one last piece of honey-dipped *feteer* before wiping her hands on a napkin and joining him. In the distance, rows of palm trees bordered the rest of the farm, and a man was climbing one of them, using a rope tied in a loop that encompassed him and the tree trunk, reminding Gameela of the Hula hoop she used to play with as a child. He leaned back, his bare feet planted on the trunk as he held on to the looped rope with both hands, one on each side of his torso. Swinging closer to the trunk, he would then ease the rope's tension just enough for him to fling it upward in a jolting motion and then climb a step, striding the trunk with feline nimbleness. Once he reached the top, he would prune the tree, sending brown, dried-up leaves raining down.

"Every time I see one of the climbers going up a palm tree, I'm afraid he will fall. It's crazy how high they go."

"At least he is going somewhere," Fouad replied.

Silently, they watched the man until he made it all the way to the top. He did not fall.

BEFORE HEADING OUT, Gameela changed into wide-legged, flowy pants and a long-sleeved T-shirt, tying a scarf around her head but leaving her neck bare, an indulgence she allowed herself only while on the farm. She looked at her reflection in the tall mirror attached to the armoire's door, admiring the way her floral head scarf sat on her head, a turban-shaped crown of light blue and white flowers. Only three years ago, she would never have worn a head scarf that did not cover her neck, just as she would never have shown her hair to any foreign man. But she had done so when Mark visited last, deliberately choosing to leave her head bare at her parents' home, even in his presence. She had noticed his startled look when he first saw her, but said nothing. How was she to explain to him that her religiousness had followed a curve that reminded her of the sensation of jumping into a pool feetfirst: a deep and speedy plunge in, followed by a slower, gentler journey up, until she finally reached the surface and, gasping for air, trod water with unexpected comfort. Her dive into the *hijab* followed a similar curve: rapid, at first, rigid in her eagerness to be fully submerged in obeying God, followed by a gentler bobbing up, not away from God but toward a more lenient devotion to His commands. She would never, ever abandon her head cover; but she had grown to see her *hijab* more as a sign of her acquiescence to a loving God than as a measure of avoiding His wrath. As such, it became a symbol of religiousness similar to a nun's habit or to an Orthodox Jew's yarmulke. As such, showing a bit of her neck or even allowing her brother-in-law to see her hair seemed like an offense too minor to worry about.

Besides, if a woman's dress needed to be modest by the standards of her society, then baring her neck was perfectly acceptable at the farm, since all the peasant women did just that, covering their heads with a scarf that they tied at the nape of their necks, leaving their throats exposed. That's how Maymouna wore her head scarf. She was the wife of Nasr, the servant who had been running the house for the previous thirty-five years, since Fouad moved to the farm. Now, with the house gaining a mistress, Nasr sent Maymouna to clean up and cook while *the woman* was there.

On her way out of the bedroom, Gameela stopped and looked in on Maymouna, who stood in the kitchen washing dishes.

"We're heading out, Maymouna."

"*Belsalamah,*" Maymouna said, wishing them a safe outing.

"What are you cooking for dinner tonight?"

"I have a pair of fresh hens that I was going to grill for you," Maymouna said. She placed the plates on a plastic rack and turned around to face Gameela, drying her hands on a dishrag.

"That sounds good. And some of that pasta you made last time on the side?"

"Yes, madam."

"Good. And no need to bake dessert. We'll have some fresh fruit today."

"Yes, madam."

With a quick nod, Gameela walked out of the kitchen, feeling the woman's eyes on her back. On the front porch, she found Fouad talking to the estate manager. They were sitting on the bench on the left side of the porch, so she sat on the one on the right side, acknowledging the tradition of separation of the sexes that she knew prevailed in the countryside, watching her husband examine a set of invoices the manager was presenting to him. He was sitting with his left side facing her, just as he had that first day she saw him five years ago, when she walked into Marwa's parents' apartment and found him sitting slouched forward, his elbows resting on his knees, listening with intent concentration as Marwa's father told him what they had witnessed in the previous three days since the start of the revolution: the tens of thousands flooding Cairo's streets, demanding the end of then President Mubarak's thirty-year rule; the antiriot forces trying, and failing, to hold protesters back, teargas canisters flying in the air everywhere; that one antiriot van that got toppled over by the sheer force of the protesters' hands. She had stood in place, the excitement of having just emerged from among thousands of marching, chanting revolutionaries dampened by the sight of a stranger sitting in her best friend's living room, but then he had looked at her and she had realized he was older and had relaxed a bit, taking him for one of Marwa's father's friends. She smiled now, remembering her instant dismissal of Fouad based on his age. To think that she had once considered him old.

"I thought you said you didn't have much work to do today," she said when he finally approached her. "Everything okay?"

"Just had a couple of peasant issues to take care of." He held his hand out to her and she took it, rising from the bench.

"Farm business?"

"Personal. Mahmoud's youngest is sick. We're sending him to Cairo to see a pediatric surgeon."

They walked down the dirt road that connected the farm's deeper acres to the main avenue up front, heading toward the watering stream stocked with tilapia. Gameela inhaled deeply, taking in Rasheed's mildly humid air, the scent of the Mediterranean close by faintly detectable, tingeing the air with a salty iodine undertone that she never experienced in Cairo.

"Now I understand what they mean by the old saying: *Air so fresh it prolongs one's life span.*"

Fouad laughed. He walked with his hands in the pocket of his utility shorts, the sleeves of his crisp, white shirt rolled up to reveal tanned, muscular arms. Gameela liked to think he paid more attention to the way he dressed when she was around. "If this were true, all the farmers here would live to be a hundred. But the fresh air doesn't stand a chance against the lack of medical care, I'm afraid."

"I thought Rasheed had plenty of doctors."

He nodded. "It does. It's a big enough town. People here are just not educated enough to take any preventative steps. By the time they go see a doctor, it's often too late."

They passed by a solitary guava tree standing in a rare patch of open land. Gameela hopped to the tree, touched its trunk, and Fouad laughed. She knew it was his favorite tree, knew he sat under its shade in the afternoons to drink his tea, knew that he would bring her here later, when Nasr would have spread a clean kilim for them to sit on and brought the tray of tea and sugar, and all this knowledge thrilled her, the result of years of slowly progressing intimacy that had accelerated exponentially during these last three months since she became his wife, his closest companion. Now, in early July, the tree was bursting with flowers, its halo of green leaves sprinkled with white blossoms and, in some spots, small green fruits that would not ripen for months. Gameela had never seen the tree bear fruit before, and she was looking forward to September, imagining herself reaching up and picking the sweet, yellow treats she loved and which she knew would have to taste heavenly, when picked fresh. For now, she jumped up and plucked a flower, sniffing it as they walked on. She could feel Fouad's smile as he trailed behind her, watching her, but she didn't look back.

BY THE STREAM, the fishing rods were ready and waiting, a woven basket filled with miniature bait shrimp placed in the shade of an umbrella between the two folding chairs. Fouad picked her fishing rod up, checked the line and the float, baited it, and handed it to her. She let him do all of that, not because she was incapable of baiting her own hook, but because she knew he liked to do it, just as he liked to walk right next to her with one arm spread behind her when they marched the streets during the 2011 protests, protecting her from the masses around them, or when he chose the seat next to her everywhere they went, not bothering to answer the inquisitive look in Marwa's eyes. Gameela cast her line and watched the red float. Perhaps if they had not gone through those weeks of the revolution together, she might never have understood the allure of this life he chose, of days spent fishing and walking through rows of trees, inspecting leaves for disease, pulling weeds. If she had not seen that one protester lose an eye to a rubber bullet, she would not have so relished the sun reflected on the stream's surface, causing her to squint as she looked at the bobbing float. She glanced at Fouad and saw him slouched in his chair, looking at the water's surface.

"When is Mahmoud taking his son to see the doctor?"

"He has an appointment on Wednesday."

She knew Fouad made the appointment for his farmhand's son, knew he was paying the doctor's fee, but suspected he would not want to admit it. Still, she could not help but make one remark.

"You know it's a lot of *thawab* to help the sick," she pointed out, reminding him of the religious merits of coming to the aid of those in need, of the multitude of blessings Allah would doubtless bestow on him in return.

"It's the right thing to do," he said.

She went back to watching her fishing line, edging her seat to the side to position herself more fully in the shade. Years ago, when she embarked on the religious education that her parents neglected to provide for her, she had learned that the intention, *al-neyyah*, was the most important part of any deed, that all good deeds needed to be done with the intention of pleasing God for them to count as steps toward grace. Fouad's good deeds, she had learned in the five years she had known him, were countless, but his intention still needed some tweaking. She pulled her line out of the water, checked for the bait—still intact—and threw it back in. She did not push the matter any further, but she knew that if she persisted in giving him subtle hints, she would be able to realign him, adjust his intentions to make them match his capacity for good, get him to see that good deeds are best done with the aim of pleasing God, not simply out of a desire to follow a code of ethics laid down by mortals. She would need to work on this. And on his prayer habits. Get him to pray five times a day, as he should. She believed that, deep down, he was a very good Muslim, even if he didn't quite know it yet.

Next to her, he lurched, and she watched him pull his line out, a fair-sized fish dangling from it.

"Dinner!" he said, a bit too excitedly, childishly.

She laughed. The fish flopped in the air, glistening in silver-green hues in the morning sun.

HIS MOOD MIRRORED the length of her stay, day by day: elated on the first day, less so on the second, even less on the third. On her last morning on the farm, he did not eat breakfast. Sitting across from her on the balcony, he lit up a cigarette, though he had promised to quit.

"You know I can't help it," she said.

"Of course you can."

"I can't stay away for longer than this without arousing suspicion."

"You could if you were honest with your parents." He extinguished his cigarette, crushing it into the ashtray with more force than was necessary. "We are not children, Gameela. *I* am not a child." He looked up at her. "We don't need to hide."

"We don't have to go through this every time I come here."

"Yes, we do. We will." He slouched forward, closer. "I'm fifty-seven years old. I don't have to sit here and patiently wait for my own wife to visit me once a week. How long do you think we can keep this up?"

"Only until I get a chance to break this to them gently. I don't want to hurt them. I just haven't found a good opportunity yet."

She knew she had claimed so before. He leaned away from her, watched her with narrowed eyes, then got up and walked into the farmhouse.

IN THE BEDROOM, Gameela packed her laundry, leaving fresh clothes behind for her next visit. Fouad paced the bedroom, and she watched him walk up and down as she folded a pair of pants.

"This situation has to change."

"Please don't start a fight now. I'm leaving in half an hour."

"You shouldn't leave. Not in half an hour, not ever." He walked up to her, grabbed her by the wrists, and pulled her down next to him. They sat on the bed facing each other. The sun shining through the bedroom window illuminated his face, and Gameela again had to wonder at the miracle of being here, alone with this man, so close to his curly hair and tanned skin. She reached over and placed one hand on the side of his face. He pulled her hand down, holding it in his.

"Call them now. Say you'll be late. That you had to stay one more day. Or let me come with you and tell them we're married."

"I will tell them myself, *habibi*, I promise. Just give me a little bit more time, okay? Please?"

He huffed, let go of her, and sat in place, looking at her. "I should never have agreed to this to start with."

She feigned shock. "You regret marrying me?"

"No, no. Of course not." He grabbed both her hands, lifted them to his mouth, kissing them. "Of course not."

When he looked up at her, his eyes were softer, the undertone of anger gone, even though the sadness prevailed. She wanted to pull him closer, to hug him and comfort him, but she did not.

"I can't be late," she said instead, getting up and placing the pants in her duffel bag. He reached over from behind her, put both hands on her waist, but she pushed them away.

THE NEW HIGHWAY from Rasheed to Alexandria was smooth and wide. Gameela reached Alexandria in less than an hour, stopped at a McDonald's for a quick bite, and then continued to Cairo. By the time she arrived at her parents' apartment three hours later, she had rehearsed what she would tell them: that she was married; that even if they had the right to stop her, they were too late; that she loved them and wished for them to accept her choices; that they had nothing to worry about.

She walked through the front door, her duffel bag hanging off her shoulder, and found them sitting in the living room.

"Gameela is back!" her mother yelled, arms thrown in the air.

Gameela dropped her bag and rushed to her mother, giving her a hug. "I missed you, Mama."

"I missed you too, *habibti*."

"How much longer do you have to travel?" her father asked as she hugged him, too. "Did they tell you anything?"

"Not much longer, I hope." She lifted one hand and tucked her hair under her head cover, remembered she was already at home, and started taking the scarf off.

"I was just telling your aunt Samya about how hard you work. You know your cousin Osama lost his job again?"

"Again? Why?"

Her mother shrugged. "Who knows? She says his boss didn't like him, but that's the third job in two years. He must be doing something wrong."

"Did you get anything to eat?" her father asked.

"I grabbed something on the way."

"Junk food." Her mother got up and headed to the kitchen. "I saved you some dinner."

"I'll eat later, Mama. Just sit down and let me tell you something."

Her mother turned around. "Whatever it is, it can wait until after you eat." She walked out of the room.

"I'm not hungry, Mama!" Gameela yelled after her mother.

"Nonsense!" her mother yelled back.

Gameela raised her arms and let them drop again, turning to look at her father.

"Let her fix you some food. She just wants to take care of you. Here," he patted the sofa next to him, "have a seat. Tell me about your day."

She sat down, dropping the head scarf by her side. Her hair was limp from being covered all day, and she flipped it down, ran her fingers through it, loosening the strands. Faintly, barely detectable, she could smell the farm air on her hair: a scent of orange and guava blossoms. She inhaled deeply.

"You must be exhausted after this long drive," her father said.

"Yes, Baba."

"They should let the company driver take you."

"I'd rather drive."

Her father patted her on the back, giving one shoulder a quick rub.

"So what did you want to talk about?" her father asked.

"It can wait."

Her mother emerged with a tray covered with food. Gameela could already smell the cubed beef in brown gravy, the pasta in béchamel sauce. Her father followed her to the dining room, where Nora was placing the food and filling a cup with guava juice. Gameela stared at the cream-colored drink.

"Come on. Sit down!" her mother ordered her, pulling out a chair and sitting, too. Her father brought his newspaper over and continued his crossword puzzle.

"So how is work?" her mother asked.

Gameela sat down, cut a piece of beef, and lifted it to her mouth. The warm food made her feel unexpectedly tired. "Okay. Nothing new."

"I have some news. Rose is getting another paper published. The second one this year!" Nora's voice was jubilant. She smacked a palm on the table to emphasize Rose's achievement.

"Oh," Gameela said, stabbing her fork into three pieces of penne.

"It's very important for her to get as many publications as possible. She thinks the Met is going to have an opening for an assistant curator next year, and she is building up her résumé and hoping they will hire her, once she is done with her fellowship. Wouldn't that be wonderful, if she got a permanent job there? I can just imagine her business card: Dr. Rose, Curator at the Metropolitan Museum of Art."

"You mean Dr. Hatfield, Assistant Curator?" Gameela corrected her mother. The pasta, drenched in sauce and cheese, was delicious—soft, warm, and comforting. Maybe she was hungry after all.

"Same thing," her mother said.

"I never really liked this Western tradition of having a wife change her last name to match her husband's," Ahmed chimed in. "What has the husband's family ever done to deserve such recognition? She should have been Dr. Gubran, not Dr. Hatfield."

Gameela pushed her food around the plate, picked up a few pieces of pasta, and dipped them in gravy before chewing on them, closing her eyes to focus on the added layer of taste.

"Mark did help her a lot. You have to give him some credit."

Ahmed shrugged. "And she lived under my roof for twenty-seven years. She should have kept her maiden name."

"That's not how it's done in the U.S.," Nora said.

Gameela got up, carrying her plate to the kitchen.

"You haven't eaten anything!" her mother protested.

"I ate enough, Mama. Thank you."

"But what did you want to talk about?" Nora asked.

"Nothing important."

IN HER ROOM, Gameela pulled her laundry out of the duffel bag, placed it in the laundry bin, and noticed one of Fouad's T-shirts among her things— an item grabbed in error. She folded the T-shirt and tucked it into the inside pocket of her duffel bag. Suddenly exhausted, she wished she were back in Rasheed, where it was certainly cooler than Cairo, where she would have been sitting on the balcony again, the crickets' hypnotizing chirps replacing the current cacophony of cars, Cairo's incessant sound track. Where she would have been with her husband, the man she chose to spend the rest of her life with, as was her God-given right. At the bottom of the bag, she found a package—a cardboard box, a cube barely the size of her palm. Opening it, she found one of Fouad's teacups inside, the yellow butterflies dancing on its edge, a folded note sitting in the cup: *Come home*.

She imagined him all alone on the farm, reading in bed, silent and morose. Outside, she could hear her parents chatting, and she considered walking up to them, blurting it all out, and then heading back to Rasheed, reaching the town by dawn, surprising Fouad in bed, waking him up with a kiss. She glanced at the clock—9:00 P.M.

She tucked his note in her wallet, deciding that this will be her reminder of where she truly belonged until she could stay there and need no further reminding. She imagined the day she finally moved into the farmhouse, pictured pulling the note out and showing it to him, telling him that she was home and tearing the note in pieces to seal the permanency of her arrival. One day, she would do that. Soon. For now, she wrapped the cup back in its packaging, hid it in the corner of the upper shelf of her armoire, took her pants off, and huddled in bed in her T-shirt.

Lying still in bed, she tried to tune out her parents' chatter but could not help catching scattered words that repeatedly included her sister's name. She pulled a pillow from under her head, placed it on top of her face, and pressed the sides to her ears. The frustration and anger that, four months earlier, led her to suggest that she and Fouad elope, content themselves with the *orfi* marriage certificate with all its stigma, was back now, and she took a deep breath in through the pillow's feathers.

The words her parents spit at her back then played again in her ears, stinging with renewed vehemence.

"You're out of your mind if you think we'll allow you to marry a man twice your age!" her mother had yelled.

"And with an arrest record. And no college education. A farmer, for God's sake, Gameela. What are you thinking?" her father had pleaded.

Gameela had stood in the middle of the living room, furious with Marwa's mother for calling her parents and professing that she suspected her crazy nephew, old enough to be Gameela's father, was infatuated with her, toying with her mind and heart, dragging her with him all around Cairo until people saw them together and reported the news back to her. Ameera had listed every single reason she thought Fouad was not a good enough match for Gameela. No wonder Ahmed and Nora were having a meltdown. Gameela suspected that her friend's mother had sniffed a scandal about to break out and rushed to exonerate herself of complicity, eager to assure Nora that she had not betrayed her trust and that she had been watching over her daughter all those times she visited with her family, as she was expected to do. Still, Gameela had allowed hope to creep in, had told herself that maybe it was all for the best, that she could now plead her case and bring the relationship out in the open.

"He was imprisoned for participating in protests at eighteen! For political charges, not for some lowly felony. He was merely idealistic—trying to defend the rights of the poor. We can't blame him for that. It's not his fault that he got dismissed from college. And what's wrong with being a farmer anyway? It's a peaceful, productive life. It saved his sanity."

Everything she said fell on deaf ears. She knew very well what her parents feared: the censure of their friends and family, the scandal that would ensue as people whispered how the doctor and his wife allowed their daughter to marry an old peasant with an arrest record. On the side table in the living room stood a framed photo of Rose with her American husband, the Christian who converted on paper only to marry her, the one who, apparently, was a better match than Fouad. Gameela thought their logic was so flawed, their objections so unfounded, that there was no point in arguing with them any longer. She remained in place, motionless, letting their words fall flat around her. She allowed them to finish all they had to say, nodded in implied resignation, then locked herself up in her room and called Fouad.

"We wouldn't be doing anything wrong," she told him over the phone, talking him into getting married anyway.

"But why not a real marriage certificate? Why *orfi?* We don't have to hide!"

"I can't get my father to sign off on a real certificate, which, as you well know, is legally required. A marriage is valid in front of God as long as we both intend for it to be. The *orfi* certificate is religiously legitimate, and that's all I care about. I'll do anything I want to do as long as it doesn't go against God's laws."

"I'm too old to be hiding and marrying you in secret. I'm not afraid of your parents. I'll come talk to them. I can convince them."

"I don't want or need their approval. We are both adults, and we'll do what we want."

He argued for weeks, but she would not budge. She refused to allow him to humiliate himself and face her parents' inevitable rejection, and she refused to allow them to dictate her life. She persisted. Eventually, he stopped arguing.

Now, lying in bed in her room, alone again, Gameela thought of her husband and her sister and her parents and how unfair life could be and screamed into the pillow that was still smothering her face.

She resented her parents for their constant preoccupation with Rose, her American husband, and her American job, when all Gameela wanted to do was talk to them and get them to listen.

She resented Rose for her unfailing ability to garner her parents' pride and approval.

And she was mad at herself for again failing to be the best person she could be, again allowing petty jealousy to fill and paralyze her. For again being too cowardly to tell her parents about her marriage and make them accept her choices, the way Rose had done, and again being—she had to admit it—too judgmental of her parents.

She needed to forgive them their weaknesses. They, like many upper- and middle-class Egyptians, were conditioned to see all things Western as superior, a version of Stockholm syndrome often manifested en masse in postcolonial societies. They were also conditioned to crave the approval of their peers, to mold their lives to fit into what other well-to-do Egyptians deemed suitable for people of their rank. No wonder they preferred the American son-in-law to Fouad with his farm, his arrest record, his lack of a formal education, and his relatively advanced age. They may have forgiven him one or two of these failings, but four was too much for them to swallow. Gameela knew that. She tried to summon the compassion that, in the previous months, she kept reminding herself to feel toward them. But she could not get over the bitterness of knowing that they could never understand her, never see that those classist, self-loathing attitudes were among the main forces that drove her toward embracing a religion that promised equality, that did not rank people based on such superficial attributes, but that instead embraced all who embraced God.

How exhausting, to try to reinvent herself. To build a set of values so different from her parents'. How lonely.

She tossed and turned, unable to sleep, not even after their voices faded away. An hour later, fatigued to the verge of tears, she got up, pulled Fouad's T-shirt out of her duffel bag, and put it on. Back in bed, she wrapped herself in the oversized garment, pulling her knees to her chest and stretching the T-shirt until it covered her toes. Only then did she fall asleep.

18

By the time Saaber was released from jail, eighteen months after his arrest, he had learned to see his imprisonment as a blessing, to believe that, just like the prophet Yusuf, his time in detention was a necessary step toward the glory he was meant to achieve.

That was the first thing Badr taught him: to recognize his fate; to embrace his destiny.

Badr was one of the twenty-two inmates sharing a cell with Saaber after he got transferred to prison. They took turns sleeping on the bare concrete floor, lying on their sides to make room for others. For the first two nights Saaber slept only in interrupted fits. On his third night, he found himself facing Badr.

"You are the boy who was in the American newspaper," Badr whispered, his voice tinged with awe.

Saaber nodded.

"I can always tell when someone is destined for glory. I see it in your brow," Badr said, pointing above Saaber's left eye.

For the first time in weeks, the fist clutching Saaber's lungs loosened its grip.

EVERY FIFTEEN DAYS, Saaber would face a judge who would flip through his file, declare there was no progress made yet, and renew his temporary detention. The first couple of times, Saaber went to the hearing with high hopes despite his fellow detainees' reassurances that no one was ever released that quickly and that some of them had been going through this process for over two years. Yet each time Saaber faced the judge, he tried to explain how the orderly had fallen, how he had not pushed him, how he certainly had no contact with foreigners with an intention to harm national security, how he was unfairly imprisoned. The judge, facing a dozen other cases after Saaber's, would nod, scribble a note, and declare that Saaber's detention was to be renewed.

His mother came to visit him.

"Feed the pigeons," he ordered her.

"After I figure out how to feed your four siblings," she retorted.

"I need a good lawyer."

"And what am I supposed to pay him with? Your pigeons?"

"Call someone," Saaber said vaguely, unsure who the someone could be. "Call Fouad," he remembered, scribbling his name and number on a piece of paper.

His mother looked at the paper and sucked at her lips.

WEEKS PASSED.

"It's not fair," Saaber would tell Badr.

"It's all part of your trials. Great men have to be forged by fire."

"Don't listen to this lunatic," an inmate sitting close by told Saaber. "He's been here for years. Isolation has rotted his brain."

"I, too, am here for a reason, Hisham," Badr replied. "I'm here to guide him." He nodded toward Saaber.

Hisham snorted. "The blind leading the blind. Since when did you become a teacher?"

"Since I understood my destiny."

"Your destiny is to die in jail," Hisham said, laughing.

"And yours?" Badr asked, smiling calmly.

"Is to make fun of you." Hisham reached over and slapped Badr, his palm making a popping sound when it met Badr's cheek and neck.

Badr's smile did not fade away. "Trials," he whispered to Saaber once Hisham's attention drifted away from them.

"But he humiliated you!" Saaber protested.

Badr shook his head. "Everything happens for a reason. Humiliation is nothing but a path toward glory." Badr turned to face Saaber, looking him straight in the eyes. "Shall I explain?" he asked.

Saaber nodded.

"To UNDERSTAND ANYTHING about how life works, one must see it as a short prelude to the afterlife," Badr said. "If you think of life as fleeting, a period as short as one day and one night when compared to the eternity of the afterlife, then you will see that nothing that happens to you here truly matters. What matters is how this life prepares you for eternity."

Saaber nodded.

"Sometimes, in rare cases, people get special treatment, a life designed to prepare them for an eternity of glory. Prophets all had such lives. Ayyub is a perfect example," Badr said, scratching his chin as he remembered the prophet Job. "God took everything away from him just so that he could find his faith instead of focusing on earthly possessions. And the prophet Yunus was swallowed by a whale so that he, too, could find God. God tests those whom he loves best. Trials are there to remind us that life is fleeting, and to show us the way to an eternity in heaven."

"Stop filling the boy's head with your bullshit, Badr," Hisham chimed in.

Badr smiled at him. He waited until Hisham returned to speaking to two other inmates before he continued in a whisper.

"Take your own life, for example. You are clearly chosen for a different life than most. Your father is imprisoned wrongfully. He dies in jail. That's injustice. Then your brother gets killed by the police, the same group of people who caused your father's death—another injustice. Then the American journalist finds you and writes a story about you, recognizing your uniqueness." Badr stressed this last word, his voice getting momentarily louder with excitement, which made Hisham turn their way again. Badr paused.

"And for that you get turned in to the police by the same people who caused your father's arrest. More injustice. Then the police come to your home, assault you and your family, and then imprison you when you defend yourself."

"I wasn't even defending myself," Saaber said. "The orderly's fall was an accident."

"You should have defended yourself!" Badr exclaimed. "What's wrong with self-defense? Are you supposed to let people walk all over you? To allow them to take your life, your freedom, and do nothing?"

Saaber looked down at his feet, examining his toes in the prison-issue sandals. For the first time, he wished he truly had pushed the orderly. If he had, Badr would have seen him as a hero. He would have taken this as confirmation of Saaber's glorious destiny.

THE ATTORNEY FOUAD hired explained to Saaber that he was facing two accusations: communicating with foreign elements with the intent of compromising national security, and attempted murder. He thought he could get both charges dropped, since there was no evidence to support either one and since there was no way to prove intent in the case of the orderly who, after all, hadn't died, which, luckily, rules out manslaughter. The attorney said he just needed time.

"I'm going to be here for years," Saaber complained to Badr once he was back in the cell.

Badr shrugged. "So what? Everything happens in God's good time."

"I don't want to die in jail."

"You will not." Badr emphasized his words with a gentle squeeze of Saaber's wrist. "This is one step in your path, one hurdle you have to cross. Have patience, and try to see what God is preparing you for."

According to Badr, God was preparing Saaber to be one of His soldiers on earth, and as such, He needed to toughen him up. This explained everything, from the various injustices Saaber endured outside of jail to the multiple injustices he endured within, including the occasional beating by the jail guards who branded Saaber as a cop killer, even though the orderly had not died, as Saaber repeatedly told them. When they refused to believe him, saying that Saaber had tried to kill the orderly in cold blood, Saaber remembered how Badr had stressed self-defense as a legitimate cause for fighting, and instead of trying to convince them of his innocence, Saaber proclaimed that he had pushed the man in self-defense, which produced more beatings by the prison guards.

"Trials, my friend," Badr repeatedly whispered as Saaber put pressure on his swollen eyelid. "Trials."

"You know why you are different from these people?" Badr asked Saaber one day, nodding toward the inmates sharing the crowded cell with them. "Because you have the power to be heard. Because you have already taken the first steps toward fame, and if you play your cards right, you can revisit this path. You can do glorious things and let the world know about them, not just people here in Egypt, but the entire world, even America! You can remind people that God has soldiers on earth that make sure His justice is served. You can be God's ambassador to the world—as close as anyone can get to being a prophet."

"But what can I do?"

"You can kill two birds with one stone. You can avenge your father and brother and your wrongful imprisonment, and be God's instrument in bringing justice to the police who brought all of this upon you in the first place, who brought this upon all of us," Badr whispered, nodding toward the other inmates again. "You're afraid of the judges, but you don't realize that you can be the judge. You can decide who lives and who dies. You can gain fame in this life and an eternity in heaven, too."

"How?" Saaber asked, his eyes widening.

Badr smiled.

"I NEED TO talk to you." Hisham pulled Saaber by the arm, taking him to the corner of the yard where they were let out to walk for an hour once every couple of days. The yard was enclosed by a tall, concrete wall, its top embedded with shards of glass that glistened under coils of barbed wire.

"What's Badr been talking to you about all this time?"

"Nothing." Saaber's heart raced. Hisham was a broad-shouldered man with a plain, clean-shaven face that would have looked harmless on a shorter man, but that in his case made him look menacing. Saaber remembered what Badr had told him: how deceptive Hisham was; how he would try to make him believe he was protecting him in the prison's hierarchy when he was only trying to secure his loyalty; how he claimed he got convicted of manslaughter for accidentally killing a man during a street fight when, in reality, he had been a hired assassin. Badr assured Saaber that Hisham's family rolled in the wealth of his blood-tinted money. Saaber looked at Hisham's white jogging suit, not the prison-issue one, but a more expensive one his family had bought for him, one that felt soft and downy when his fingers brushed against Hisham's arm. Saaber hated that suit.

"Don't 'nothing' me, boy. I've seen him talk to you, and I've heard some of the bullshit he's been feeding you. I'm this close to reporting both of you to the guards." He held his pointer and thumb half an inch apart. "I would do it, too, but I know what they'll do to both of you if they found out. I don't give a crap about him—would be good riddance, if you ask me—but you're still young. You'll probably be out of here in a few weeks. You have your entire life ahead of you. Don't waste it."

Saaber swallowed. "I don't know what you're talking about."

Hisham sighed. "You know why Badr is in prison? He defrauded old women of their money. He would find some poor old woman with a few pennies saved and would convince her to donate her money to some imaginary orphanage he was building. Carried photos of kids with him all the time. You know what he did with the money he collected?"

Saaber shook his head.

"One of the women had a nephew who cared enough about her to alert the police. They raided Badr's apartment and found money stuffed in mattresses, in boxes under the bed, in old suitcases stacked in a corner. All small bills, all the life savings of these women. He was just keeping it all there while the poor old women starved. He had been doing this for years. The police are still trying to track them down to give them their money back, but they probably won't find them. They believed they were giving the money to God. It's not like they would have reported it missing."

"He was saving up to build the orphanage. He just didn't have enough money to get started yet."

Hisham snorted. "Is that what he told you?"

"I believe him."

"Of course you do."

Saaber glanced around and saw Badr standing a few feet away, in the shade of the wall, shifting his weight from foot to foot, his gaze so intently focused on Hisham that he didn't see Saaber look his way. Hisham followed Saaber's glance.

"Get lost," Hisham yelled at Badr, flicking him away with one wave of his hand.

Saaber looked at Badr's back as he slowly walked away.

"I'm only trying to protect you," Hisham said. "The man is a known crook. Nothing good can come out of spending that much time with him. He is not being kind to you. He is using you."

"What would he be using me for? I have nothing to give him."

"You have more to give him than you realize."

"He is a man of God."

Hisham snorted again. "Based on what? His beard? Any idiot can grow a beard."

"He knows a lot about religion."

"And how do you know that what he's telling you is true and not some bullshit he is making up?"

"I just know."

Hisham shook his head. "Not everyone who talks religion knows religion, Saaber. Nothing is easier than sounding religious. All you need is a beard and some *inshaa Allah* and *mashaa Allah* scattered between your words and people will swallow all you say. If you really want to learn about religion, I can get you some books. Or I can hook you up with someone to teach you, once you get out of here. I have a close friend who graduated from Al-Azhar, a real scholar. I'll have him contact you, if you want."

"Yeah, sure," Saaber said, scanning the yard again for Badr. He saw him sitting on the ground, his back against the wall, his legs pulled up to his chest, staring at his feet. "Sure," Saaber repeated, inching away from Hisham. "I'll contact your friend once I get out of here."

"We need to be more careful," Saaber whispered to Badr as they stood in line to get back in.

Badr nodded. "I know. The devil is already sending his followers to stop us. I expected that. I *told you* it would happen."

Saaber nodded. Badr had, just the day before, warned him of Hisham, who had settled down too close to them as they spoke, obviously eaves-dropping.

"You know what that means, don't you? They are starting to realize how powerful you are. They, too, are recognizing your destiny, your potential for glory." Here Badr stopped, nodded toward another inmate ahead of them, who had turned around and given him a stern look. Badr slowed his pace, and Saaber followed his lead until the inmate was out of earshot. "We just have to be more careful. Trust me, Saaber: this only proves my point about how important you are. You think Hisham would have spared you a minute of his time if you weren't?" He looked at Saaber, who shook his head. "Of course not. He is noticing you only because he is afraid you'll overshadow him. Here, within these walls, he is the big shot, and he wor-ries that you will be even bigger, you will reach more people, you will be more powerful than he ever can be. But guess what?" Here Badr stood in place and turned to look straight at Hisham, who was farther behind in line and who had stepped aside, clearly looking at them. "You will," Badr said, holding Hisham's gaze, not budging. "You will."

LYING DOWN TO sleep that night, Saaber did not mind the concrete floor anymore, nor did he find the walls around him constraining. When he thought of the police orderly, of the prison guards, of the judge stamping his file with the renewed detention, of the injustice done to his brother and his father, of Hisham trying to sway him from his destiny, he felt a hatred harder, more solid, than anything he had ever experienced before, but his hate did not constrain his chest, like it used to when he first came to prison, when he focused only on the injustice and not on how he could fight it and bring balance to a life out of kilter.

He had power, he now realized, smiling. When he closed his eyes, he remembered the look on his face when it once graced the pages of the

American newspaper, how even then he had seen something in his own eyes that he had never noticed before: determination, a sense of purpose. He remembered the neighbors huddling around the TV as the news anchor held up the article featuring his photo, remembered the way the kids looked up at him when he passed by, and he knew why Badr had recognized this quality in him, this ability to make things happen, to galvanize people just by being himself. Before drifting away to sleep, Saaber realized that, for the first time in his life, he liked the person he was turning out to be.

19

When the text messages started, they did not stop for three days. Fouad's phone pinged once, then again, then multiple times in a row, and then it slowed down to a steady trickle of one ping every hour or so, until he turned it to silent mode.

"What's up with all the texts?" Gameela asked. Four months into their marriage, she was still unsure about boundaries and did not want to fit the stereotype of a meddling wife, but thought the repeated messages warranted an inquiry, especially since that last one had happened after ten in the evening, when the farm was doused in the deep countryside darkness and she and Fouad were already in bed.

"It's Saaber. I can't shake him off."

"He's not in trouble again, is he?"

"No. He hasn't been in trouble since he got released, as far as I know."

"What does he want?"

Fouad picked his phone up, read the last message, and then put the phone facedown on the nightstand. "He keeps asking me to go to Cairo and meet with him. I told him I can't travel right now, especially since he won't tell me what he needs me for. It's ridiculous of him to expect me to drive all the way there just because he asks me to—it's not like we're old friends. I hardly know him. I'm not at his beck and call."

Gameela turned to face Fouad. The pillows on his bed were the old-fashioned, cotton-stuffed ones, and she had to adjust hers to prevent her neck from hurting. She beat the pillow down with one hand, hoping to create a groove in the stiff filling. "Maybe he needs something but is too embarrassed to ask?"

"I offered to send him money, and he refused." The phone vibrated on the wooden nightstand. Fouad, puffing, picked the phone up and turned the vibration off. "I don't know what else I can do. I've endured this for days. I've even called him to try to understand what he wants, and I got nowhere. All he says is *I need to see you. I need to see you. Come to Cairo.* I would block him, but I want him to be able to reach me if he truly needs something. If he changes his mind about the money."

"You've helped him out enough already."

"Hiring that attorney was the least I could do, considering I caused Saaber's troubles to start with."

"No, you didn't."

"I put him in touch with Mark."

"Only because I asked you to. You only know Mark through me. And you didn't tell Saaber to push that orderly off the building!"

Fouad turned to face her. He held her hand in his, and she fell silent.

"You're too kind, Gameela. I could set Cairo on fire and you'd find an excuse for me."

She could not decide whether she was flattered or offended, suspecting him of being condescending, talking to her as if she were a child and he the old, wise man. Behind him, the phone's screen lit up, creating a halo of pale light, which lasted for a few seconds before disappearing.

FOUAD HAD A faint scar on his forehead, a silvery line that would have been invisible had it not cut straight across his brow, leaving in its wake a line where hair stopped growing. In the mornings, whenever Gameela woke up before he did, she remained still, staring at the faded scar, sometimes reaching over and gently touching it, making sure she didn't wake him up. It took her years of sleuthing to get him to explain the scar to her, to take one more step toward trusting her, which he allowed in such slow progression that she was often brought to tears of frustration. He was her greatest unsolved mystery, but she was cracking this case, one step at a time.

Her life before she met him felt so distant now that she barely remembered it. On the day she first saw him five years ago, nothing special had happened to signal that this was the day her life was to change forever: no wedding processions passed by her parents' apartment building on their way to the Marriott next door; no deafening drumbeats announced the arrival of the bride and groom. Only an older man sitting in Marwa's living room, a man who looked at her as she walked in and then casually looked away, as if nothing had happened.

Later, she would realize that she missed the biggest sign of all: the Egyptian revolution bursting all around them, changing the country's destiny and, in the process, changing her own fate as well.

As the streets between Gameela's parents' apartment and Marwa's filled with protesters pushing against the forces of the riot police, as people spread across the Qasr El-Nile Bridge, praying under the downpour of the water police hosed them down with, Gameela, Marwa, her brother, and Fouad watched from the sidelines, sometimes venturing into the midst of the marching masses, shouting slogans requesting social justice, other times stepping into the entryways of random apartment buildings, hiding in stairwells as the riot police shot rubber bullets at protesters around them.

"We barely see you for twenty years," Marwa told Fouad as they walked back into her parents' apartment building, Gameela and Mustafa in tow, "and then a revolution happens and we can't get rid of you. Since when were you interested in activism anyway?"

"Since before you were born," Fouad replied, stepping aside to let Gameela pass.

Later, after the military cleared the streets, when the revolution was relocated to the TV screens people were glued to, watching power being transferred from the army to the Muslim Brotherhood and back to the army, arguing ceaselessly about who was on the side of justice, Gameela started her gentle inquiry into the life of the man who, to the astonishment of his family, would not go back to his beloved farm. He had stayed in Cairo for a full year before disappearing for that dark, dark month without notice, a move he later confessed was supposed to cure her of any infatuation with him but that, instead, had made her more obsessed with him than ever. Later, after he came back, after he started joining her in her forty-five-minute walk back to her parents' place, after they started spending hours of each day together, Gameela had basked in his ability to focus solely on her, to sit in a room full of people and stare at her until she caught him doing it and then, rather than look away, to continue staring anyway.

"I still don't understand what you see in me," she asked him three years after they first met, when their daily meetings had settled into a routine that neither one questioned. She was sitting across from him on the porch of the Studio Masr restaurant, the gardens of Al-Azhar extended before them, the mosque of Mohammed Ali visible on top of the Mokattam hill in the distance, the mosque's two tall minarets and multiple white domes jutting into Cairo's clear blue sky.

"I see myself thirty-five years ago. Does that make me narcissistic?" he asked, smiling.

"Probably. What's the difference between younger you and current you?"

He looked at the vast gardens ahead, tapped one finger on the white tablecloth. "Thirty-five years."

It would be another full year before she learned what happened to him: how he had participated in the Bread Riots of 1977, when the government attempted to remove the subsidies on basic foodstuffs and found itself squelching a spontaneous revolt, with thousands of people flooding the streets, fearing they could no longer afford to feed their families. Gameela learned how Fouad's eighteen-year-old self requested justice for the masses of poor people he was not one of, how he got arrested, how he got that scar: in jail, under interrogation, denying that he was a communist.

"It breaks my heart to think of how unfair life has been to you," she would later whisper as she sat next to him on the balcony in the evening, weeks after they got married.

"It's not unfair anymore, is it?" he would ask, kissing her temple, one arm wrapped around her shoulders.

And it would not be, because she would not allow it to be. That was the vow she'd made to herself when she decided to marry him against her parents' wishes; that was the vow she still lived by. She would bend life to meet her desires; as long as she was not doing anything to offend God, she would pursue what she wanted. No one would stop her.

EVERY DAY, she reinvented her life, using the farm as a brand-new, spotless canvas. She was Gameela, mistress of the manor, ordering Maymouna around, making everyday decisions about evening meals, furniture layout, which corners needed dusting. Gameela, lover of nature, who walked around the farm during the day, following her husband as he inspected his vast grounds tree by tree, reaching over and sniffing the sweet orange blossoms, collecting ripe mangoes for the evening's dessert. Gameela, amateur sleuth, gently probing her husband to discover everything about him: his morning routine; how he liked his tea; how his eyes wrinkled when he laughed; the true tone of his skin, visible beneath the T-shirt's tan lines; the feel of his biceps, kept strong by the manual labor he still insisted on doing, helping transplant young trees, pushing carts loaded with bags of fertilizer around the farm, getting dirt stuck under his fingernails, brushing them clean each night.

She loved her multiple new identities, the freedom of self-invention.

Gameela the lover, in silk negligees that glistened in the faint evening light of her husband's bedroom.

"This farm is a piece of heaven," she whispered one night, lying on her back on their bed, staring at the ceiling fan softly swishing above.

Fouad chuckled. "I wouldn't take it that far. But it certainly was a haven to me when I first came here."

"I love how quiet it is here at night."

"It's isolated, yes."

"It's peaceful."

He nodded, saying nothing. She turned to her side and reached over, holding his hand. Closing her eyes, she imagined him thirty-five years ago, out of prison, too young to have his life so ruthlessly upended because of a simple decision to participate in a protest, such a large price to pay for wanting to set things right.

On the nightstand behind him, the phone buzzed again. Fouad turned around and grabbed it.

"Enough is enough. I'm blocking him."

Gameela watched the screen go black. Saaber was just about the same age Fouad had been when he got out of prison, and he was obviously reaching out for help. Gameela eyed Fouad's phone, connected to its charger on the nightstand. Pity no one was helping the poor boy.

20

The pigeon house was deserted. Saaber stood in the center of the abandoned structure, examining the empty cages. He wondered how long it had taken the pigeons to realize no one would bring them food and water anymore, whether they had taken off all together in a mass exodus, or whether they had left one by one.

A minor pang gripped his chest as he thought of the birds waiting in vain for someone to feed them. He hoped they had all found new homes, immigrated to other, established pigeon houses, but feared that some may have stayed behind and died of hunger and thirst. Opening the cage doors, he found no traces of dead birds, no heaps of bones and feathers. That, at least, was a relief.

If he were to replenish the supply of food and water, some of the pigeons might come back, but he no longer desired that. In the midday sun, in Cairo's suffocating heat, he could clearly see how wrong it had been for him to be so attached to material things, to brute animals, to the possibility of becoming rich. Badr had been right when he insisted that the real life was the eternal afterlife, not this fleeting mess where all suffer. No one dies in heaven, unlike here, where every human being will die, sooner or later. So what if some die a few years sooner than the rest?

Mahadesh beymout nakes omr. No one dies before his time. One of the sayings his mother often repeated. Surprisingly true.

When his mother had cried that the jail had not provided his father with proper treatment for his diabetes, the officer had assured her that no one died before his time.

When, years later, she had fallen to her knees and wailed in front of her dwelling's door, lamenting Houda's death, the neighbors had gathered around her, reminding her to accept God's will, assuring her that no one died before his time.

Dying is simply stepping into the eternal life. It's not the end; it's the beginning, Badr had told him.

Everything Badr said made sense.

A flutter of wings announced the arrival of a bird, a single pigeon that landed on the corner of the cages over his left shoulder. Saaber looked at it, examining the blue, green, and silver sheen of the feathers protecting its long neck and puffed-up chest. Then he shushed it away, watched it fly off in a surprised flurry.

THOUGH HE MISSED Badr's guidance, Saaber did not need him anymore. Not as long as he had the internet, that mine of information begging to be explored.

After his release, Saaber spent months visiting multiple internet cafés, educating himself on the injustices facing Muslims everywhere and on various ways to fight those wrongs, to be God's soldier on earth, as Badr had repeatedly described him.

He liked the image of himself as an avenging warrior, an instrument of God's wrath.

He imagined himself standing in front of God in the afterlife, basking in His praise for his selflessness, his willingness to fight for what God deemed right.

The more he read, the clearer everything seemed. Simpler. Now he could easily recognize that people fell into two categories: good and evil.

The evil ones needed to be punished.

The good ones, if they suffered, got rewarded for their suffering in the afterlife.

Everything made sense.

———

YEARS BEFORE, a man had posed a question to the sheikh at the mosque where Houda used to go for his weekly lessons, dragging Saaber along with him.

"But how about all those people? The innocent ones? The ones he killed?"

They were discussing Osama bin Laden. The sheikh had paused, nodded. "Martyrs, of course. All of them. No excuse for taking any life. Ever." And the sheikh had recited the verse from the Qur'an about how if one killed one soul it was as if one had killed the entirety of humanity, and how if one saved one soul it was as if one had saved the entirety of humanity.

"A soul is sacred," the sheikh had said. "Note that Allah did not specify the soul's race, religion, or devotion. The soul of an atheist is just as sacred as the soul of the most ardent believer in Allah."

Later, the man who had posed the question had stayed behind after the sheikh was done with the lesson. Saaber had pretended to read from the Qur'an as the man talked to Houda.

"But if those killed as collateral damage are martyrs and go straight to heaven, then what's the harm in killing them?"

Both men had chuckled. Saaber gazed intently at the verses in front of him, but he saw nothing.

ONLINE, Saaber learned that Muslims were being persecuted everywhere: in Israel, in Burma, even in Islamic countries like Syria and Iraq, where sects of Muslims were killing other sects, apparently backed up by foreign financing, all part of the big conspiracy targeting Muslims everywhere. With increasing horror, he flipped through photos of mangled bodies, of rows of dead children wrapped up in white burial shrouds.

He remembered Houda and his heart swelled with anger.

Badr had explained this to him, underscoring how true believers were oppressed everywhere, but Saaber had not imagined the magnitude of what his mentor described. The websites opened his eyes. They also taught him ways to fight. To right what is wrong.

THE INSTRUCTIONS WERE EASY. Again and again, he went back to the internet café and used a notepad to copy them down step by step so that he would not have to print them and risk having someone see the images as they rolled out of the printer. When he saw that he would need only pieces of pipe and nails and some basic wiring skills he almost fell to the ground right there to thank God, because wasn't that a sign, too? The years he spent jumping from one apprenticeship to the other were not in vain. Badr was right: his entire life so far was leading him to this, preparing him for his moment of glory. He could almost weep with joy.

He sat in a booth by the corner. Someone pointed at him and made a crude joke about him being on porn, but he pretended he had not heard that.

THE MORE HE THOUGHT about life, the clearer everything became to him. Walking down the dirt alley leading to his mother's dwelling, his notepad clutched tightly under his arm, Saaber looked at those around him and marveled at their inability to see what he now so clearly saw: that life was going off-kilter, that injustice was rampant, and that, contrary to what they had been told their entire lives, there were effective, legitimate ways to fight this injustice, to sew together the scattered pieces of existence until everything aligned perfectly again.

Violence can be fought only with violence.

Pity filled his heart. If only people could see what he saw.

Badr had seen it, of course. Badr had also noted how Saaber had the unique ability to make himself heard.

Close to home, Saaber remembered the day the American had interviewed him. He was still proud of how determined his face had looked in the photo, but he regretted having wasted this opportunity talking about pigeons. If only he had known then what he knew now—he could have revealed so much to the world. If only he had had Badr's guidance earlier, he would have recognized how remarkable it was that Fouad, one of dozens of rich men in whose apartments he had worked, would remember him and bring an American journalist right to his doorstep. That had doubtless been another sign, another way God had singled him out for greatness.

At the door, his mother blocked his way.

"When are you going to go back to work?"

He squeezed past her. "I'm already working."

"Where is the money you've earned, then?"

He looked up at her, almost pitying her, too. "There are rewards greater than money, Mother."

She stared at him, her hands on her hips, then she turned her head and spat to the side, her spit hitting the dirt floor, marking it with a circular bull's-eye.

IN THE PIGEON HOUSE, sitting in the center of the clearing, surrounded by the empty cages, Saaber started writing down his vision, documenting all he had learned, explaining how perfectly all the pieces of his life now fit together: the deaths of both his father and brother; his imprisonment; even the wrong step the orderly had taken before he plunged down and landed on the roof of the neighboring building.

Everything happened according to God's plan so that he, Saaber, could fulfill his destiny.

The words flowed out of him, lines slithering one after the other on the paper, covering sheet after sheet.

Fouad stopped responding to his texts, which angered Saaber until he remembered Badr's words: Everything happens in God's good time.

If Fouad didn't respond now, it meant only that the time had not yet come.

Saaber kept texting him.

The more he read online, the more things made sense. The more he wrote about his thoughts, the clearer they became.

God knows what's in everyone's heart. *Alaamalu belneyyat.* Works are judged based on the intentions behind them, on the purity of one's heart.

His intention was clear: he was to avenge his father, his brother, and all those killed by the police, directly or indirectly. In prison, Badr had told him story after story of *mujahideen* dying by the hands of the police, of freedom fighters imprisoned under terrorism charges when all they wanted to do was fight for God's cause, as he did. Badr had explained that the riot police had killed Houda, which meant that the police were murderers.

The Qur'an legitimized punishing murderers. Clearly, the riot police had killed his brother. Therefore, punishing the police was the right thing to do. Technically, the only ones allowed to inflict such punishment were those in authority, but the judge who had overseen Houda's case had let his killer roam free, citing lack of evidence. The authorities were not upholding justice. Therefore, it logically followed that Saaber should be allowed to take things into his own hands. Badr was certain God would agree with this logic, and Saaber concurred.

His actions would bring police atrocities to the world's attention. Perhaps if the American journalist had not interviewed him, his actions could easily have been dismissed. But that interview had made him famous. People would have to take note.

That, too, was a sign from God. Fouad had brought the journalist to him because God had guided his hand.

All things led to this.

He needed to make the loudest statement possible. The noise he made would speak more clearly than any words, but putting his wisdom into words certainly would not hurt, just in case people failed to understand his actions.

He texted Fouad again.

I need to see you. When will you be back in Cairo?

He got no answer.

He contemplated traveling to Rasheed to meet with Fouad, but he was afraid the police may be following him. Every day he saw people looking at him as he walked down the street, felt certain he was being watched, remembered Badr's words about the devil sending his followers to stop him. If the police saw him leave the city, they would probably harass him, search him. He couldn't risk getting arrested again.

Everything happened in due time, he reminded himself.

He kept texting Fouad.

AND IF ANY innocent lives were taken?

Well, since no one died before his time, their deaths would have been predetermined anyway. He was merely the instrument implementing their fates. Besides, those souls would become martyrs and go straight to heaven, be spared this world's pain and sorrow.

Everyone gains. And he would be known for having fought to restore justice, to avenge those mistreated. His face would again grace the front pages of newspapers worldwide.

He, too, would be a martyr. Because God deals in intentions and God would know that his intentions were to restore justice on earth.

The verse in the Qur'an about killing innocent souls would not apply to him. The verse about the rewards of martyrs would.

And all the martyrs live on forever. Any innocent bystanders will live forever. He, too, will live forever.

It all made sense.

WHEN HE FINALLY got a text from Fouad, he saw that as the sign he had been waiting for. From a nook under his bed, he pulled out the money he had wrapped in a sheet of butcher paper, a gift Badr had arranged for him to receive on his release and that Saaber had kept hidden since then, reaching for it only when he absolutely needed to. Most of the thick stack of bills was still untouched. Consulting his notebook, he wrote down a list of supplies. Then he went shopping.

IN THE SHADE of the abandoned wooden structures of the pigeon house, Saaber worked patiently, consulting the instructions, until he created a perfect prototype. He sat in place, gazing at the piece of pipe in front of him, marveling at his ability to create such a thing in mere hours.

He wrapped it in multiple pieces of cloth, carefully placed it in a backpack, and took the bus out of Cairo and toward the 6th of October City, one of the suburbs built on the edge of the desert. Once there, he got out, but instead of entering the community of apartment buildings and villas, he continued walking on the edge of the road until he passed the entire suburb, and then he turned into the desert and walked for close to an hour, making sure he was out of sight.

Carefully, he took his creation out of the backpack he had been hugging close to his chest, set it up, extended the wire to what he thought was a safe distance, and, hiding behind a sand dune, pushed the trigger.

The boom was so loud that the sand dune shook under its waves, sand flying up and then raining down on Saaber, who crouched with his head between his elbows, a high-pitched tone ringing in his ears. After the sand settled, Saaber could still hear his heart pounding, its beat jovial, proud.

Badr was certainly right. Why wallow in hopelessness when he could become an instrument of justice, a beacon of hope for all those who suffered as he did?

Saaber knew, right then, that he was destined for glory.

21

Of all the sleuthing she had ever done, this last endeavor was among her most brilliant, a feat so intricately planned that it furthered her conviction that she had earned the Irene Adler nickname.

Gameela, getting dressed after breakfast at the farmhouse, examined her reflection in the mirror and could not help but smile.

"You seem cheerful," Fouad said. Sitting in a chair in the corner of the room, his left leg violently shaking in a nervous habit she had gotten used to, he had watched her change and pack her things, the morose expression that haunted his face whenever she got ready to leave tinged with an undertone of anger. "So excited to go back home?" he asked with obvious sarcasm.

She turned to face him. "I *am* home. Here more than anywhere else. You know that."

"This is useless."

He got up and walked out of the room. From the window, she watched him climb down the front steps and walk away, heading toward the farm's deeper acres. Biting her lip, she contemplated chasing after him and getting him to turn around, look at her, and tell her he was not upset, that he was willing to be patient for just a few more days, a few more weeks, at the most, until she figured out how to break the news to her parents without breaking their hearts. Without making them think ill of her. She opened the window, leaned out, and called after him.

He did not turn around.

IN THE CAR, Gameela tried to not let Fouad's petulant behavior ruin her mood and to focus, instead, on her plan for the day. It was barely ten in the morning, the sun already high up but the day still not too hot. She rolled her window down, letting the fresh air lap against her face as she turned out of the farm's gates and onto the main avenue. She drove alongside the farm for a few minutes, its sprawling acres bordering the road. Glancing sideways, she looked between the trees to see if Fouad had made his way there, if, perhaps, he was standing in the shade of the mango trees, watching her pass by, but she could not see him.

On the highway, she rolled her window back up and pressed the pedal, zooming in her cool, air-conditioned Kia past trucks overflowing with hay and minibuses loaded with passengers. She had a good five hours before she was supposed to meet with Saaber, but she had hoped she would have time to stop at home first. She scolded herself for not leaving earlier, for being late to everything. But she was not going to be late to this appointment.

She pressed the pedal harder, zoomed past lazy drivers clogging the road. A decrepit maroon sedan, its backseat crammed with kids, rattled next to her as she passed, and glancing at it, Gameela saw a young girl watching her, one hand holding on to the ledge of the opened window, her eyes wide with curiosity, not blinking despite the wind that swept her hair.

FOR DAYS she had been troubled by Saaber's incessant messages. She pitied the boy and felt guilty about her role in what happened to him. After all, she was the one who asked Fouad if he knew anyone whom Mark could interview for his series of profiles. Fouad would never have brought Mark to Saaber were it not for her. She had a moral obligation to help the boy. More important, she had a religious obligation to do so. For the previous days, she had been reassessing her religious journey so far. After the initial dive into devotion and the subsequent calmer, more content bobbing at what she believed was a less strict level of religious adherence, she was now ready to move past the phase of obsession with the rituals of Islam and into a more proactive phase, one where she could do things, act and see material results of her actions. This, to her, was the true meaning of *jihad*—this constant striving to do good in the world. The revolution of 2011 had given her a taste of the adrenaline rush accompanying action, of the power one felt when one could initiate change. That chance was gone now—striving for political change seemed futile. But personal change was still doable. She hungered for it, itched to mold her character into a stronger, better version of herself, one who helped others even if all those around her were content with complacency. She would change Saaber's life, too. She would help him—how, she wasn't sure. But she would respond to his call for help, even if Fouad refused to do so.

Besides, she had to admit that she was devoured by curiosity. Every time the phone beeped, she had to resist an urge to pick it up, call Saaber, and ask him to reveal, in great detail, why he was so insistent on seeing Fouad.

"We can go meet him together. I already travel to Cairo every week; you can come with me one time, see what he wants, and we'll drive back to Rasheed together a couple of days later," she had pleaded with Fouad as he walked around the farm, inspecting the newly raised bed of a couple of acres, she trailing behind him.

"There is nothing more I can do for him. I already told him this repeatedly."

"But the poor boy keeps texting you."

"I can't help that he doesn't take no for an answer."

"But what if he truly needs something? What if he is in some great bind that only you can help him get out of? What if he has no one else to turn to?"

"If he was in a bind, he would have said so by now. He did it before, when he had his mom ask me to hire him a lawyer. But he refuses to explain why he needs to see me. It's insane to expect me to take off and go all the way to Cairo to meet with him without knowing why he needs me. He can't order me around without providing an explanation."

"He must have his reasons!"

Fouad stopped, turning to face Gameela. "So you're asking me to trust the judgment of a boy who just spent a year and a half in jail on terrorism charges?"

"Not terrorism, conspiring with the enemy," Gameela corrected him. "And he was never charged. He merely got in trouble over that poor orderly he pushed off the roof."

"Merely!" Fouad shook his head. "He is merely homicidal?"

"He says it was an accident!"

"Even if. I don't need to be anywhere near this boy. Neither do you."

Gameela looked up at him, arms crossed. "You're just afraid, aren't you?"

"Afraid to mess with someone doubtless watched by the police? Yes. As I have every right to be," he hissed, leaning closer to her. "Afraid to have you anywhere near a boy who has a talent for trouble? Yes."

"It's not right, Fouad. Abandoning him that way."

"I did all I could for him."

"He is just a young boy who got in trouble with the police for speaking his mind. You of all people should understand that."

"I, of all people, totally understand that. Which is why I'm not going anywhere near him."

"Easy for you to say. When *you* got out of jail, you had all of this waiting for you." She raised both arms, gesturing at the sprawling farm around them. "Pity the poor boy doesn't come from a family of landowners."

"Enough, Gameela," he grimaced, waving a dismissive hand her way. "I've humored you long enough. This has already been settled."

"*Humored me?*"

He walked off, not turning to see if she followed him. Gameela stood in place, marveling at how easily Fouad had slipped into a superior attitude, a rare but reoccurring theme, she was noticing, of him playing his age card as if that brought any argument to a definitive stop. He had not acted so superior back in 2011, when she was the one leading the way into the protests as he marched behind her, echoing the chants that she initiated. Back then, they had been peers, fellows in a fight for justice. Now that they had a chance to act again, he was backing off and expecting her to follow suit, hide with him in his small piece of heaven, sit under the shade of his guava tree and pretend that those who suffered did not exist.

But Fouad was a hapless victim of a society that told him that his gender and age elevated him above her. She did not question his authority over her—religiously, she was expected to obey her husband once she got married—but she was seeing now, clearer and clearer each day, that there were ways around this. That when dealing with matters of justice and of what was right versus what was wrong, her obedience to God overruled her obedience to her husband. And God ordered humans to help each other.

FINDING A WAY to implement her will was so easy, she marveled again at why she spent so many years listening to others, when she could do whatever she knew was right and pass it under their noses without their noticing.

For example, breaking into Fouad's apartment that time he disappeared and seeking out all the assurances of his return that he refused to give her.

For example, getting married despite the disapproval of her parents, who rejected Fouad based on unfair, classist criteria.

For example, texting Saaber from Fouad's phone, pretending to be Fouad, agreeing on a meeting time and place, giving him her own phone number as a "new contact number" that he should be using from now on, and then deleting the entire text exchange. She even remembered to check Fouad's laptop to make sure no texts were forwarded there.

Simple. Child's play. Now she would be meeting with a young man who, she knew, would not have agreed to meet with her had she not pretended to be Fouad. She doubted he would have remembered her, and even if he had, she was certain he would not have agreed to receive help from a woman. Just like Fouad, Saaber, too, was a victim of a society that told him that men had to be strong, that cries for help were signs of weakness, especially if those cries were directed at a woman. She would change that, too, in her journey to change herself. Challenge it. She would exercise her God-given right and obligation to help others, even if they were too stubborn to realize they needed her help.

She felt invincible. A more modestly dressed but just as powerful incarnation of Irene Adler, a woman who can outwit all men.

Including this poor boy, who was now walking into the street café where she had been waiting to meet him. On seeing her, Saaber took a step back, as if he had just set eyes on Medusa, and froze in place.

"*Assalamu aleikum*, Saaber," she said, getting up, remembering to use the Islamic greeting that she favored anyway and that she knew he would, too. *Peace be upon you.*

"Where is Fouad?"

"He's not feeling well and couldn't be here, but he didn't want you to come and find no one, so he sent me instead." Which was not a total lie—he had not been feeling well this morning, refusing to say goodbye to her. Walking out into the fields as if he were Heathcliff on the dunes.

"Why did he send *you*?"

Gameela ignored the condescending tone. "Because he trusts me." Then, after a moment's hesitation, "I'm his wife."

Saaber looked her up and down, apparently reluctant to believe her. "He should have called me."

"Why don't you sit down for a while? I'm sure I can take care of whatever it was you wanted of him."

He stood in place, shifting his weight from foot to foot, not making eye contact with her, which was typical of religious men who thought that looking at a woman's face was sinful. But he did not look as obviously religious as he had when they'd last met, two and a half years earlier. His beard was gone, and he was wearing blue jeans and a polo shirt, which would have made him look younger, had his face not aged so. Gameela scrutinized him, his hollow cheeks noticeable without the protection of the beard, his eyes baggy and dark.

"I can't stay," he finally said.

"Not even for a few minutes? I made the trip specifically to meet you. I'm sure I can be of help."

He looked at her but still did not sit down. She took a deep breath in, telling herself to remain calm—she had been right in assuming he would never have met with a woman, especially one as young as she was. If she were an older man, he would have been pouring his heart out by now.

"I'm sure I'm quite capable of taking care of whatever you need." She tried to keep her voice as friendly as possible. "If you would just tell me why you wanted Fouad to meet with you, I can help." Then, rethinking his ability to accept help from a woman, "Or I can convey your message to Fouad, and *he* can help."

He looked at her with resigned disappointment. "I guess." He sighed. "Whatever God proclaimed shall be."

"Exactly. Sit down. Please."

He pulled a chair out, carefully placing his backpack on his lap.

"Can I order you something to drink?" she asked, signaling for the waiter to come.

He shook his head. "Do you know the American journalist?"

"Yes." She took a sip out of her minted lemonade, the cold glass covered with condensation. She wiped her hand on her jeans.

"You know how to get in touch with him?"

"Yes." She left it at that, not mentioning her sister's marriage, knowing the stigma associated with a marriage between a Muslim woman and a foreign man, even if he converted. Saaber would distrust her if he found out her sister had transgressed so.

"Would you be able to give him something?"

He was already opening the front compartment of his backpack, pulling out a yellow manila envelope and handing it to her. Gameela took it.

"He will know what to do with this. You must give it to him."

"Yes, of course. But—"

"Swear you will."

"Excuse me?"

"Swear."

He was staring straight into her eyes, his own eyes wide but strangely out of focus, as if he were looking through her and at something directly behind her.

Gameela sighed. "*Wallahi al-Azim* I will give it to him. But there must be something *I* can do for you. I really would like to help you in any—"

Already he had zipped his backpack shut and picked it up, lifting one strap to hang it off his shoulder. "I don't need anyone's help."

"Seriously?" Gameela stared at him in disbelief. For days she had imagined countless scenarios of the moment when she finally got to meet him and prove herself useful, do something that she could be proud of in front of God. She had not imagined that thing was as common as delivering a package. "You texted Fouad for weeks just for this? You dragged me all the way here just for this?" She waved the manila envelope at his face, getting up, too. "What do you think we are? Your personal homing pigeons?"

He looked up at her, taken back. An older man sitting at a table next to them glanced away from his newspaper. Gameela shot him an angry glare and he looked back down. She turned to face Saaber again.

"Because if all I am is your mail carrier, you can have that back." She held the envelope up to Saaber's face. "There is such a thing as a mail service, you know. Just mail it to him."

"But I don't have his address!"

The sudden panic in his voice and eyes, mixed with his failure to read anything beyond the literal meaning of her words, assuaged her anger. Suddenly, he looked young again. She pulled the envelope back to her chest.

"You don't know how to reach him?"

He shook his head.

"That's why you kept texting Fouad?"

He nodded, wiped the sweat dripping off his forehead on his wrist. Gameela examined his black curls, moist with perspiration, and couldn't bring herself to tell him that he could have googled Mark's name and he would have gotten his email address. Then again, the boy surely didn't speak English, let alone write it.

"Can we sit down for a while?"

"Are you going to take this to the journalist or not?"

She narrowed her eyes, standing straight. "No. Not unless you talk to me first."

He tilted his head, peering at her with apparent contempt. "You would break your own *helfan*? Take God's name in vain, refusing to do that which you have sworn to do?"

"I will fast for three days to atone for the unfulfilled promise," she retorted, feeling a bit childish.

"I should have known better." Behind them, a pair of older men playing backgammon burst into laughter, and Saaber glanced at them. When he turned back to face her, he seemed calm again. "You're probably lying. I bet you don't even know the journalist. And I bet you're not married to Fouad. What are you—his mistress?"

Gameela's face flushed. "I am married to him! And I do know the journalist. In fact, I was the one who introduced them."

Saaber snickered, shaking his head.

"The journalist is married to my sister," Gameela could not resist saying. She pulled out her phone, scrolled through the hundreds of photos she had on there, and found an old one she had kept since her sister's wedding: Rose in her wedding dress, Mark next to her, and Gameela next to Rose, her arm around her waist. She held the phone up to Saaber's face. "See?"

Saaber squinted at the screen. "Your sister is married to the American?"

Gameela, already regretting having revealed that piece of information, added, "He converted. He's a Muslim."

She expected the information to relieve Saaber, but instead, she saw something change in his face, a cloud she could not understand. He still stared at the phone. She pulled it away, tucking it in her pocket.

"Now do you believe me? I only want to help you."

Saaber looked at her, his eyes narrow. She tried to decipher his face. Was he angry? Upset? She couldn't tell. She was usually good at reading people's faces, and his opaqueness suddenly scared her. She remembered Fouad's words: *that boy has a talent for trouble.*

"All I want is to help you out, if I can," she repeated, both to reassure him and to remind herself. "Please, just let me help you. I feel I owe it to you."

Saaber said nothing. He remained standing, his backpack hanging on his shoulder. She waited.

"Let me think about it," he finally said.

"Yes, please do. You can reach me at the phone number I sent you," she said, then realizing her mistake, added, "Fouad's phone number, that is. I have his phone."

Saaber nodded. "Yes. I'll think about it."

SHE DIDN'T HEAR back from him for three days. Lying in bed in the morning of the third day, spread-eagled, the covers kicked off, she stared at the ceiling fan as it whooshed on. The restlessness of the previous days had reached a peak so high, she felt paralyzed by anxiety, certain that her arms and legs would refuse to obey her if she tried to move them. She was due at the farm that day, and she couldn't decide whether to go back or wait in Cairo. *I'm not at his beck and call,* Fouad had said of Saaber, and Gameela now empathized.

The whole thing had lost its edge. The burning curiosity that had consumed her the entire time Saaber was texting Fouad had fallen flat, now that she learned he only needed to get that envelope to Mark—such a meaningless request. Once she got home after her meeting with Saaber, she had opened the envelope, toiled through reading the first few pages, and then set it aside on her nightstand, where it still lay. The boy's handwriting and his Arabic were both pathetic, and he went on and on about all the injustices done to him, which she truly sympathized with but which she felt Mark had no need to read and could do nothing about anyway. It's not as if publishing that would erase the boy's one and a half years of imprisonment; on the contrary, it might get him in even more trouble. Besides, the whole thing was in Arabic—all twelve pages. What was she supposed to do? Translate it before sending it to Mark? She guessed she could contact him and ask if he wanted it, but she couldn't fathom why he would be interested in a dozen pages of self-pity. She wondered whether she should contact Rose instead, but decided against it.

Rose. Gameela watched the ceiling fan, tried and failed to discern its movement, which was too fast for her eyes to follow. She glanced at the bed next to hers, where Rose used to sleep. They often fought over this same ceiling fan—Rose, perpetually hot, wanting it on all night, Gameela resisting. Gameela picked up her phone, started to text Rose, then hesitated. How would she start? I miss you? I'm sorry I was such an asshole about your marriage? I now know how it feels to love someone? I understand?

Maybe start small. She began to type a simple good morning, then remembered the time difference: 9:00 A.M. in Cairo; 3:00 A.M. on the East Coast. She put the phone down. She would text Rose later.

She got out of bed, went into the bathroom, showered, then walked back to her room, her wet hair wrapped in a towel, and started packing her duffel bag. Not until she had zipped it up, placed it next to the front door, and walked back into her room did she notice the text notification on her phone.

Did you give the journalist the envelope? Saaber asked.

She glanced at the envelope sitting on her nightstand.

Yes, she lied.

Good.

She waited. Minutes passed before he texted her again.

If you still want to help, meet me today at the same place at noon.

That was it. In a moment, her hesitation of the previous days vanished. She texted Saaber back.

Of course I still want to help. I'll see you today inshaa Allah.

Then she sent a message to Fouad.

Going to be a bit late coming home today.

He did not respond. He had been giving her the silent treatment since she left the farm, and she was sick of his childish behavior. She was tempted to send him some words of reprimand, but decided against it. She would take care of that face-to-face. For now, she had more important matters to attend to. The boy needed her, and she was going to help him. She imagined him overcoming his pride and asking her for her assistance in some specific, useful way that could set his life straight after that awful period of imprisonment. Perhaps he had trouble finding a job—who would hire a recently released Islamist?—and needed connections to get one. In Egypt, everyone needed connections, and Gameela had them, both on her family's side and on Fouad's. Already she was making a mental list of acquaintances who would not deny her such a simple request. She had two hours before she was to meet Saaber, and she needed to get ready. She ran into the bathroom, dried her hair, ran back into her room and changed, put her head cover on. She was about to walk out of the room when she stopped and considered the envelope on her nightstand. Perhaps she could show it to Fouad. It would be a peace offering, a way to include him in her efforts to help the boy. She was certain Fouad would be eager to assist him in any way he could, once he read through these pages and understood how wronged Saaber had felt. Maybe that would lead Fouad to work with her as a team again, to actively try to right the wrongs of society, just as they had done during the revolution, just as Fouad had done during the Bread Riots. She walked back to her nightstand, picked the envelope up, stuffed it in her backpack, then walked out of the bedroom. On her way out, she passed by her parents' room—the door still closed, both probably still asleep. She considered knocking but didn't want to wake them up. Softly, she passed by the door, picked her duffel bag up, and walked out of the apartment.

SAABER SAT AT a table in the corner of the coffee shop, his backpack on his lap, staring at the entrance.

"You're late," he told her.

"You only gave me a two-hour notice, and I had to drive here all the way from Zamalek. I got stuck in traffic."

She had just sat down when she saw him get up.

"I just got here!"

"We're not staying. You said you wanted to help, right?"

She nodded.

"Are you absolutely sure?" His words were slow, his lips curled in a smile that, again, Gameela could not decipher.

"Of course I am!"

He nodded. "Let's go."

He walked out of the café and kept to the sidewalk, his step brisk. She followed him, sprinting to keep up. At times, she felt as if he had forgotten she was there with him, walking ahead of her, gaining distance that threatened to separate them in Cairo's busy streets. He stopped at a traffic light, and she stopped, too, catching her breath.

"Where are we going?"

"You'll see."

Walking the Cairo streets in the suffocating August midday heat was never a good idea. She pulled a tissue out of her backpack, used it to wipe the sweat already pooling on her forehead.

"Are we almost there?" she asked, stepping up until she was walking by Saaber's side.

"Ten more minutes."

"Can you slow down a bit? I'm getting out of breath."

He slowed down. For a couple of minutes, they walked on in silence, Gameela struggling to remain by his side amid the pedestrian traffic. She could not imagine why he would need to bring her somewhere. Was he taking her to a prospective place of employment? Using her as a character reference? Certainly there were ways to do so without dragging her with him, but still, she was too curious to learn their destination to object to tagging along. Besides, walking together provided a good chance for talking.

"I wanted to apologize to you, Saaber," she started, going through the words she had rehearsed many times in the past few days. "I feel I was partly responsible for getting you in the trouble you ended up in."

He did not look her way, but she did not care. Already she was feeling part of the load she had carried for two years lifting, her words picking tiny weights off her conscience.

"I had no way of knowing all of this would happen, of course. I thought that I was helping Mark out when I got him in touch with you, and I told myself I'd be helping you out, too. Getting your story out there. Neither one of us could have known this simple story would get you in trouble. I know Fouad and Mark both felt really bad about it."

He stopped, turning to look at her. "They felt bad? Then why didn't the journalist get me out of jail? Why did Fouad stop responding to my texts?"

"Mark couldn't have gotten you out. How could he?"

"He's an American. They can do all they want."

"Not when it comes to the law!"

He snorted, started walking again.

Gameela followed him. "And Fouad did help. He got you the lawyer who got you out of jail."

"I would have gotten out of jail anyway. They had no case against me."

"That's not fair."

"He didn't help when I needed him. He wouldn't meet with me."

"But he sent me in his place." She was glad to be able to maintain that lie, if only to defend Fouad.

"Yes, he sent you to me." For the second time since they met, she saw that same smile curl his lips. "He sent me his wife, the journalist's sister-in-law. I've been thinking about this for the past two days. It's amazing the signs God will send his true believers to show them they are on the right path, to give His blessings, to assure them that all who wronged them will be punished, that all will be avenged."

"What path?"

"I wasn't planning on this, you know. Having anyone with me. I thought everyone had a role that God assigned them and that my role was different. But then you showed up and I didn't know you were related to both Fouad and the journalist and I thought about it and I thought God was sending me another sign." He turned to face her, his eyes gleaming. "I have to follow God's signs. You understand that, don't you?"

"I'm sorry, Saaber, but I have no clue what you're trying to tell me."

"It's okay." He walked on. "We're almost there."

He fell silent again, his steps getting faster. Gameela scurried to keep up, fighting a sudden urge to stop right here, turn around, and abandon him altogether. But she still wanted to see where they were going. Besides, she felt that leaving now would get him off the hook too easily. He owed her an explanation. Or, at least, he owed her a chance to do something worthwhile to justify all the trouble she had gone to, all those lies that she had permitted herself only because her intentions were good.

She stayed close, walking next to him, her shoulder to his. Whether he liked it or not, she was going to make things go her way.

THE ROAD LEADING to the police headquarters was blockaded on both ends, with no traffic allowed except for a trickle of pedestrians who had to go through the metal detectors installed in the middle of the road. Saaber stepped up to the line leading to the gate, and Gameela stood behind him. Over a dozen people separated them from the metal detectors. Gameela stepped aside, trying to see ahead, but all she could discern were two female officers chatting off to the side, their navy head covers matching their uniforms, and the officer sitting in the shade of an umbrella next to the gate.

Gameela could not fathom why Saaber had brought her here, of all places. Surely, he was not seeking employment at the police headquarters. Was he in trouble with the police again? Did he need her to testify on his behalf? To tell them that she was the one who brought Mark to him? That he had not sought out the American journalist?

"What are we doing here?" she whispered to his back.

He did not answer.

The early afternoon had turned suffocatingly hot, and she was sweating profusely under her head cover, her hair sticky and itchy. To her utter embarrassment, she was also getting nervous about going through the security checkpoint with the boy's envelope in her backpack. She remembered the stories flooding her social media feed in the previous three years since the Muslim Brotherhood president got thrown out and the state tightened its grip on all forms of dissent: the fifteen-year-old kid arrested for wearing a T-shirt with "NO TO TORTURE" printed on it, thrown in jail for years under terrorism charges; the young man who got detained for a sticker on his laptop denouncing the military rule. She had only read through the first few pages, had not even glanced through the rest. What if the rest contained similar material? What if the officers at the security checkpoint read through the boy's scribbles?

Still a good five or six people away from the metal gate, Gameela tore the envelope open, pulling out the dozen sheets inside. Ahead of her, Saaber looked straight in front of him, never turning around. Gameela folded the envelope, stuffed it in her purse, then looked at the sheets.

Pages and pages covered with notes lay in her hands, fanned out, the white of the sheets blinding in the bright daylight. Gameela squinted, held the sheets up to her face. The boy's handwriting was a tightly wound scrawl, the words written in black ink often too close to each other to decipher. She removed the first three pages, the ones she already read, and flipped through the rest. No way she could read all of this before arriving at the gate. She stepped aside, let one woman pass in front of her, still keeping an eye on Saaber, afraid he would make it through and she would lose him. She got back in line and frantically scanned the pages.

At first, all she found were stock prayers: declarations that God will always be on the side of those defending His laws; that this life was for the vain; that eternity was the true life. She skimmed through the next paragraph, then the next.

Then she got to the paragraph about the police.

Reading through the first two sentences, Gameela immediately got out of the line and stepped to the side. The boy had gone on a two—no, three-page rant against the police, accusing them of murdering his brother and his father, of killing his pigeons (his pigeons!), of holding him unjustly. He went on to blame them for every protester who died during the revolution, for helping the army throw out the legitimately elected Muslim Brotherhood president.

Gameela took another step away from the line, glanced at the two female officers, making sure they couldn't read the pages over her shoulder, and then at Saaber, who was just two people away from the metal gates.

This stuff was enough to get her arrested. To get him arrested again.

She wondered what he had in his backpack, hoped he didn't carry more copies of this to distribute, imagined him walking around the police building handing out flyers. She wondered if he realized he would be searched.

Ahead of her, one of the two policewomen was looking through a lady's purse.

Chances are, they wouldn't really look through all the papers in his backpack.

But what if they did?

She took another frantic glance through the pages, skipped a few paragraphs ahead.

What on earth did Saaber think Mark would do with this, a watered-down, not very eloquent version of those angry posts the supporters of the ousted Muslim Brotherhood president had flooded Facebook with for the previous three years?

She kept skimming through the pages.

What finally caught her eyes was a pronoun. "It."

Because God has sent me signals that I was called upon to do it.

Do what?

She skimmed back up, looking for an explanation she may have missed, a reference, or an elaboration.

This deed that I have committed is a testimony to my faith in God, my responsibility to do His bidding, my determination to set things right.

Was he going to the police to confess a crime he had committed? If so, why did he need to drag her with him?

Frantically she scanned the paragraphs, reading them backward one by one, skipping some then going back to them, glancing at Saaber to see if he had made it to the front of the line yet. Nothing. She went back to the spot where she had originally left off reading and continued from there. Muddling through Saaber's inconsistent, poor prose, she struggled to find a clue she had previously missed, anything that would explain what that deed was that he referred to, what it was that he felt needed twelve pages of justification.

Did he refer to pushing the orderly off the roof? Was this an admission of guilt?

Was he, perhaps, feeling responsible for his brother's death?

Did he feel a need to apologize for his interview with Mark? But why would he? After all, he had explicitly asked her to get the pages to Mark. Doubtless seeking more exposure.

What was it, then?

Because God rewards those who embrace jihad *in His name.*

Gameela looked up, her heart racing.

After years of studying Islam, she knew what *jihad* meant: striving to be pious, to spread goodness on earth, to act every day in the knowledge that God was watching all one's deeds, to live in the hope of attaining grace.

She knew perfectly well that this was not what Saaber meant when he used the word *jihad.*

For a moment, she felt the clarity of vision that she had always longed for but never grasped, the pieces falling into place: Saaber's senseless manifesto, his anger with the police, with Mark, and with Fouad.

Her presence here. The cherry on top of his revenge cake.

In her burst of revelation, she felt utterly, completely stupid.

"Saaber!" she yelled.

He did not respond.

Gameela's heart raced. She considered running to him and pulling him away—he was right there; she could reach him in a few skips. But she should not run toward a security checkpoint. All three police officers were armed. She took one slow, hesitant step toward him. One of the police-women turned and gave her an inquisitive look.

"Get back in line," the policewoman ordered her.

Gameela retreated.

"Saaber!' she called one more time.

But he had already made it to the front of the line.

She watched him try to walk around the metal detector, between it and the barricade set up close by. The police officer shouted at him to get back.

He got back, paused in front of the metal detector, then stepped through it, and it beeped, a shrill, loud noise.

Gameela took one step backward and, mirroring her, Saaber took a step back, too.

Then he turned his head to look her way.

For a split second, she thought she saw a youthful look flash in his eyes, a look of fear, of hesitation, of indecisiveness, just like that look she always saw in the eyes of the young peasants' kids at the farm when they had to pick between two fruits she offered them, wanting both, wanting every-thing, but believing there could only be one choice.

She clung to that look, her eyes wide, hoping it would last.

But a second later it vanished.

Part Five

22

For two months, the box containing Gameela's things sits in the corner of Rose's living room, untouched. She passes by it each morning on her way to the kitchen, sits next to it in the evenings when she and Mark watch the news, even occasionally places a book or magazine on its closed lid. The box shares the room with Rose and Mark, but Rose is determined never to look through it again. On the lid, she has tacked an orange sticky note with the words "Pandora's box" written on it in black Sharpie, followed by three exclamation marks—reminders of the perils of asking too many questions.

Weeks earlier, she had allowed herself one last question, posed to her parents on the phone a few days after she found out about Gameela's marriage:

"Did Gameela have any suitors? In the last year or so?"

On the other side: silence. Then her father's slowly uttered words.

"There was a man, yes. Some older guy she was infatuated with. One of those hopeless cases she always fell for."

"You know how your sister always thought she could save the miserable and depressed," her mother added.

Rose remembered two of Gameela's former relationships: a college friend, a recovering addict whom she believed she could keep sober until he relapsed and his parents shipped him off to rehab, and the older son of one of her mother's friends, a widower who could not get over his wife's death, a young father with a child Gameela knew she would become the perfect mother to. Neither relationship had lasted.

"We found out she had been prancing all over Cairo with him for some time, so we confronted her about it. She told us he wanted to ask for her hand in marriage," her father continued. "We refused, of course."

"She got over it, with time," her mother assured her.

Rose closed her eyes, started counting till ten, arming herself against the surge of anger she expected would assault her, but surprisingly, the anger didn't come. She opened her eyes. Perhaps she was not capable of being angry with her old, bereaved parents, who, after all, thought they were looking out for their child's best interest. Or perhaps anger was a finite emotion, and Rose had overdrawn her credit limit. Either way, she felt only numbness and asked no more questions, neither of her parents nor of her sister's belongings, which, she was convinced, punished her inquisitiveness with increasingly painful revelations.

At night, she woke up sweating, imagining she had discovered how her sister ended up next to the suicide bomber, only to find out that the terrorist had, in fact, been her own sister, or that she, Rose, had been standing in the shadows, her finger poised on the button that detonated the bomb.

She couldn't handle any other discoveries.

She placed Gameela's wedding certificate back where she found it, folded and tucked between the pages of Rose's childhood book on archaeology, her sister's dream nestled inside hers. That book, too, sits in the box, hidden from sight by the container's opaque plastic but still palpable, as if it were emanating radioactive waves that make Rose's eyes itch and the hairs on her arms stand on end whenever she glances in its direction.

Mark never mentions it, though Rose has caught him staring at the box when he thought she was not looking.

ON A SATURDAY a couple of weeks later, Mark leaves early in the morning and returns with a rental car. "I'm taking you to the beach," he tells a pajama-clad Rose.

"In December?"

"It's a warm December day! Besides, beaches are not just for swimming."

They drive to Staten Island. Rose has seen the Verrazano Bridge from Brooklyn but has never been on it. She looks out the window at the suspension cables, then through the sunroof as they pass under each of the two towers.

"This is beautiful," she says, thinking of ancient monuments and new marvels of technology, pyramids and skyscrapers. "Beautiful."

They park by a wooden boardwalk overlooking a sandy beach. Rose follows Mark to the wide walkway bordered by a white-painted iron railing. They stand together, Rose's gloved hands and his bare ones resting on the railing, looking out on the sea.

"Welcome to the Franklin D. Roosevelt Boardwalk. Not exactly Alexandria, but still a beach. Close enough, in my book."

Ahead of them, gentle waves crash on the beach. Rose lifts both hands and puts one open palm on each side of her face, blocking her peripheral vision. Now all she sees is water and sand. Too much sand—Alexandria's beaches are narrower than this. She tilts her head up until she sees only a narrow strip of sand, then water and sky. "Now I'm in Alexandria."

It's warm enough to pass for Alexandria in the wintertime. Rose closes her eyes, allows herself to indulge in this fantasy for a few minutes, but the sounds and smells are all wrong, and she knows it. She opens her eyes and drops her hands. "Then again, I haven't been to Alexandria in years. Who knows how it looks now." She remembers family vacations when she was a child, trips to El-Agamy beach with its fine white sand. Gameela's hair inevitably bleached golden by the sun and the salty water; Rose's remaining stubbornly black.

"Let's walk out on the sand," Mark says.

They climb down the stairs and walk up to the waterline, then stroll toward a fishing pier in the distance. Rose inhales the fresh air, letting it fill her lungs. Next to her, Mark is silent, hands in his pockets. Her sneakers scrunch on the wet, compacted sand by the water, and Rose looks behind at her footprints and at Mark's.

"It's not fair that your stride is so long. I have to take four steps for each three of yours."

He laughs. "The advantages of being tall."

Ahead of them, fishermen are sitting on the pier, casting their lines into the ocean. Mark and Rose walk back to the boardwalk and onto the pier, stroll toward the blue-roofed pavilion at its end. On their way, they stop and watch a fisherman unhook a large, round, hard-shelled marine creature from his line. He flips it over, handling it with gloves.

"What is this?" Rose asks.

"A horseshoe crab," Mark answers. "Also called a living fossil because they go back four hundred and fifty million years. So right up your alley," he smiles.

Rose watches the creature. Upturned, it shows multiple legs and a threatening-looking tail. The fisherman is struggling to free the crab, and when he finally does, he flips it right side up and looks at Rose, smiling. "Want to touch him?" he asks.

"No, thank you." Rose does not hesitate.

He laughs. "Harmless creature, really. Doesn't bite or sting or anything." Gently, he lifts it by the sides of its shell, carries it over the railing, holds it there as if ready to drop it into the water, then hesitates. He turns around, carries the crab all the way to the end of the pier, off onto the boardwalk, then down to the water, where he releases it. In a moment, the crab is gone. Rose watches the man as he walks back. Probably in his sixties or seventies, his pace slow, hunched forward as he approaches his fishing gear. He smiles at her before he takes his seat, and Rose smiles back.

They resume their walk toward the pavilion. There, they lean against the railing again, this time looking out at the ocean that stretches in all directions.

"Thank you," Rose says. "I needed this."

"I thought you'd like a change of scenery."

"A new place to add to my list of places?"

"Why not? One more step toward feeling at home."

Rose watches a couple of seagulls dive down toward the water then swoop back up. In the shade of the pavilion, the day feels suddenly colder, and Rose shivers. Mark takes his jacket off, steps closer to Rose, wraps his arm around her shoulders, and throws his jacket around both of them. The lining of his jacket smells like his aftershave: sporty, familiar.

"We should have brought a quilt," Rose says.

"Maybe next time."

"Yes. Next time."

THAT NIGHT, Rose inches closer to Mark in bed. He is asleep with his back turned to her, his chest rising and falling softly with each breath. She presses herself as close as possible to him. She wants to whisper something into the back of his neck, something deep and meaningful, maybe that home is not only a place but a person, too, but it sounds both silly and superficial, like an attempt to label something that should not be constrained by a simple definition. She thinks of Gameela's home or homes, wherever they were, and of the person she felt most at home with. For a moment, the ongoing, persistent ache that has never left her since her sister's death parts just slightly enough to allow one ray of light to seep in: that her sister was married, that she must have loved her husband, that she had, even if only for a short time, someone to inch closer to at night, someone to hold on tight to. With this one thought, one of the endless pebbles that have weighed down her heart for the previous months seems to pop, disappear, leaving a shimmer in its wake, as if it were a bug that flew into an electric zapper, illuminating the area around it for the second it took for it to die.

Her heart felt suddenly lighter. One pebble gone, many more to go.

Mark stirs. Rose is still not sure whether her anger with him has fully subsided or whether it ever will. He has played a part in Gameela's death, even if unwittingly—that's a fact that will not change. She still looks at his sleeping back and wants to stay as close as possible to him—that, too, is a fact. For a moment, she thinks that maybe there are multiple versions of her, too, just as there are multiple versions of him and multiple versions of Gameela, and that her different Roses will have to learn to coexist, that Gameela's sister and Mark's wife cannot go on believing that they are enemies, citizens of warring countries.

The night is calmer than usual, and Rose glances at the clock: 3:00 A.M. She reaches over Mark's torso, finds his hand, and grabs it in hers. She squeezes his fingers, and in his sleep, he squeezes hers back.

THE NEXT MORNING, Rose walks into the kitchen for coffee and notices sunlight trickling through the window and drawing playful shadows on the kitchen countertop. She places her palm on the countertop and the shadows bend and break over her skin, the surface's warmth welcoming her outstretched hand. Taking her coffee with her, Rose opens the window and listens to the birds chirping, watches Mrs. Kumiega sit on her bench in the backyard and play with her cats, and she feels a new, partly exciting, mostly calming kind of peace.

She feels at home.

When she walks back to the living room and looks at the plastic bin, she no longer detects that near suffocation that had made itself quite comfortable in some nook of her chest for the previous months. She waits for it to peek out, announce itself, but it has vanished.

When Mark wakes up, he finds Rose sitting at the kitchen table, the plastic bin opened next to her, Gameela's things stacked in neat piles on the table's glass top. She looks up at him and smiles.

"Come. Help me decide what to do with this stuff."

They sit at opposite sides of the table, sifting through the things. Rose looks at each paper before discarding it, reads all the mail she had not yet opened, rubs the edges of sheets between finger and thumb to make sure they are not stuck together, hiding anything from her view. Because she is now ready to find anything—documents proving that Gameela was an international spy; that she was the leader of a ring of terrorists; photos of her on top of the mountains of Saint Catherine or diving with sharks—she finds nothing. Shortly, the garbage bin she has placed on the floor next to her overflows with old bills; work documents that Rose decides cannot be important; copies of academic articles.

Mark has separated the photos in two piles: those with people in them, and those without—snapshots of building sites, exposed metal beams and concrete perpetually waiting to dry. He lets Rose look through the photos containing people, but he has already pulled one out and now slides it across the table toward her.

"Keep this one," he says.

The photo shows Rose and Gameela in their teens. They are standing at the beach (Alexandria, perhaps? Rose is not sure), pants rolled up to their knees, their backs to a visibly stormy sea, waves breaking behind them, their arms laced. Rose's hair is cropped short, a mass of black curls, while Gameela's, longer, auburn, flows sideways behind her, like a single wing extended. They are both laughing and looking at the camera.

In one of her desk drawers, Rose finds a new frame, carries it back to the kitchen, and puts the photo in it. The frame is too large for the photo, which stands crooked, Gameela's side of the snapshot higher than Rose's.

"I'll fix that," Mark says, reaching into one of the kitchen drawers behind him for Scotch tape. Moments later, the photo stands perfectly centered in its wooden frame.

Rose places it in the middle of the bookcase in the living room, in the section where the East meets the West. She stands looking at it.

"Feels like a lifetime ago. It's like I'm looking at a different person."

Mark walks closer, places one hand on her shoulder, squeezing it. "Not a different person. An earlier incarnation of the same person."

She leans against him for support, her shoulder resting on his chest.

"I wish I had known how things would turn out. I would have changed so much. I would have spoken to her more often, at least."

Mark holds her tighter, closer to him. Rose looks at the two smiling girls in the photo, their arms entangled, frozen in a moment that is now forever theirs.

AT WORK, Rose dives into the preparations for the new exhibit with renewed fervor. Dr. Winkenstein has been back for two months, and while he did not disapprove of including evidence of communication with the dead in the exhibit, he wants her to present this as part of a section on ancient Egyptian religious rituals. Shifting the focus to highlight celebratory traditions, Dr. Winkenstein suggests she include holidays such as the annual Khoiak Festival, celebrating the myth of Osiris. During the festival, Osiris's death and resurrection were reenacted in processions that marched across Egypt, and ordinary people made figurines of the dead god. The University of Chicago owns multiple such figurines in bronze, and the Boston Museum of Fine Arts has one as well, a corn mummy made as a replica of Osiris's mummy. Dr. Winkenstein is sure the Met would be able to borrow some of those for the duration of the exhibit.

Rose puts the letters to the dead aside and starts researching the celebratory figurines of Osiris.

AT HOME, a couple of weeks after their trip to the beach, Mark presents Rose with a sheet of paper. The paper lists an address and a phone number, both in Egypt.

"What is this?"

"Fouad's contact information."

Sitting in her living room, her legs extended on the coffee table, a book in her lap, Rose stares at the paper but does not move.

Mark brings it closer to her face. "Take it. It's not going to bite you."

"How did you get this?" Her voice is hoarse. She notices Mark's still-outstretched hand, reaches over and takes the paper.

"I am a reporter, remember?" He smiles, obviously proud of himself.

She looks up from the paper at his face, feels she should say something, but is not sure what. "How did you get this?" she asks again.

"I had a friend from the Cairo office do some investigating. Not hard to do if you have the right connections in Egypt."

"You didn't call Marwa, did you?"

"No, of course not. Don't worry." Mark sits down next to her.

They had discussed that before, the possibility of asking Marwa about Fouad, but Rose had opposed it. She didn't want to risk revealing her sister's secret, and she couldn't be sure Marwa knew about the marriage.

"How did you find him?" she asks one more time.

"We assumed Gameela lied to your parents when she said she was traveling to Rasheed for work after she had quit her job, but then I remembered that she had said Fouad had a farm in Rasheed. He even mentioned the English name: Rosetta. That's how I knew it was the same town. So I thought maybe she lied about the purpose of her travel, not the destination. I had a friend make some phone calls and, sure enough, there was a Fouad Salem Sedky in Rasheed. A big landowner, apparently. We're lucky it's such a small town."

"How do we know it's the same man?"

"My friend's source is on the local police force." Here Mark hesitates. Softly, he adds, "He said the man had always been secluded but had grown more so since he recently lost his young wife in a terrorist attack."

Rose stares at the sheet of paper in her hand. "Now what?"

"Up to you. But at least you have a way to contact him, if you ever choose to do so."

"ANOTHER TRIP?" Dr. Winkenstein asks.

"Just for a few days. Three days and a weekend. Maybe four. Certainly not longer than a week, I promise. I'll aim for the New Year weekend and the first couple of days of January. And I'll take it out of my annual vacation time."

"I know it has been a difficult time for you, Rose, but there is a board meeting coming up. I need to have something to report to them about the exhibit's progress."

"You will. I'll work on it while I'm there. I'll work weekends when I come back. I've already done so much since the last meeting. I probably even have enough for you to report right now, if you wish."

He sighs, pushes his glasses back, and looks at her. "I don't know."

"There is someone there I need to see," she pleads, softly. "Someone I didn't get to see the last time I was there. Please."

He looks down. Rose scoots to the edge of her seat. On his desk lie stacks of papers, documentation of his ongoing research that Rose has been helping him with as well, in preparation for the exhibit.

"I'll stop by the Egyptian Museum and take multiple photos of the entire cabinet holding those Old Kingdom embalming tools," she says, pointing to a sheet of paper on his desk.

"You don't need to bribe me." He looks at her above his glasses.

"I really need to go, Dr. Winkenstein."

He nods, sighing. Rose makes a mental note to add this to the ever-increasing list of things she owes the kind man, promising herself that, at some point soon, she will throw propriety through the window and give him a peck on the cheek.

ON HER LAST DAY before heading to Egypt, Rose wraps her work up early, and, instead of going straight home, she walks into the Egyptian art wing of the museum and finds the Temple of Dendur. Again she marvels at how grand this minuscule temple looks in its large exhibit hall with its wall of slanted glass, which keeps the temple doused in clear but placid light. This room is Rose's favorite: an Egyptian temple to the goddess Isis set in the heart of Manhattan, the multiple layers of her various homes overlapping. She finds a spot on the low partition encircling the temple, sits down looking at its walls, tries to imagine them painted in their original bright colors, not in the uniform beige of the two-thousand-year-old blocks. All around the temple, visitors are walking in awed silence, and Rose, as always, cannot help but feel proud. She does not begrudge the museum this temple, which would have been flooded under the waters of the Aswan Dam in the 1960s, had the U.S. and UNESCO not helped rescue it. It is a legitimately earned piece of Egypt's history, not like the bust of Nefertiti, housed in the Berlin museum for decades since it was illegally smuggled out of Egypt, just like many other artifacts that should never have left their country.

But things smuggled out of Egypt often find their way back home, Rose knows.

She gets up and walks to the temple. Passing through the columns, she turns left and looks at the graffiti, at the names of various European visitors who came to the temple in the nineteenth century and, perhaps inspired by the structure's ability to survive those who built it, carved their names on its walls, leaving their own marks that outlasted their short lives: *Leonardo, 1820; D. Gallone, 1821; L. Politi, 1819;* someone from 1891 with enough national pride to mark the name of his home city: *NY, US.* Rose marvels at the time it must have taken to carve those names, the care some of the vandals took in making the letters uniform, deep, large. The inescapable allure of immortality.

The boy who thought that blowing himself up would grant him an eternal life.

Beside Rose, a young girl stands looking up, not at the graffiti but at the tall ceiling above.

"Look how high it is, Mommy!" She pulls at her mother's hand. "But it's cracked!"

Rose, too, looks up. The ceiling looks as if it's cracked, the seams between the stones visible, but Rose knows these are merely the effects of time, eroding the ancient structure's cosmetic surface, leaving the secrets of its inner workings bare.

"Don't worry," she tells the young girl. "It's not going to fall."

23

Fouad peels oranges using a Swiss Army knife that he pulled out of the pocket of his cargo pants. Rose watches him. Her first impression stands: he looks older than she had expected, closer to the midsixties than to fifty-seven. Then again, the man seems to have never known sunscreen. His skin is blackened with exposure, his original skin tone peeking from under his chambray shirt's neck opening and rolled-up sleeves, which reveal arms quite toned for his age. Maybe he isn't in his sixties. She can't decide. He hands her a peeled orange and she takes it, starts separating the segments.

He watches her eat. He has a probing, attentive look, and she thinks she understands why her sister would have found this older man attractive just based on the way he handed her that orange, on the intensity in his look as he watches her eat.

"Did you tell your parents? About Gameela and me?" he asks.

She shakes her head.

He nods. "Better leave it this way."

"Yes."

Rose bites at the last segment of the orange. Already he is peeling another one for her.

"These are good oranges," she says.

"Yes."

"I wish she had told me about you."

He does not respond.

"Why didn't she tell me?"

"We didn't tell anyone."

"I'm her sister. She should have told me."

He places another peeled orange on a plate in front of her and starts peeling one for himself. With every peeled orange, he produces one long spiral strip of orange skin, uniform in width, which he then gently places on a plate. The orange peel holds its shape, a hollow globe. The plate is cream colored with butterflies on the edge, a piece of fine china that certainly did not belong on a kilim spread on the dirt in the shade of a guava tree. Yet, the plate did not seem out of place.

"I think she regretted the way she reacted to your marriage. It must have made it difficult to confess to a match that was arguably even more inappropriate," he smiled.

"You're not a foreigner."

"I'm twenty-nine years her senior. And I have an arrest record. Political charges. But still. Anyway, your parents certainly thought it wasn't a good match for her. I can't say I blame them."

Rose separates another segment of orange, bites it, and lets the juice fill her mouth.

"These are good oranges," she says again.

"Yes. I grow guavas as well. And dates, and mangoes. The mangoes are the best. Do you like mangoes?"

"I love mangoes."

He nods. Gameela loved mangoes, too. She knows that he knows that, that he is thinking of it. But he says nothing.

"I can't talk about her to anyone," she says. "Not really."

"I know. I can't either."

"Mark blames himself." She stops short of saying that for a long time, she blamed him, too.

"Tell him to join the club."

"It wasn't your fault," she tells him.

"I introduced her to the boy. I'm the one who suggested his name. He worked for an electrician who replaced some of the wiring in my apartment in Cairo a few years ago, and the electrician told me his story, how his brother was killed in the protests. I thought he would be a good one for Mark to interview. I never imagined . . ." He trails off.

"You couldn't have known what he was capable of." She takes the segments of the second orange apart, arranges them like a flower on the plate. "Do you know anything about how she ended up there? With him?"

He shakes his head. "I couldn't figure it out. He had been trying to get me to go meet him in Cairo, but I wouldn't do it. I imagine he must have found a way to reach her." He pauses before adding, faintly, "She was very eager to help him. If I had listened to her and met with him, then maybe none of this would have happened."

"It wasn't your fault," she tells him again, thinking of Mark. "She was a grown woman. She was responsible for her own actions."

He smiles. "She certainly knew how to make things go her way."

"Did she like it here?"

"She did. Sometimes I felt she was playing housewife, enjoying the novelty of life on the farm a bit too much. Would she have liked it in a year or two? I'm not so sure. But I was taking my blessings as they came to me. I didn't care if she eventually got tired of me."

"I don't think she would have."

He looks up at her, still smiling. "How do you know?"

"She is my sister. I know."

He nods, his eyes watering, then looks back down at the orange in his hands.

"I have something for you," she says.

FROM THE TRUNK of the rental car she pulls out the plastic bin she has carried all the way back from the U.S., her sister's things neatly stacked in it. She puts it down on the floor, takes out the floral scarf, wraps it around her neck, and then carries the box back to the porch of the farmhouse, where Fouad is now sitting, waiting for her.

"I took some of her things from her room, the last time I was in Egypt. I want you to have them."

She places the box on the floor in front of him. He sits straight up in his chair, leans forward, then opens the lid, peers inside, not touching anything. She can see his hands are trembling, but then he laces his fingers, his elbows dug firmly in his thighs, and, still looking down, stays perfectly still. She looks away, peering into the house through the window that opens to the porch. It's an old house, built like all farmers' houses are, its white-plastered clay walls reflecting the afternoon sun. Inside, she sees a wooden staircase leading to the upper floor, and she imagines Gameela walking down the stairs, greeting her.

"I'm keeping the scarf, if that's okay." She touches the scarf around her neck, looking away from the staircase.

He looks up, his eyes moist. He nods.

"Is there anything else you would like me to get you? Any of her things?"

He shakes his head.

"May I walk around the farm for a little while?"

"Of course," he says, standing up. "Give me a few minutes, and I'll join you." Carefully, he places the lid back on the box, picks it up, and walks into the house, disappearing inside.

PASSING BY THE GUAVA TREE, Rose stops and grabs a few red dates and one long strip of orange peel. She munches on the dates on her way to the stream in the distance, the fresh fruits bloodred outside but cream inside, crunchy and sweet. Never in the years she has spent in the U.S. so far has she found these fresh dates for sale, not the red ones, nor could she find the exact same kind of guavas that now dangle off every tree she passes: the white-fleshed fruit with yellow skin, not the ones that are green outside and pink inside she has sometimes found in Asian grocery stores in New York. The dates are relatively small, and whenever she bites one side off and reaches the elongated, brown pit, easily separated from the flesh, she shakes it off into the globe of orange peel resting in her cupped left hand. By the time she reaches the stream, she has gone through all the dates and is left with the pit-filled orange shell, which produces a muffled rattle whenever she shakes it.

The stream is not too wide, about six feet, she estimates, and is overgrown on both sides with bamboo shoots. One strip has been cleared of the shoots and provides easy access to the water. Standing there, she watches the shallow stream, spots a couple of fish swimming close by.

"They don't bite when they are swimming near the surface this way," Fouad says, joining her. "They just tease you."

She smiles. "I'm sure that's not their intention."

"Who knows about intentions? Maybe it is. Maybe they do it on purpose."

She removes the circular top of the orange peel, picks one date pit from within, and tosses it at the fish, which scatter with impressive speed.

"There. Now they won't tease you anymore."

They stand in place, watching, until the fish appear again.

"Evil fish," he says.

"You know, ancient Egyptians used to think that the heart was the source of intellect and passion, housing the good and evil within us. They believed that, when one died, the heart was weighed against the feather of Maat, the goddess of truth and justice, and one would be allowed to pass into the afterlife only if the heart weighed the same as the feather. If the heart was contaminated with even a trace of evil, it would weigh more."

"And if it did?"

"It would be devoured by a god with the head of a crocodile and the person would lose his chance at a second, eternal life."

"Ouch."

"At least that's better than an eternity in hell. You were merely deprived of that second chance at living." From the orange peel in her palm, she picks out another one of the seeds, throws it in the water but far from the fish.

"I'd like a chance at a second life."

"Wouldn't we all."

"A totally pure heart seems unattainable, though."

"I think it was meant as something to aspire to, like an upcoming test of purity people would be motivated to prepare for."

"I wouldn't pass that test."

"Neither would I." She tosses a few more seeds into the water. "But it's only a myth anyway."

"Gameela probably would have passed it," Fouad says.

Rose hopes he did not see her grimace. For weeks now, she has marveled at the different versions of Gameela that existed: the highly efficient, organized one her work colleagues saw; the religious, pious, obedient one that her parents knew; the judgmental, harsh one that Rose had been angry with for years, the one who declared Mark a hypocrite and Rose a transgressor. And then that other one, the one Rose had tried to build a shrine to when she collected those things a few months earlier, the one who died young and thereby erased all her sins from the memories of those who loved her, the one Fouad was probably thinking of now. Various incarnations of Gameela, like a Lego set that promised the ability to construct three different contraptions using the same pieces.

Across the stream, a pair of ducks appear, one leading, the other following. The first, adventurous one finds a way down the steep bank and onto the water, and shortly afterward, the other one follows. Rose watches them swim by.

"Can you believe I've been inside the tombs of Pharaohs and on three different continents but never once on a farm before?"

He laughs. "Gameela hadn't either."

"It's so peaceful here."

"She loved it."

Rose nods. "I imagine she would have, yes. I'm glad she did."

The orange peel in her hand is now empty. She holds it by the topmost part and lets it unfurl, a curl of orange and white, bouncy, light.

AT HER PARENTS' APARTMENT, Rose sits cross-legged in the corner of the sofa, notepad in lap, and sketches an idea for the exhibit: an interactive game for kids, perhaps on a touchscreen, where they empty a model of a heart of tiny cubes representing malice until the heart become as light as the feather it is being weighed against. It's the kind of game she hopes her own kids will enjoy one day. She has been drawing models of it for close to an hour now, even though she is not sure the museum is interested in a kids' section.

Her mother, sitting next to her, watches her draw.

"Don't you think that's a bit too dark a theme for kids?" She points at the small cubes Rose has labeled with words like "hate," "malice," and "revenge." "Judgment." "Why don't you get them to do something more fun? Dress up like Cleopatra, for example?"

"What is it with the Cleopatra obsession? She was Ptolemaic, not truly Egyptian. Why not dress up like Nefertiti instead? Or Hatshepsut? She was a strong, fearless woman who ruled Egypt as an actual Pharaoh at the height of the empire's power, centuries before Cleopatra."

Her father, sitting in the armchair on her other side, chimes in. "Cleopatra was of Ptolemaic origin; that doesn't make her less Egyptian. She ruled the country and obviously loved it. You, of all people, should not be such a purist when it comes to ethnic origin."

Rose looks up, contemplating this. She wonders why she never thought of it before—Cleopatra, the immigrant, the descendant of immigrants.

"I think people are obsessed with Cleopatra because she used a poisonous snake to kill herself," Nora says.

"And don't forget the milk-and-honey baths," Ahmed adds.

"And the affairs with both Caesar and Mark Antony," Nora responds.

Rose's phone vibrates in her pocket, and she gets up, heads to her room, and, closing the door behind her, calls Mark back.

"How was your visit?" he asks.

"Good. Cathartic. And sad. And exhausting. I can't believe she made the drive there as often as she did."

"Did you find out anything new? About how she ended up at the site of the attack?"

"No. He didn't know."

"I'm sorry."

"It's okay."

She looks around the room she once shared with her sister. For the previous two days, she has been sorting through things, giving piles of old possessions away, both hers and her sister's, and now the room looks bare and feels cold, more so since the temperature has dropped to the low sixties, as it often does in the evening in the winter. She rubs her arms, warming herself up.

"Have you told your parents anything?"

"No. I told them I had to go do some fieldwork for the museum for the day. They don't need to know about her marriage. It would only make them feel guilty, and we have enough guilt floating around for a lifetime. No need to add them to the club."

Mark is silent. She wants to tell him about Fouad, how he, too, blames himself, and how she has decided no longer to blame anyone, but she is not sure this is quite true or feasible. Instead, she asks, "Do you remember that conversation we had when we first met about Nefertiti being more Egyptian than Cleopatra? Well, I just realized that as a naturalized American citizen, I'd be a hypocrite to claim that Cleopatra was not truly Egyptian, even if none of her ancestors were Egyptian. So there. You win."

"Does that mean you get to dress up as Cleopatra next Halloween?"

"Not on your life."

He chuckles.

Rose thinks of the different versions of her that her pieces would build: Rose the Egyptian and the American; the one who cared so little about tradition that she married a foreigner but cared so much that she made him wear a silver wedding band; the one who could not believe her sister had a secret life yet found it easy to keep secrets of her own. She looks at her wedding band, examining the tiny scratches that it has incurred over the years, its original, dazzling sheen swapped for a calm, subtle luster.

On the phone, Mark is silent again, but she thinks she can hear his breathing. She closes her eyes, tunes out the noise of the honking cars rising from the street, the faint sound of the TV her parents just turned on in the living room, and tries to focus only on Mark's breathing, imagining his chest rising softly with each breath, his heart, pure or not, beating with the same soft rhythm that she loves to listen to whenever she tries to fall asleep.

"Are you still coming home this Sunday?"

"Yes."

"Can I wait for you at the airport this time?"

"Yes," she says, nodding. "Yes."

Author's Note

Over the years of working on this novel, I've collected many publications on Egyptology, all of them so passionately written that I've often wished I could go back to school to study the rich history of my country of birth. These books and scholarly magazines now sit on my shelves, bursting with sticky notes, marked with stars in the margins next to fascinating tidbits of information and loopy ovals penciled around all the excerpts of ancient Egyptian literature that I thought I could use as I was writing the novel. Most prominent of these books and scholarly articles are Jan Assmann's *Death and Salvation in Ancient Egypt*; the revised edition of *The Egyptian Book of the Dead: The Book of Going Forth by Day*, edited by Ogden Goelet, Jr., et al.; Benjamin Hinson's article on the tale of Sinuhe in the 2013 volume of *Current Research in Egyptology*; Gene Kritsky's *The Tears of Re: Beekeeping in Ancient Egypt*; Miriam Lichtheim's *Ancient Egyptian Literature: The New Kingdom* (Volume II); R. B. Parkinson's *The Tale of Sinuhe and Other Ancient Egyptian Poems, 1940–1640 B.C.*; David P. Silverman's *Ancient Egypt*; John H. Taylor's *Death and the Afterlife in Ancient Egypt*; and Emily Teeter's *Religion and Ritual in Ancient Egypt*.

To the authors, translators, and editors of these books and, by extension, to academics everywhere: Thank you.

ACKNOWLEDGMENTS

I am sincerely, humbly grateful to the following people, without whom this book would not have existed:

Jane Hill, my mentor, friend, first reader of every single draft, and guardian of my sanity.

Lynn Nesbit, whom I instate as the most wisely and kindly supportive literary agent in existence.

Everyone at Viking: Allison Lorentzen, my anchor of an editor, whose impeccably sharp and yet unfailingly gentle guidance always steers me in the right direction. Brian Tart, Andrea Schulz, and Kate Stark believed in this novel and brought it to life. Lindsey Prevette and Theresa Gaffney worked tirelessly on its publicity. Jane Cavolina meticulously copyedited every single line. Beena Kamlani gave the book a thorough read. Brianna Harden gave it a gorgeous cover.

Essam Marouf, who allowed the use of the breathtaking artwork that graces the jacket.

The list of writers and poets I am indebted to includes: Ann Beattie (always), Bob Hill, Marie Manilla; my fellow Missfits (Laura Michele Diener, Wendi Kozma, Greta Rensenbrink, Kristin Steele, and Tracy Proctor Williamson); Molly Fuller and Jill Treftz, whose hilarious posts about PhD struggles inspired the prospectus chapter; the West Virginia writers who have all embraced me as one of them; and the entire faculty, past and present, of Marshall University's English Department.

Finally, my family: my parents, Raafat and Laila (I miss you, Mama); my sister, Dina; my nephew and niece, Omar and Malak. And, of course: Sarah and Yousef, my sweetest blessings, and Kamel: I followed you to the U.S. twenty years ago, and I would still follow you anywhere you go. I build my home wherever you are.

Join a literary community of
like-minded readers who seek out
the best in contemporary writing.

From the thousands of submissions Sceptre
receives each year, our editors select the books
we consider to be outstanding.

We look for distinctive voices, thought-provoking
themes, original ideas, absorbing narratives and
writing of prize-winning quality.

If you want to be the first to hear about our
new discoveries, and would like the chance to
receive advance reading copies of our books
before they are published, visit

www.sceptrebooks.co.uk

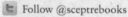 Follow @sceptrebooks

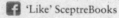 'Like' SceptreBooks

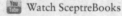 Watch SceptreBooks